Here is the 9th Quest of that modern knight-errant in slightly tarnished armor, that amiable Florida boat bum, that left-handed savior of damsels in distress . . . Travis McGee.

Here's what they're saying about

JOHN D. MacDONALD

"Absolutely top-notch and eminently readable. In our opinion, the man can do no wrong."

—THE TOLEDO BLADE

"MacDonald is the thinking mystery-lovers' answer to Ian Fleming and Mickey Spillane."

—BAKERSFIELD NEWS BULLETIN

". . . one of the most creative and reliable writers . . ."

—THE NEW YORK TIMES

"A crime writer who never lets the customer down."

—SATURDAY REVIEW SYNDICATE

JOHN D. MacDONALD

Pale Gray
for Guilt

"Perhaps no one can be really a good appreciating pagan who has not once been a bad puritan."
—BOURNE

A FAWCETT GOLD MEDAL BOOK

Fawcett Publications, Inc., Greenwich, Conn.

One

THE NEXT to the last time I saw Tush Bannon alive was the very same day I had that new little boat running the way I wanted it to run, after about six weeks of futzing around with it.

So on the test run I demonstrated one of our contemporary maladies: You can't just go out and ride around in car, boat, or airplane—you have to have a destination.

Then you feel purposeful.

So in the early morn on a flat, calm, overcast day I stocked the ice chest on the little *Muñequita* from my ship's stores on *The Busted Flush,* locked up the *Flush,* dropped down into my new playtoy, and, as what faint breeze there was seemed to be coming out of the southwest, I stuck my nose out of the pass to see if I could run north outside. The long, slow gray-green lift and fall of the ground swell was all of a towering five inches high, so I took it a mile off the beaches and fooled with the rpm and the fuel flowmeter, until she was riding right and sounded right and just a hair under 3,000 on each of the OMC 120-horse stern-drive units. I then turned the steering over to the little Calmec autopilot, took a bearing on the Lauderdale Municipal Casino and noted the time.

That, of course, is one of the fussy little enchantments of a new boat—new being either brand-new or second-hand new. What you are hunting for is the optimum relationship between fuel consumption and distance. You tell yourself that maybe someday you are going to get caught very short, and you are going to have to squeak back into port with no more than half a cup of fuel left, with luck, and it would be very nice to know what rpm leaves you the least chance of running dry.

But like the exercise of caution in almost every human activity, the fusspots who make it their business to know are the ones least likely to ever have that ticklish problem. It's the ones who never check it out who keep the Coast Guard choppers busy.

The little boat was aimed back up the Florida east coast toward Broward Beach, where I had picked her up on an estate sale from a law firm. She'd belonged to a Texan named Kayd whose luck had run out somewhere in the Bahamas.

It's a funny thing about boat names. She had that *Muñequita* across the stern in four-inch white letters against that nice shade of Gulf Stream blue when I brought her on back to Bahia Mar. Spanish for "little doll." One night Meyer and Irv Deibert and Johnny Dow and I sat around trying to dream up a name that would match *The Busted Flush*. Little Flush? Inside Straight? Hole Card? The Ante? And I forget which one we decided was best because when I got around to changing it, I looked at the name it had and I decided that trying to match it to the name on the mother ship was a case of the quaints and the cutes, and I liked the name just fine. It was a little doll and had begun to acquire in my mind a personality that could very well resent being called anything else, and would sulk and wallow.

I switched the FM-UHF marine radio to the commercial frequencies and tried to find something that didn't sound like somebody trying to break up a dogfight in a sorority house by banging drums and cymbals. Not that I want to say it isn't music. Of course it is music, styled to accompany teen-age fertility rites, and thus is as far out of my range as "Rockabye Baby." FM radio was a great product when it was servicing a fringe area of the great American market. But it has turned into a commercial success, so they have denigrated the sound, and they have mickey-moused the stereo, and you have to really search that dial to find something that isn't either folk hoke, rickyticky rock, or the saccharine they pump into elevators, bus stations and Howard Johnsons.

As I was about to give up I found some pleasant eccentric, or somebody who'd grabbed the wrong record, playing Brubeck doing Cole Porter, and I caught it just as he opened up "Love for Sale" in a fine and gentle manner, and then handed it delicately over to Desmond, who set up a witty dialogue with Joe Morello.

After telling myself that ten of eight in the morning is beer time only for the lowest types, I cracked a bottle of Carta Blanca and stood in the forward well, leaning through the center opening where I'd laid the hinged windshield over to port, out of the way, forearms on the smoke-blue foredeck shell.

Well, I was on my way to see old Tush after too long, and I had wind in my face like a happy dog leaning out a car window. The wake was straight. The engines ran sweetly in sync. I could feel the slow rise and fall in the imperceptible ground swell. The overcast was starting to burn off, the sea starting to glint. I could see pigmy figures over on the beach by Sea Ranch. Even with the investment in the playtoy, I still had a comforting wad of currency back in the cache aboard *The Busted Flush* at Slip F-18, Bahia Mar.

It had been a fine long hot lazy summer, a drifting time of good fish, old friends, new girls, of talk and laughter.

Cold beer, good music and a place to go.

That's the way They do you. That's the way They set you up for it. There ought to be a warning bell on the happymeter, so that every time it creeps high enough, you get that dang-dang alert. Duck, boy. That glow makes you too visible. One of Them is out there in the boonies, adjusting the windage, getting you lined up in the cross hairs of the scope. When it happens so often, wouldn't you think I'd be more ready for it?

I took my right-angle sight on a water tower just beyond Ocean Ridge, one that measures almost exactly thirty miles north of the Municipal Casino, and my elapsed time was sixty-two minutes. I wrote that down, along with fuel consumption, so I could do the math later, breaking it down in the way that to me is easiest to remember, statute miles per gallon at x rpm.

The wind was freshening and quartering into the south, and though I was still comfortable, I decided it wasn't going to last very long, so I went through Boynton Inlet into Lake Worth. The OMC's were still green enough so that too much constant speed wasn't the best thing in the world, so as soon as I had a nice open straightaway

7

up the Waterway without traffic, I pushed it up to 4,200 rpm, estimating it at about 45 miles an hour. I estimated I had fifty if I ever needed it, and hoped I'd never get in a bind where I needed it. I held her there for five or six minutes, then dropped it way back, getting it to that minimum rpm that, depending on gross weight at the time, would just hold it on the plane. It wasn't a rig I was about to take out and see if I could get to Nassau ahead of Wynne and Bertram and those people, taking those thirty-foot leaps and turning your spine into a concertina every time you smash back into the sea, pulping your kidneys and chomping your jaw into the foam rubber tooth guard. The little *Muñequita* would have had to be turned into a racing machine, with a hundred more horses in each mill, special wheels, a lot more bracing and reinforcement to keep the engines in her, and then she would not be much good for anything else.

Besides, I had been talked into trying it once. I think you could maybe argue the point that it is a little more fun than a hungover, carbuncled cowboy might have while trying to stay aboard a longhorn in a dusty rodeo, but it would be a close decision.

When I reached the bay north of Broward Beach, I had to look at the chart to see at which marker I should leave the Waterway to hit the mouth of the Shawana River. So it was ten thirty of that Tuesday morning, or a little later, when I eased up to one of the finger piers at Bannon's Boatel, put a line on a piling and cut the engines off.

I stepped high onto the pier decking and looked around. He had a dozen outboards tied up, and maybe half as many inboard-outboard rigs, two smallish cruisers, and, neatly aligned in their slips, the dozen rental houseboats, outboard rigged, fiberglass, white with orange trim. I saw that he'd put up the in-and-out storage he had told me about the last time I'd seen him, over a year and a half ago. Fifteen racks wide and three high. The forklift could tuck forty-five boats in there on monthly storage, but only the bottom row was full, and the middle layer half full.

Up the river from his place and on the other side, where it had all been marshland the last time I was there, I could see, maybe a mile away and more, some squat, pale, technical-looking buildings and a glinting of cars in the industrial parking lot next to them.

There didn't seem to be anyone around the little marina building, or around the white cement-block motel with the red tile roof that sat parallel to the river and parallel to State Road 80D, and about a hundred feet from each of them. I remember Tush talking about how he was going to expand the motel from ten units to twenty.

"Now that there's the three kids, me and Janine are taking up two units, and having just eight rentals, I couldn't tell you the times we've had to turn folks away, Trav."

The slab had been poured for the extra ten units, and the block had been laid up to shoulder-high on about three of them, but some kind of a coarse green vine had taken hold and had crawled along fifteen feet of the wall, spilling tendrils down.

Some of the dock pilings sagged. The pennons on the marina building were bleached gray, wind-ripped and tattered.

"Hey!" yelled Tush. "Hey, now! Hey, McGee!" He had come around the corner of the motel and came toward me in a kind of Percheron canter. A big man. Almost as high as I am, and half again as big around.

Long ago and far away we'd been on the same ball team. Brantley Breckenridge Bannon, second string offensive fullback. First string if he could have gotten into his stride quicker, because he was hard to stop when he was in gear. The nickname had started as BeeBee and had been shortened to Beeb, and it was that season it suddenly turned into Tush. He was a man totally incapable of profanity. The most we ever heard from him, even in the most hideous, unlucky and painful circumstances, was a mumbled "Durn!"

Then in one game we tried running a play that was designed to make up for his slow start. They set him out to the right, and on the snap he had to run to his left, go behind the quarterback who had taken some quick steps back and who had faked a handoff to a wingback slanting right, and who would then spin and stuff the ball into Bannon's belly on a half cut and an off-tackle slant left.

The first time we ran it, and I was offensive left end at the time, a linebacker thought he smelled a pass,

9

blitzed through, saw what was happening, and rolled his shoulders right into Bannon's ankles. The second time we ran it, he had a good head of steam but there was absolutely no hole at all, and as he tried to spin along the line and find one they tore him down. The third time we tried it, we were fourth and two at their eleven, so late in the game that we had to go for six points, being four points behind. He got a fine start. We got a good jump and cleared him a big hole. But as he went through the hole he was juggling that ball, hand to chin to chest to forearm to hand, too busy to keep from getting hit, and was hit from the side and the ball floated into the hands of their squatty defensive center, who after a considerable pause to realize he actually had a football right there in his hands, took off in a lumpy little grinning gallop out to their forty before he got pulled down from behind. Bannon, on his knees, ripped off his helmet, whammed it against the sod, stared skyward and yelled, "Oh . . . TUSH!"

When things went badly for him on one play in the next game, about four of us yelled, "Tush!" And Tush it became, then and forever.

After he was converted to a tackle, he stayed with an AFL team four years, during two of which, being married to Janine, he saved his money. A pinched nerve in his neck turned him into an insurance salesman and he did well but got sick of it, and then he sold houseboats, and then he bought the ten acres on the Shawana River on which to act out and work out the American Dream.

So after the obligatory thumping upon each other, our words of greeting were drowned out by an oncoming roar, deep and grinding, and three big orange Euclids went by on their six-foot tires of solid rubber, loaded high with yards of wet marl, kicking up a powdery dust that drifted north, across the palmetto and scrub pine flats on the other side of the state road. I saw then that the blacktop was gone, and the right of way widened.

"We're being improved around here," he said in sour explanation. "Everything is going to be first-class. By and by." He stared west, after the fading roar of the big earth movers. "Worries me the way they bucket through here. Janine should be on her way back from town by now, and there's some bad places where she could meet

10

up with them. She does more than her share of driving now that the school bus can't come down here."

"Why can't it?"

"They can't use roads that are officially closed, that's why." He looked toward his waterfront. "What'd you come in. You can't get the *Flush* upriver in this tide."

"Wasn't there a good deep channel?"

"Until they did a lot of dredge and fill upriver. Now the first half mile from the bay up toward me is pretty bad. They say they're going to scour it out, but they won't say when."

We walked out and I showed him the *Muñequita*. He knew that good honest T-Craft hull, the semi-V that Rodney Thompson makes in Titusville. When people from the Kansas flats get the marine fever, it is a dreadful addiction, and Tush had a bad case. He looked over the custom installation of the two dual-carb OMC's and listened to my explanation of why I'd pulled the Chrysler-Volvos the original owner installed. He was intrigued by the special engineering of the Teleflex panel and control system.

I heard myself talking too much. Things were going well for me. And the world was a little sour for my friend Tush Bannon. In repose his broad, heavy, freckly face sagged. So when it happens like that, you talk too much. The small breeze stopped, and the October forenoon heat leaned hard, in that 95°-95 humidity that makes the sweat pop out.

So we went up to the motel and sat in the kitchen alcove under the rackety-clatter of an overworked little window air-conditioner, drank beer while he said Janine was fine, the boys were fine, and we talked about who we'd heard from and who we hadn't, and who was doing what. I stood by the window with the cold can in my hand and said, "What's all the big industry over there, up river?"

"TTA," he said with a tangible bitterness. "Tech-Tex Applications. A nice clean industry, except every now and then any fool fish that comes up the Shawana turns belly-up and floats back down. And sometimes there's a funny little smell, sort of like ammonia, and the tears run down your face. But they employ four hundred people, Trav. Big tax base. They gave 'em the keys to the county to move in here."

"But I thought this county had pretty fair zoning and pollution control and all that. I mean Broward Beach is a——."

"Don't you know where you are, boy?" he asked. "You're a good mile west of that county line. You are in Shawana County, Mister McGee. A garden spot. Go right over to Sunnydale, to the County Courthouse, and ever' one of those happy, smiling five commissioners will tell you a man couldn't pick a better spot to live and raise his kids and grow with the county." He astonished me. I had never thought of Tush as being capable of irony. He was a big, amiable, beefy man, with mild blue eyes and stubbly pale lashes and brows, and a pink, peeling, permanent case of sunburn.

I heard a car drive in. He went to the window on the road side and looked out and said, "Oh . . . *no!*"

I followed him out. Janine had gotten out of the car, a very dusty pale blue sedan about two years old. At twenty paces she still had the gawky, leggy look and stance of a teen-ager. She stood in an attitude at once defiant and disconsolate, staring at the left rear corner of the car, which squatted expensively low. Their youngest, about two and a half, stood nearby, scowling, giving the intermittent snuffle of tears not long ended. Janine wore bleached khaki walking shorts and a yellow halter in a coarse fabric. The shorts were darkened with perspiration around her narrow waist. She had cropped her black hair very short. With her deep tan, and the length and strength and slender delicacy of her face, her dark eyes, she looked like a young man, Mediterranean, ready to guide you to the Roman ruins, pick your pocket, sell you fake heirlooms, send you out in a leaky gondola with his thieving cousin.

But the shape of the ears was girl, and the corners of the mouth, and the elegance of the throat, and from there on down no doubt at all, even were she clad in a loose-fitting mattress cover, no doubt whatsoever. And I knew her maiden name was Sorrensen, and she was Wisconsin Swede, and she birthed towheaded Swede kids, and so she was one of the improbabilities of genetic mathematics, of maybe one of the Scandinavian raiders who brought home from a far country a swarthy boy to be a kitchen slave.

12

Tush got down behind the car and rolled onto his back and wormed his way under it. She said, "It was just a half mile this side of the hard top. I guess the rains dug it out and then the dust drifted into it, and I swear, honey, nobody could have seen it."

He slid out. "Spring shackle."

"She *hit* me!" the little kid said. "She hit me awful hard, Pop."

"Were you going fast, Jan?" he asked her.

She stared at him. She raised a helpless arm and let it flap down. "Oh, good Christ, I was making better time than Phil Hill, laughing and singing because the world is so sweet, and I was probably all boozed up, and I was trying to break the goddamn whatever it is!"

She spun and went by me, giving me a sudden and startled glance of recognition, but too trapped then in the compulsions of the quarrel to deviate from the planned exit.

He shouted after her. "You can say hello to my friend! The least you can do is say hello to my friend!"

She walked ten more strides, shoulders rigid, and then turned at the motel doorstep and, with no expression on her face or in her voice, said, "Hello. Hello. Hello. Come on, Jimmy. Come with mother."

The kid went plodding after her. The door closed. Tush looked at me and shook his head and tried to smile. "Sorry, boy."

"For what? There are good days, medium days and bad days."

"We seem to be getting a long run of one kind."

"So, for starters let's fix it."

He ran it down to the marina shed, where the tools were. We used the forklift to raise the back end. It took two gallons of sweat apiece to punch the busted pieces out, hacksaw some bar stock, clumsy it into place and peen the ends over. We set it down and it sat level, no longer looking like a spavined duck. I stepped on the rear bumper and it didn't come back up as it should. It oscillated, good proof the shocks were nearly gone, and from the way he sighed I was sorry I'd done it.

I got fresh clothes off the boat, and Tush gave me a motel unit to shower and change in. I was just buttoning the clean shirt when Janine knocked at the door. I let her

13

in. She carried a clinking pitcher of iced tea, and her apologetic pride. She wore a little pink cotton shift and a pale pink lipstick.

She put the pitcher down, put her hand out. "Hello the right way, Travis. Like welcome. Excuse the bad scene." Her hand was long and brown and slender, and her grip surprisingly strong. She poured the two tall glasses of tea and gave me one and took hers over and sat on the bed. I counted back and realized that this would be the fifth time I had seen her. And, as before, the chemistry was slightly off, as it so often is with the friend who knew the husband before the husband met the wife. It can be a kind of jealousy, I guess, because it is a reminder of years she didn't share, and of an acceptance of the husband's friendship, which was in no way her decision. She seemed to relate to me with a flavor of challenge. Prove yourself to me, McGee. But you can't, McGee, because you aren't housebroken. Your life isn't real. You drift around and you have your fun and games. You make my husband feel wistful about the debts he has and the girls he hasn't. When you come near my nest, just by being here, you remind my man of the gaudy grasshopper years, and somehow you turn me into some kind of guard, or attendant, or burden.

With some of the wives of old friends I have been able to quench that initial antagonism. They soon find out that I am aware of what every single unwed person knows—that the world is always a little out of focus when there is no one who gives the final total damn about whether you live or die. It is the price you pay for being a rambler, and if you don't read the price tag, you are a dull one indeed.

Jan had obvious warmth. She seemed to have the empathy to realize that I meant her well. But the antagonism wouldn't melt. She could hide it pretty well. But it was there.

I toasted her with tea, saying, "That was a mere snit, Janine. One of the tizzies you get during the hot months."

"Thanks," she said, and smiled. "Tush gobbled and ran. He took over the child taxi service. Come on over in about ten minutes and I'll have a sort of a lunch."

She finished the glass of tea, then poured herself another to take with her. As she moved toward the door she shook her head slowly and sadly. "You know, I think it

14

was guilt mostly. Poor darn little Jimmy kid. What's wrong, Mom? What busted, Mom? Will it run, Mom? So I swatted him a dandy. Much too hard, without thinking. Taking it out on him." Beyond the wry smile her eyes looked wet. "I don't know what's happening to me lately. Oh, how I hate that goddamn car. That goddamn stinking car. How I hate it!"

Two

As I WAITED, sitting in the full huff of the air-conditioner, gulping down the tea, I thought of the little dreamworld called Detroit, fifteen years behind the rest of America, as usual.

Janine had nailed it. People hate their cars. Daddy doesn't come proudly home with the new one any more, and the family doesn't come racing out, yelling WOW, and the neighbors don't come over to admire it. They all look alike, for one thing. So you have to wedge a piece of bright trash atop the aerial to find your own. They may be named after predators, or primitive emotions, or astronomical objects, but in essence they are a big shiny sink down which the money swirls—in insurance, car payments, tags, tolls, tires, repairs. They give you a chance to sit in helpless rage, beating on the steering wheel in a blare of horns while, a mile away, your flight leaves the airport. They give you a good chance of dying quick, and a better chance of months of agony of torn flesh, smashed guts and splintered bones. Take it to your kindly dealer, and the service people look right through you until you grab one by the arm, and then he says: Come back a week from Tuesday. Make an appointment. Their billions of tons of excreted pollutants wither the leaves on the trees and sicken the livestock. We hate our cars, Detroit. Those of us who can possibly get along without them do so very happily. For those who can't, if there were an alternate choice, they'd grab it in a minute. We buy them reluctantly and try to make them last, and they are not friendly machines anymore. They are expensive, murderous junk, and they manage to look glassily contemptuous of the people who own them. A car is something that

15

makes you whomp your youngest kid too hard and then feel ashamed of yourself.

I had just been through the bit. My elderly Rolls pick-up, *Miss Agnes,* was as agile as ever, which meant about 40 seconds from a dead stop to sixty miles an hour. And she had the same reluctance to come to a stop once she was humming along. So she and I were slowly becoming a highway hazard, the narrow shaves getting narrower. So I had gone shopping, test driving, and found they all had fantastic acceleration, and they'd all stop on dimes, and they all bored me to hell.

So I went looking for a boat I could use as a car. I would keep *Miss Agnes* for back roads and the *Flush* for open waters, and use the *Muñequita* for errands, and if I had to have a car, there was Mr. Hertz trying hard, and Mr. Avis trying harder, and Mr. National hoping they'd run each other into the ground. Anything in Lauderdale that I wanted to buy, and I could lift, if I couldn't buy it right at Bahia Mar, I could go off in the *Muñequita* and buy it. And it was nice to poot along an urban waterway and hear the distant clashing of fenders, gnashing of bumpers, and the song of the ambulances.

Janine and I ate ham and cheese sandwiches at the breakfast bar, and every time Jimmy came stomping by, he got a couple of loving pats from his mother. I had forgotten the names of the older two boys and had to pick them up out of her conversation. Johnny and Joey. Joey was the big kid. Six. Johnny was four and a half.

I realized I hadn't seen Tyler around, the Negro who had been working for them the other times I'd been there, a tall, stringy, cheerful, ageless man, dark saffron in color, and with a scholarly face, plus an uncanny knack of diagnosing the ailments of marine engines. I asked her if it was his day off.

"Oh, Tyler quit us . . . it must be eight months ago. Tush was very upset about it. You know how good he was around here. But now . . . it's just as well, I guess, because we couldn't afford to pay him anyway, the way things are."

"On account of the road?"

"And a lot of other things."

"Such as?"

"I think if Tush wants you to hear the tale of woe, he better be the one to tell you. But I'll tell you one thing, Travis McGee!" Her eyes narrowed, and she thumped her fist on the formica counter top. "We are *not* going to be run off this place!"

"Is somebody trying?"

"You'd best talk to Tush about it."

"Can you get a sitter for tonight?"

"Huh?"

"Wear your pretties and the three of us will go run-abouting into Broward Beach and track down some booze and some meat and come home late, singing all the way."

Her narrow face lighted up. "I would *love* it!"

And when Tush got back with the other two towheads, he approved. The sitter was handy. Jan explained they had made a special rate on a houseboat rental to a couple. Young kids. About twenty-one years old. They were in the houseboat where the old yellow station wagon was parked. There was a retired couple in the one on the far end. Those were the only two rented at the moment.

"Arlie and Roger Denn, their names are," Janine explained. "They're a little on the weird side. Sort of untidy-looking. He makes little funny figurine things and he makes shell jewelry. She does handweaving and she paints these insipid little seascapes, and when they have enough, they fill up the station wagon and go around and sell them to gift shops. Sometimes it takes two days, and sometimes it takes a week."

Arlie Denn arrived for sitter duty right on time, and I could agree about the untidy part. She was a soft, doughy, pallid girl with a long tangle of dark blonde hair, wide, empty, indifferent blue eyes, a little sing-song voice and a mouth that hung open. She wore a man's white shirt, dirty. Pale blue denim walking shorts, ditto. Bare feet, also dirty. I could see why Janine had fed the kids before we left.

Once I had the little boat away from the dock, I turned it over to Tush. And with the sun lowering behind us, we skimmed down the long, broad curves of the Shawana River, past the mangrove and the white herons, and out into the big bay where, corny as any postcard, a ketch was moving northward up the Waterway, sun turning the sails orange, while a ragged flight of pelicans passed diagonally in front of her, heading for the rookery, pumping then soaring, taking the cue from the flight leader.

With his big paw on the twin throttles Tush raised a questioning eyebrow, and I made a shoving motion with the heel of my hand. Janine sat on a life cushion on the transom engine hatch, in her pretty yellow dress, her short black hair snapping in the wind, her face alight with the pleasure of speed and change and the rush of the soft evening air after the heat of the day.

At the city marina Tush slowed and we went up the channel and under the bridge, and along the bay side of the beaches. I took it into a place called Beach Marine, where the man said nobody would mess with it. We walked three blocks to a good place I knew. Thirty feet from the restaurant entrance Jan balanced herself with one hand on Tush's big shoulder while she changed from the zoris to the high-heeled shoes she was carrying in her straw purse.

The drinks were good, the steaks were good, the evening was almost good. Every marriage at one time or another is going to run through some heavy weather. Heavy weather comes in all kinds of flavors. Slowly going broke, slowly losing the whole stake instead of making it like you thought you would—that can erode the happiest of hearts. With the two of them it wasn't a continuous thing. It just kept cropping up now and again, and clouding the fun and games.

There was just enough said for me to see the shape of the running quarrel, or argument, or regret. Over a year ago, when they had a chance to pull out, when they had a buyer for the place, Jan had wanted to take the loss and get out. Only about a ten-percent loss on what they'd put into it, but that didn't count all the hours of their brute labor. But he'd insisted it was just a run of bad luck. Nobody was really trying to stack the cards against them. Things would get better. Things always got better.

Except when they get worse.

Tush didn't want to talk about it at all. To him it was like whining. He would let it go just so far, and then he would reach out, grab the conversational ball, and throw it the hell into center field.

But they seemed to have a good time, on average. Maybe a better time than in many months. It was overcast, and there was pink lightning on three sides of us when we went hurrying back across the bay. Tush picked up the markers for me with the hand-held spotlight, with its 45,000 candles and its narrow one-mile beam. We got the boat tied up and the first fat drops were speckling the dust as we made it to the motel. The rain roar was coming. The fat sitter went cantering and bobbling off to her rented houseboat.

Maybe three inches came down in the hour we sat at the Bannon's breakfast bar and drank kitchen whisky and told lies.

Back in my borrowed motel unit, after starting to get ready for bed, I decided I'd better check the *Muñequita* and see if the automatic bilge pump had handled the heavy rain and turned off, as promised. The air was washed clean, and the hungry mosquitoes hadn't begun to roam. The wind was rain-fresh, and from the west. The boat was fine, and, as I turned, the bulk of Tush Bannon standing in the night startled me.

"I miss the sound of that old hump-back bridge when the wind's from upriver," he said. "Not much traffic over it, but the timbers would rumble. You get so you don't even hear a sound like that, and then you miss it after it's gone."

"They put a new one there?"

He sighed. "Not there. Three miles further upriver. That hurts. It lost me most of the business I was getting from the people that live on the other side. TTA wanted it taken out. They wanted the road to it officially abandoned. We went to the Public Hearing and made a lot of noise, but what TTA wants from this county, TTA gets."

"Tush, if you need any help hanging on here until things pick up . . ."

"Forget it. Thanks, but forget it. It would just take that much longer to run down the drain."

"Is it all going to go?"

"Probably."

"Can you sell?"

"Sell what? Our equity? Go ask the bank what they think our equity is." He yawned. "Hell, I can always get a pretty good job selling. I can sell pretty good. Trouble is, I hate the work. 'Night, McGee. And thanks again. It was a good evening. It helped. We needed it bad."

I left the next morning. And that was in October, and I kept thinking about them and wondering about them, but I didn't do anything about it. I didn't run up there again. I wish I had. There are a lot of things in this life I wish I'd done, and a pretty gamey collection of things I wish I hadn't done—but the things you don't do leave the remorses around a little longer somehow.

The last time I saw Tush Bannon alive was the weekend before Christmas, late on a Saturday afternoon. It was by the kind of accident so unlikely, one has the temptation to call it fate. My friend Mick Coseen was awaiting a very important phone call from Madrid, and he had given my phone number aboard *The Busted Flush.* So when it was delayed, he asked me if I'd take his car and run down to the Miami International and pick up his date, Barni Baker, a Pan-Am stewardess due in from Rio for a Miami layover. As I was the only other one in the group who knew her by sight, it was more efficient for me to go down.

For company I toted Puss Killian along in Mick's rental convertible. It was a cool, bright day, and the time of year when the gold coast is as empty as it ever gets. Nervous little men who own points in the big beach hotels brood about their fifth mortgages, and the retailers give fervent thanks that the Christmas pressure on the locals makes up for the lack of snowbird money. Puss is a big, stately, random redhead, a master of the put-on and the cop-out, who believes the world is mad, so she is the best of companions if you can keep up with the slants and shifts of her conversation, and merely irritating and confusing if you can't. A little herd was assembling, and it was shaping up party time.

We put the car in the lot and went in and checked the board, and the man said that 955 was just touching down. After the passengers had been herded off and aimed in the right direction, Barni, with her peer group, came brisk-clicking along, button-big, button-bright, a little candy-package blonde with eyes of widest innocent blue, eyes casting right and left, searching for Mick, finding me as I moved to intercept her. Big smile, gracious and wary acknowledgement of the introduction to Puss. I told her about Mick and his call, about an independent wanting somebody to take over the camera crew because

20

their chief cameraman had racked himself up on a bicycle in Madrid traffic, and Barni Baker said to give her fifteen minutes, and I said we would be up at the bar on top of the International, and she said just fine and went tap-tapping away, moving firm and well in her uniform.

In the big blue windowed room high in the air, the cocktail business was still thin, because of the hour, and a familiar face was working the quiet and elegant bar, and he remembered The Drink, and seemed so pleased with himself in remembering, that we each had one, sitting and watching the deftness with silent and respectful attention. Two ample old-fashioned glasses, side by side, filled to the two thirds line with cracked ice. A big, unmeasured slosh of dry sherry into each glass. Then swiftly, the strainer placed across the top of one and then the other, as with a delicate snap of the wrist he dumped the sherry down the drain. Then fill to the ice level with Plymouth gin, rub the lemon peel around the inside of the rim, pinch some little floating beads of citrus oil on the surface of the drink, throw away the peel, present with small tidy bow and flourish to the folk. "Two McGees," said he.

"Thank you, Harold," I said.

He had two new customers and when he moved away, Puss hoisted her glass, tinked it against mine. "The instant drink," she said. "Instant stupidity, or instant rape, or instant permission. Me, what I get is this instant numbness around the chops. Here's to flying quail."

"To what?"

"To stewardesses! You're slow today, lover. You're not relating now and again."

"It's just that I was looking at you. Then I don't hear so well." And looking by chance beyond her, I saw Tush Bannon sitting at a deuce against the wall, the shoulder bulk hunched toward a still-faced girl who sat across from him. She had long, straight auburn-brown hair, a pouty, impassive little face. She seemed to be listening to him with a thoughtful intentness, and she bit at the heavy bulge of her underlip and closed her eyes and slowly shook her head in a prolonged No.

That is not the point where one goes ambling over to the old buddy and whacks him on the shoulder and asks how Janine is. It was a private conversation, so private and intense they seemed to be inside an overturned bowl of thinnest glass, almost visible.

"Know them?" Puss asked.

"Just him."

"I'd say he's going to get called out on strikes. He's lost his cool. The hard sell makes a gal nervous these days."

"Hey!" said Barni Baker, and put her overnight case down and climbed up onto the stool on my right. She wore a little pale green sleeveless blouse with a high collar, a darker green short skirt, and she had little gold ladybugs in her pierced ears, and she wanted a bourbon sour.

Puss leaned forward and spoke across me, saying, "Gad, it must be the most marvelous, exciting, romantic thing in the world, jetting around to marvelously romantic places! It's really living, I bet. Those fascinating pilot types, and mysterious international travelers and all. I guess you realize how jealous of you all we earthbound females are, Barni."

There was just the slightest narrowing of Barni's eyes, gone in an instant. She leaned in from her side and said breathlessly, "Oh, yes! It's all my dreams come true, Miss Killian. To fly to all the lovely places in the world." She sighed and shook her pretty little head. "But it seems so . . . so *artificial* somehow to have to use an airplane, don't you think? But with my little broom, I can just barely get above the treetops. Have you had better luck?"

"I think having to carry that damned cat makes the difference," said Puss without hesitation. "And wear that stupid hat and the long skirts."

"And it's hard to enjoy the moonlight when you have to keep up that dreary cackling, don't you think?" Barni asked.

Tush came up behind me and said, "Talk to you a minute, Trav?" He turned and walked away before I could introduce him. The gals did not notice. I excused myself and followed Tush. Barni Baker moved over onto my stool. As I went out into the corridor, before the glass door swung shut, I heard the contralto bark of one of Puss's better laughs, in counterpoint with a silvery yet somehow earthy yelp from Barni. Knife-fighting among the females can spoil party time, and it was nice to know that this pair would get along.

I went with Tush past the elevators to the empty men's room.

"I would have said hello, but you had a friend."

"Friend! With friends like that, who needs, and so forth. She left. Look, I haven't got much time. I've left Jan alone with the kids for three days and I want to get back. She said a year ago there was a pattern in this whole thing and we should get out, but I wouldn't believe her. Okay. I believe her now. It's a business deal. A land development deal. And we got in the way."

He was as big as ever, but his face looked oddly shrunken. His big hands were shaky. His eyes had a starey look, somewhat like the eyes of people who wear glasses when they have their glasses off.

He tried to laugh. "I thought somebody wanted my marina. So I used money I couldn't spare to get a local lawyer to see what he could find out. Young guy. Steve Besseker. I thought maybe he was the only lawyer in Sunnydale who wouldn't scare. I told him everything that had happened to me, and he agreed it couldn't be coincidence. So he nosed around. Nobody wants the marina, Trav. They want to put together a parcel of four hundred and eighty acres. And my little ten acres is right in the middle of all that riverfront land they want."

"They?"

"All that area is zoned as an industrial park ever since Tech-Tex came in, across the river. Big high lines come in with all the power anybody would need. They're going to dredge the river and the channel so barges can come in from the Waterway. Some big corporation wants to come in, apparently, and they'd pay a nice price for the land."

"So who's putting it together?"

"A local real estate man named Preston LaFrance owns the fifty acres right behind me. Besseker found out La-France has an option on the two hundred acres just east of me, at a price of two hundred dollars an acre. It's owned by an old boy named D. J. Carbee, an early settler. On the other side of me, to the west, there's two hundred and twenty acres owned by something called Southway Lands, Incorporated. Besseker found out that

Southway is one of Gary Santo's operations. Do you know him?"

"I know *of* him. Like everybody else in south Florida." A few years ago Santo had been the dramatic young swinger, with the touch of gold. Now he is the not-so-young swinger, moving in mysterious ways behind many scenes, behind barriers of privacy and money. The name in Miami has the flavor of penthouses, pipelines, South American playmates, mergers and acquisitions, private jets, and well-publicized donations to local drives in the art and culture areas.

"I don't know the exact relationship between Santo and Preston LaFrance, Trav. Maybe LaFrance is just acting as Santo's agent. Maybe it's a joint venture. Bessecker heard a rumor that the plant location experts nosed around the area a year and a half ago and recommended that the big company that wants it could go as high as eight hundred thousand! Seventeen hundred dollars an acre. About the time I learned all this, an old friend came out and told me he couldn't help it, and didn't want to do it, but he had to pick up the houseboats. I still owed on them. He told me that one of the Shawana County Commissioners, Mr. P. K. Hazzard—they call him Monk Hazzard—had hinted that if my friend repossessed his houseboats, he'd get a favorable ruling on a zoning application. So when I told that to Besseker, he said that Monk Hazzard was Preston LaFrance's brother-in-law, and there wasn't any way to prove a thing. He acted funny. He said he had a lot of things coming up and he couldn't promise to give me any more time. They'd gotten to him too, I guess. He has to make a living there."

"All just folks," I said.

He stared at the paper towel rack. He shook his head. "You know my style, Trav. I don't like all this round-and-about stuff. Direct confrontation. I'd seen Hazzard at a couple of those public hearings where they'd messed me up, like about taking that bridge out, but I hadn't talked to him. So I tried to make an appointment and he kept stalling, and finally I took Jan with me and we sat there outside his office until finally he saw us. Smallish man, with a long neck and a little bit of a round head, and big goggly eyes behind his thick glasses. Face sort of like a monkey, and a squeaky voice. I said we were

24

citizens and taxpayers and landowners, and he was a public official, and it was his ethical and moral duty to see that the machinery of government wasn't used to shove me into bankruptcy so his brother-in-law could make a few bucks. You know about humiliation, Trav?"

"I keep getting a little every once in a while."

"He strutted around and he squeaked and lectured. Folks come down from the north and think it's easy to make a living in Florida. Toughest place in the world. He wouldn't look at me. He looked out the window part of the time, and at Jan's legs the rest of the time. He said it wasn't the job of local government to save a man from his own mistakes and bad judgment. He said that the greatest good for the greatest number meant the best possible land use, and maybe a marina wasn't the best use when you think of the tax base and employment and so on. He said he'd overlook the slur on his honesty because a man in trouble says things he doesn't mean. He said people just don't know how much talent it takes to run a small business, and I'd probably be happier in some other line of work. He said that he didn't know whether Press LaFrance was interested in my ten acres or not, but maybe if I could talk to him he might make me an offer, but I shouldn't expect too much because the business was in bad shape. He said that people in trouble get to thinking the whole world is against them, and just because certain necessary county improvements were hurting my business, it didn't mean it was done on purpose. He said thousands of little businesses go broke every year in Florida, and I shouldn't think I was an exception. So we left and Jan was crying before we got to the car. Humiliation and frustration."

"You're bucking the power structure, Tush. You can't hardly win."

"I thought I could. When I saw LaFrance, I went along. He gave me the same line, as if they'd rehearsed it. I told him to make an offer. He said he wasn't interested. He said maybe if it came on the market later on, he might make an offer on a foreclosure price, but he didn't think it was worth the mortgage balance. A little over sixty thousand, that is. And we put fifty-one thousand in it. So I had to open my big mouth. I leaned across his desk and told him he was never going to get his hands on my

25

property. I'd leave Jan there to run it and go back to sales work, and put every dime I could spare against that mortgage. So they squeezed a little harder."

"How?"

"First they extended that road contract another hundred days. Then they sent out inspectors from the County Bureau of Services, and they condemned my wiring, and the septic tank drain fields, and my well, and lifted my license to do business. With the license gone, the bank said I come up with the whole amount of the mortgage in thirty days or they foreclose. It's way past due. We did well for a while there, Trav. I didn't overextend. If they'd left me alone, I had enough business to pay for the boat storage rack and the motel enlargement. We were going to have one of the best little operations in that whole area. I tried to see Commissioner Hazzard again. I waited and a couple of sheriff's deputies showed up and said I could either leave or get picked up for loitering. So Jan and I talked it over and decided the best thing to do would be lay it all out for Mr. Gary Santo. We decided he was probably big enough so that he didn't even know what was going on up there, and would tell them to put a stop to it if he did know. We decided that probably LaFrance just got too eager to do a big job for Santo and do it as cheap as possible. I put it all down on paper. I guess that between us we must have rewritten that letter about nine times, and Janine typed it on the old machine in the motel office, and we sent it down here Special Delivery, marked personal."

"Any answer?"

"Verbal. From that girl I was sitting with. Her name is Mary Smith. I came down and tried to get to Santo. She was as far as I got. She said she'd meet me out here, because she had to catch a flight. Cold as a meat locker, boy. Yes, Mr. Santo had read my letter personally. Yes, he had an informal agreement with Mr. LaFrance. But Mr. LaFrance is not employed by Mr. Santo. Yes, Mr. France is under considerable pressure by Mr. Santo to produce the results promised insofar as land acquisition is concerned. Mr. Santo feels no personal responsibility for your plight. He is not running a charitable organization. I wanted to know if I could see him in person. No. Sorry. But no."

26

"Now what?"

"We lose it. That's all. The grace period is about gone. Janine is taking it hard. It's a lot of money and work and time down the drain, and nothing to show for it. I . . . I wish I'd come to you sooner, Trav, before it got to be too late. Maybe you could have figured out some kind of a salvage operation. Your kind of salvage. Squeeze them like they've squoze me." He gave me a strange, puzzled, thoughtful look. "You know, I keep thinking about how I might kill somebody. Hazzard, Santo, LaFrance. Somebody. Anybody. I never thought that way in my life before. I'm not like that."

He grimaced, whirled, kicked the big metal trash basket full of used paper towels. "Aaaah . . . Tush!" he yelled, and went blundering out.

I collected Puss and Barni. It was after six thirty when we got back to *The Busted Flush*. Mick had gotten his phone call, made his deal, and set up a Monday morning flight to Spain via New York. And so, though my mood was somewhat soured, there was song and sport, sunburn and music, beach time and nap time, old and new jokes, girls in the galley, new tapes on the music machine, lipstick and sand and the sometime kiss, and the long heavy look through curl of lashes.

Meyer trooped in and out from time to time with little groups of Meyer's Irregulars and Partisans. We had a slight overflow from the permanent floating houseparty aboard the Alabama Tiger's big cruiser.

Though it looked as it always looks—so informal you don't know who is tied up with whom—there is a protocol. There is a very real in-group unwritten list of things you do and things you don't do, things you say and things you don't say. And if you are the kind of person who can't case the scene and know by instinct what the rules have to be, then the blinds are closed, shades drawn, and the freeze is on. But sometimes, as in the case of one midday visitor on Sunday, someone is so obtuse the action has to be a little more direct.

This one was named Buster or Buddy or Sonny, one of those names, a big loud thirtyish jollyboy type, office-soft, overconfident, far from home on a business trip and out beagling for a broad, confident that he was twice the man any of these beach-bum types could be, ready for a nice little roll and scuffle that he could describe to the other JC's back in God's Country, and hide from li'l ol' Peggy staying back home there with the kids.

So he came up onto the sun deck and sprawled out next to Barni and told her she was cute as any bug in the wide world, and if she would just let him spread a little more of this here suntan juice on that cute little ol' back and this here cute little ol' tummy, why she'd be making him the happiest paper salesman in the southeast territory.

She sat up and frowned into his dumb, happy, smirking face, and as Mick started to get up to heave Buster-Buddy-Sonny over the rail she waved him back. "Music down and out," she said. Puss went to the speakers and turned the volume off.

In the silence Barni said, with a brutal clarity, "Puss? Marilee? Come here, dears. Come take a look at this one."

They came and sat close to her on her sun pad, all of them staring at Buster-Buddy-Sonny. "The type I was telling you about," Barni said. "One of the charmers that make life hell for a stewardess."

"Now, don't you badmouth me, you purty thing," he said, grinning.

Puss said, scowling, "I see. Of course. All that fatty look around the middle. And that big voice and those dim, nasty little eyes."

"You funning me, you gals?" he asked, his smile fading a little.

Marilee tilted her head. "Mmmm. The kind you don't dare turn your back on when you're on duty. A real snatch-ass Charlie."

"They have this crazy dream, I guess," Barni said, "about how you're going to fall for all that meaty charm and go back to their hotel or motel and climb right into the sack. Can you imagine?"

Puss shuddered delicately. "My God, darlings, suppose we were call girls or something and we *had* to sleep with one of those."

"Ekk!" said Marilee.

Buster-Buddy-Sonny stood up and the three lovelies looked blandly up at him.

"Coffee, tea or milk?" asked Barni.

"You lousy little bitch!" said he.

Puss laughed. "See? Just like you said, dear. Typical

reaction. Look at how red his face is! Let me guess. He'll be bald in five years."

"Four," said Marilee firmly.

"He needs glasses already and won't wear them," said Barni.

"He's going to grow an enormous belly," Puss said.

"And fall over dead of a massive coronary occlusion when he's forty-five."

"And when he falls over, it will bust his cigar and spill his bourbon."

"And some sorry wretched woman is married to him."

Barni shook her head. "No girl who ever spent any time as a stewardess would ever marry one of those. Look at that mouth on it! Imagine having to actually kiss something like that and pretend you were enjoying it!"

"And look at the dirty fingernails, will you!"

When Buster-Buddy-Sonny reappeared in view, he was eighty feet up the dock, walking briskly and not swinging his arms at all.

"You girls need your mouths washed out with gin," Mick said. "That was naughty."

"A little friendly castration never hurt anybody," said Marilee.

"Besides," said Puss, "we didn't touch on his *really* filthy habit. Given half a chance, do you know what that dreary bastard might do?"

Marilee, with a dirty chuckle, leaned close to Puss and whispered to her. Puss shook her head and said, "Congratulations, sweetie. You must be leading a full life. But I meant something much worse than that."

"Like what?" Barni asked, puzzled.

"If you were ever stupid enough to let him get just a little bit past first base, that utter spook would stare right into your eyes and he would kind of gulp and look like a kicked dog and his voice would quiver and he'd say, 'Darlin', I love you.' "

"He would! He would indeed!" cried Marilee. "The lowest of the low. He's the *perfect* type for it. A real rat-fink coward."

Meyer came out of a long and somber contemplation, hunched like a hirsute Buddha, reached a slow ape arm and picked up his queen's bishop and plonked it down in what at first glance seemed like an idiotic place, right next to my center pawn. A round little lady who was one of his retinue that week, beamed, clapped her hands and rattled off a long comment in German.

"She says you give up now," said Meyer.

"Never!" said I. I studied and studied and studied. Finally I put a knuckle against my king and tipped the poor fellow over and said, "Beach-walking, anyone?"

But before Puss and I went over, I tried once again to reach Tush Bannon at his Boatel by phone. Once again there was no answer. I felt irritation and depression. And, perhaps, the first little needles of alarm.

Three

I AWAKENED AT six thirty Monday morning thinking about Tush and his problem. If I hadn't awakened with that idea in mind, I could have gone back to sleep. But it snapped my eyelids up and held them there. And big as the bed was, the custom job that had been aboard the *Flush* when I won her in Palm Beach, Puss Killian had left me in precarious balance on the edge. She was curled, her back to me, and there was a solid and immovable feel to the warm and shapely rear that pressed against the side of my hip. She was deeply recharging all her redheaded batteries, in the deep, slow intake and humming exhalation of sleep of the heaviest and best kind.

So I gave up and got up and showered and came back, and tried to quietly get into a white sports shirt and khaki slacks. But in the muted light as I shoved my arm through the short sleeve I knocked a nightcap glass off the shelf and it smashed on the deck.

She rolled, rose up slowly, glowered indignantly at me and settled back down into her sleep, nestling onto her other side, a long, tangled tassle of red hair falling across her cheek and mouth, stirring with each breath.

I heard furtive galley sounds and found Barni Baker in a hip-length yellow robe, her hair in a kerchief, doing something to eggs. Her eyebrows went up when she saw me, and she whispered, "You too! What's *your* excuse? Don't answer. It's rhetorical. It's criminal to have to talk in the morning. I found this here good-looking roe and these here good-looking eggs, and what smells like good Herkimer County cheese, and if you want me to double the portion, just nod."

I nodded. I poured us some juice. She had the water on. I dumped the Columbian fine grind into the Benz filter paper and slid into the booth. She stared at me as I tried the egg invention. The question was in the lift of a little blonde eyebrow. The response was the circle of thumb and forefinger. When she started to tidy up, I told her to leave it until later, and I carried our coffee seconds in the white porcelain pot topsides, and she brought along the mugs.

The morning was almost cold. I dug a blanket out of the forward locker for her to use as a lap robe over her bare legs, and I put on an old gray cardigan I've had for seven hundred years. It could now be classified as a missionary barrel reject.

"I think we could have practiced on the snare drum and tuba down there without bothering those two," I said.

"Mick needs all the sleep he can get. We'll have to leave by ten o'clock to make that flight. They're going to work him to death when he gets to Spain. The picture is behind schedule."

"When do you have to go back to work?"

"Tuesday noon."

"So come back."

"Thanks, but I don't think so. I think I'll turn the car in and hole up and try to do some thinking. You make damned good coffee, Trav. How good is your advice? Like to the lovelorn?"

"The best. But nobody ever takes it."

"So here is a hypothetical case about two loners, about this little ball of fluff who is an airline stewardess who is twenty-seven all too soon, and likes to be where the action is, but lately she wonders if the action isn't getting to be all alike. And there is this very special and talented guy who is a cinematographer, and who is a tough and skeptical thirty-two, who is gun-shy from a sour marriage, and who gets so hooked on his work he can't remember the stewardess's name, practically. And they are together maybe five times a year, maybe five days a time, and it is always the rightest of the right. The workingest of ever,

31

even though they keep telling themselves and each other that it is going to wear off any minute now. So last time the camera guy wanted to marry the airline girl and she said hell no, so she thought about it a lot, and this time she brought it up and said okay and he said hell no, because he was hurt because she said no the last time. Can these two darling kids find happiness, McGee?"

"You get married when there is no other conceivable course of action, Barni-baby. You get married because you are both compelled to marry each other."

"Indeed?"

"Don't get frosty. I'm not putting down your romance. It will either get inevitable or it won't. It won't hang where it is. It will get bigger, or it will start to dry up, and either way it goes will be the right answer at that time. Don't get pushy."

After a long silence she said, "Anyway, the coffee *is* good." She shrugged. "Change of subject. This Puss Killian of yours. I *like* her, Trav. I like her a lot. But there's a funny thing about her. You think she's telling you all about herself, and afterward you know she hasn't really told you a thing. What about her, anyway?"

"I wouldn't know. Don't look at me like that. I've known her for four months. She goes away for a couple of days every few weeks. I could do some digging. But it's up to her. When and if she wants to talk, she can talk. I know that she's from Seattle, that she isn't hurting for money, that she's twenty-four or five, that she shed a husband not long before she showed up here, that I met her on the beach only because she stepped on a sea urchin and was cursing billy blue blazes and ordered me to come over and do something about it right now. I know she has enough energy for three stevedores, that she can eat three pounds of steak at a sitting, that she can hold her booze, and she would walk up and spit in a tiger's eye if she thought it would liven up the idle hour. And I know that once in a while she goes absolutely dead silent, and all she wants is for you to pretend she isn't there."

"She has a very soft look for you, Travis. When you're not looking at her."

"Troublemaker!"

I tried again and couldn't get an answer out of Tush. I had the long distance operator run a check on the phone up there, but it was reported in order. At a little after nine I thought I'd better see if Puss wanted to say her good-bye in person or let me relay it. I went in and sat gently on the bed. She was breathing faster. Her hand and arm were twitching as she dreamed, and she made a little whimpering sound. I gently thumbed the red hair back away from her face and saw a wetness of tears leaking out of the closed lids.

I put my hand on her bare shoulder and gave her a little shake. "Hey," I said. "It's not all *that* bad, is it?"

She opened wide blind eyes and snuffled and said in a little-girl voice, "But they keep saying . . ." She shook herself like a wet red setter. She focused on me, snuffled again, smiled and said, "Thanks, pal. They were about to cut me off at the pass. Whassa time?"

"Nine fifteen."

"Hmmm. If I'm reading you, McGee, I admire your thinking. It's very good. Stay right where you are while I go brush my teeth first."

"Mick and Barni are taking off in a half hour. I wondered if you wanted to wave bye-bye."

She gave a leonine stretching yawn. "Yes I do indeed. And if you had any sense at all, you big brown knuckly idiot, you'd have come smirking in here at quarter of, not quarter after. Haste makes waste, and what I have is not to be wasted, lad. So set your little clock for siesta time."

"At siesta time we're going to be up in Shawana County visiting some old friends of mine with a problem."

"Really?" She sat up, holding the sheet to her breasts. "Hmm. Then hustle the lady some coffee while she showers. And set your clock ahead."

". . . on location like that," Mick was saying, "It's the time lag that drives you nuts, not getting to see rushes, and see how the color values stand up until you're three days or four past that particular point."

And from the giant shower stall, above the sound of sloshing like unto that which a small walrus herd might make, the three of us could hear Puss in good voice: "With 'er 'ead tooked oonderneath 'er arm, she 'awnts

33

the bloody tow'r. With 'er 'ead tooked oonderneath 'er arm at the midnight hour."

"So I turned around," said Barni Baker, "and there was that sweet little old man yanking away at the lever on the cabin door thinking it was how you get into the men's room, and we're at twenty-eight thousand feet over the Amazon basin. So I got to him at a dead run and steered him gently where he wanted to go. Then he came out and stared at the cabin door and the big lever and rolled his eyes up and fainted dead away. A passenger helped me get him back to his seat and I gave him smelling salts and then I explained to him how the doors are designed so the pressurization clamps them shut so tightly ten men couldn't open them. But he just kept shaking his head and saying O Dear God."

Puss appeared just in time, wearing her big white wooly robe and carrying the half cup of coffee left from what I had taken her as she was stepping into the shower. The ends of her red hair were damp. She gathered little Barni into the big white wooly arms, hugged her, smacked her on the cheek, and told her she was all doll. We went out the aft door of the lounge and waved them off, and watched them get into the car and drive away.

"Nice ones," said Puss. "For such a raunchy old beach bum, you know a lot of nice ones. Like me, for example. I was nice enough to leave our coffee and my cigarettes right beside the bed." She went over to the phone and switched it off. She went frowning to the record bin, made a thoughtful selection of two and held up the sleeves so I could see what she had picked. George Van Eps guitar, and the Modern Jazz Quartet on Blues at Carnegie Hall. I took them from her, put them on the changer, fixed the volume where she said she liked it.

"Coming, dear?" she said with an excessive primness, and just inside the door of the master stateroom I had to step over the wooly whiteness of the robe on the deck just beyond the sill.

The day had warmed up. The *Muñequita* had run handsomely, with a deep drone speaking of a lot more power in reserve. When we had anchored for lunch in Fort Worth, well away from the channel, while we ate the thick roast beef and raw onion sandwiches and shared

34

an icy bottle of dry red supermarket wine, I briefed her on Tush, on how long I had known him, and on Janine and what Tush had told me of his problems.

"No answer at all on the phone?"

"Not a thing."

"Seems odd."

"Seems very damned odd, Puss. The thing is, he isn't a devious guy. And he's caught in the middle in a very devious situation, with large money hanging on it, and old Tush may try to bull his way through, and he could get hurt twice as bad."

When we went up the Shawana River, there was a faint, drifting acrid stink. Our eyes watered. When I came around the last bend, I was shocked at the deserted look of the place. The cheerful white houseboats were all gone. All but one storage rack on the in-and-out boat shelter were empty, and the remaining boat was, at a hundred feet, worth perhaps fifty dollars, outboard motor and all. The moored boats were gone, except for a skiff so full of water there were only inches of freeboard left, and an old cruiser hulk that had sunk in the shallows. The fork-lift truck was gone.

I tied up and we went ashore. Near the cities, all the old highways of America pass businesses that have gone broke. End of the dream. The spoor of a broken marriage can be kept in a couple of cartons on a shelf in the garage. Broken lives can be tucked neatly away in graves and jails and sanitariums. But the dead business in a sub-marginal commercial strip stays right there, ugly and moldering away, the frantic advertising signs of the final convulsive effort fading and tattering over the weeds. For every one of them was the big dream, the gala opening, the last dusting and arranging before the doors opened. "We're going to make it big, honey. Real big." Then there is the slow slide into doubt, into confusion, and into the terminal despair. "So we were going to make it real big, were we? Ha!"

It was a silent place. The acrid river slid by. Dry fronds rattled in the breeze. A sign creaked.

Even the two marine gas pumps were gone. I went to the marina shed. The tools were gone. We asked each other questions in low, graveyard voices. There was a shiny new hasp and padlock on the marina building, along with a printed notification from the County Sheriff's Department. There was another on the motel office. I could find no note fastened to anything that told how to get in touch with the Bannons.

"Now what?" Puss asked.

"There's no neighbors, nobody here to ask. I suppose we could run upriver until we come to something."

She stared around. "Gives me the spooks," she said. We'd just reached the dock when I heard a car coming. We went back around in front and saw the phone company service truck lurching over the torn-up road. As I moved to wave him down, he turned in and stopped and got out and stared at us as we approached. He looked to be about fifty, a squatty, leathery man wearing silver-rimmed glasses.

"I'd like to find Mr. Bannon," I said.

"Why?" It was a very flat and very abrupt question, and there was something about the flavor of it that made me wary. So I reached into the old bag of tired tricks and pulled out the one labeled Real Cordial.

"Well, it's like this. Quite a while back, I can't remember how many weeks, I had a bilge pump acting up, and I stopped in here and Bannon pulled it and stuck in a loaner, the idea being he'd fix it if he could or sell me the loaner if he couldn't, but I didn't get back as soon as I thought. Now it looks like he's gone out of business or moved someplace else."

"You could say that. Yes. It surely does. Let me make the disconnect and check in first, then maybe I can tell you what happened."

He donned harness and spurs with practiced ease and walked up the pole. He made his service disconnect at the lead-in terminals, clipped his handset onto the wires and called in. We could hear his voice but not what he was saying. He came down fast, showing off a little. He took off his gear and tossed it into the truck.

"Well, sir," he said, "you got here yesterday morning, you'd had some excitement for sure. You'da found Bannon right here. Promised myself I'd take a look and see where it was they found him. Maybe you'd like to come take a look, mister. Maybe the young lady should kind of wait on us."

But Puss tagged along. He went around in back and looked around, grunted and went over to a sturdy and rusty tripod made of heavy pipe, standing about fifteen feet tall. There was a manual winch with a crank, as rusty as the pipe, and a wire cable that went from the winch drum up through a pulley at the top of the tripod. A big, heavy old marine deisel, cannibalized down to little more than the ponderous block, hung from the taut cable about five feet off the ground.

The phone man sat on his heels and shook his head and said, "Sure a terrible way for a man to do himself. Look there! There's still hair and mess on the bottom side a that engine."

I had thought the stain on the packed oily dirt was merely more oil. Puss went trotting busily away about fifty feet. She stopped and bent forward and coughed shallowly a few times, then straightened up and went over and sat on a sawhorse with her back to us.

"What Freddy said this Bannon done—Freddy is one of Sheriff Bunny Burgoon's deputies and Freddy is the one that found him Sunday morning—this Bannon must have cranked that block up as high as he could get it, and then he fastened a piece of stove wire to that ratchet there on the side of the drum and lay out on his back right under that thing and give the wire a yank. The wire was still wound around his hand. Mashed him something terrible they say." He stood up, spat. "Well, you got to say one thing. It was quick and it was for certain. And I guess the poor fella didn't have much to live for."

"Because he went broke?"

"Maybe I don't have the straight of it. You know how people get to talking and every time they tell something, it comes out different. What I hear, he went off to try to raise some money fast to save the business. So when they come out here Friday with all the eviction papers and bankrupt papers and so on, just his missus is here with the youngest. She wanted them to hold off until Bannon got back, but all the legal steps had been took care of in proper order, and there was just no choice about it. They waited about an hour for her to pack up personal stuff and they helped her load the car. They say she was crying but she wasn't carrying on. She was crying without making any noise about it. She picked up the other two kids

37

from school, and she left off Bannon's suitcase and a note from her to him with the Sherf, and she just took off. She must have had some travel money saved out, because they say that yesterday after they toted Bannon's body back to Ingledine's Funeral Home, Sherf Burgoon opened that note to see where he could get in touch with her to tell her about her husband, but all it said was she was going to go stay with some girl's first name for a while, and Bannon would have known the whole name, but nobody else does."

He spat again and started to move toward his truck. I walked slowly with him and said, "He seemed like a bright, pleasant guy. He didn't seem like the kind who'd go broke. But you never can tell. Sometime it's booze, or the dog track, or other women."

He got into the truck and stared out at me. "Not this time. They run this boy off. He was in the way, and they run him off. But you didn't hear me say that, mister."

"I didn't hear you, friend."

He headed back over the lumpy road. I walked around to where Puss still sat on the sawhorse. She looked up at me. With a small frown she said, "My heart bled for you the way you went reeling around in shock, McGee. You really took it hard. Your dear old buddy has gone to the big marina in the sky. The hard way. Came to get your bilge pump! God's sake, Travis!"

I sat on my heels and squinted up at her. Dark red hair and disapproval, outlined against a blue December sky. "Win a few, lose a few, honey," I said.

"What *are* you?" she asked.

I stood up and put my hands on her upper arms, near the shoulders and plucked her up off the sawhorse and held her. Maybe I was smiling at her. I wouldn't know. What I was saying seemed to come from a strange direction, as if I were standing several feet behind myself. I said some nonsense about smelling these things out, about sensing the quickest way to open people up, and so you do it, because if you don't, then maybe you miss one little piece of something you should know, and then you go join the long long line of the dead ones, because you were careless.

"And," I heard myself say, "Tush killed himself but not with that damned engine block. He killed himself with
38

something he said, or something he did, and he didn't know he was killing himself. Maybe he didn't listen very good, or catch on soon enough. I listen very good. I catch on. And when I add up this tab and name the price, I'm going to look at some nice gray skin, honey. Gray and pale, oily and guilty as hell, and some eyes shifting around looking for some way out of it. But every damned door will be nailed shut."

I came out of it and realized she was making little hiccupy sobs and looking down and to the side, and her cheeks were wet, and she was saying, "Please, please."

I released her and turned on my heel and walked away from her. I went a little way up the road. I leaned against the trunk of an Australian pine and emptied my lungs a few times. A jay yammered at me. There were tree toads in a swamp somewhere nearby. Puss came walking very slowly up the road. She came over to me and with a quick, shy smile leaned her face into my neck and chest.

"Sorry," she whispered.

"For nothing?"

She exhaled. "I don't know. I asked you what you were. Maybe I found out, sort of."

"Whatever it is, I don't let it show, Puss. Ten more minutes and I would have been kindly Trav forevermore."

She pushed herself a few inches away and looked up at me. "Just smile with your eyes like kindly ol' McGee, dear, to kind of erase that other . . . that other look."

"Was it that bad?"

"They could bottle it and use it to poison pit vipers."

"Okay now?"

She nodded. "Sure." Her eyes were a sherry brown, almost a tan, and in that good light under the tree I could see the area right around the pupil, a corona of green. "He was a special guy?"

"He was that."

"But can't even a special guy . . . give up?"

"Maybe, but if that one ever had, it wouldn't have been like that."

We walked back toward the dead marina, my arm around her strong waist. "Call it enemy country," I explained. "He's dead, and it solves some problems for some people. And they'll want to forget all about it as fast as they can, and they won't know anything about anything."

I got the camera off the boat, a battered old Retina C-III, and put in a roll of Plus X. I hand-cranked the block as high as it would go before it wedged against the tripod poles. I got wire and pliers out of the toolbox aboard, fastened wire to the ratchet stop. I took pictures as I went along. When I yanked the wire, the great weight came down to thud against the hard dirt with a shock I could feel in the soles of my feet, while the drum clattered and the cable rasped through the rusty pulley. I craned it up and left it the way it had been.

She watched, and had the grace not to ask why.

I didn't rinse my hands in the river. I waited until we were well out into the bay.

Then I put it at dead slow, right at 700 rpm, and told her to head down the channel. I climbed out onto the forward bow shell and leaned back against the port windshield.

One approach: Go storming into Sunnydale, promising stink and investigations and general turmoil.

Or: Find some kind of cover story that might open up some mouths. See who can be conned. See who can be turned against whom.

Or: Go in fast and quietly and come out with one Preston LaFrance and take him to a nice quiet place and open him up.

Or: What if some mysterious buyer picked up the Bannon property? Then the boys couldn't put the whole two sections together. And that might bring them out of the woodwork.

The last had the right flavor, if it could be worked.

But first there had to be a first thing, and it had to be poor damned Janine. And if I couldn't get to her before the Sherf told her the bad news, I could at least arrive shortly thereafter.

So I hopped down and took the wheel and ran at high cruise to Broward Beach and tied up at the city marina. I left Puss at the drugstore counter and shut myself into a booth and made a person-to-person credit card call to Sheriff Bunny Burgoon in Sunnydale. I yapped at him in the excited tones of a whiter-wash commercial and told him that CBS news had researched him and discovered he was a truly fine law officer, and had they located Mrs. Bannon yet, and her three kids, and it was a great human interest story and we might do a little feature.

"Sure," he said. "Just before Christmas and all that. Yeh. Locate her? Well, not exactly yet, but we're doing everything that any human person could expect or ask for, and that's the truth. We got aholt of her folks in Milwaukee, and they're all upset as any human person could imagine, but they haven't heard a word from her, and they don't know any friend of hers of the name of Connie. Now if it was to go on national television, she'd turn up right off, I imagine. The name is Sheriff Hadley—that's an e-y, Burgoon, B-u-r-g-o-o-n. And I've been elected here three times as Sherf of Shawana County and——"

"Could you read me the note she left her husband?"

"Did you get the name wrote down with the right spelling?"

"I did, Sheriff."

"It's personal-like, but I see no harm in reading it to you, as any human person could tell it's a public service to find that poor lady. Just a minute. Let me see now. Here it is. It goes like this. 'Dear Tush, I'm sorry. This last thing was just the bitter end. Somehow it made me so ashamed. The boys are so upset and confused. I had to handle it alone because you weren't there, and it took the very last bit of strength and courage I had. Don't be angry with me. I'm worn out. I'm going to go stay with Connie for a while. I'm leaving this note and a suitcase with the things you'll probably need with the Sheriff. When you get the details and all straightened out, please phone me. Don't come charging up here, because I might not be ready to see you yet. I have some thinking to do, and then we have a lot of talking to do, about what's going to happen to you and me. Don't worry about me or the boys. We'll be fine. It was all so ugly, the way it happened. I suppose those men tried to be nice, and it wasn't their fault, but it was a terrible thing. Jan.'"

"I certainly appreciate your cooperation, Sheriff. We'll be in touch. Yes sir, we'll stay in close touch with developments."

I went back to the counter. Puss was sitting on the stool sipping her cola drink, eyes a bit narrow, and on her lips a dangerous little smile. A plump man with a vulgar shirt and a hairline mustache sat two stools away, blushing furiously. He tried to sip his coffee with trembling hand and spilled a dollop of it into his saucer.

"Darling!" she cried, turning toward me, her voice of such a penetrating clarity it reached all the way back to the remedies for iron-poor blood. "This dear little fat fellow wanted to show me all the sights. What's your name, dear little fat fellow?"

He clapped two bits onto the counter top. "Geee-ZUSS!" he muttered. He fled out of the cool into the midafternoon sunlight.

She gazed somberly toward the door. "Seems to have turned chicken. Have you noticed the progressive emasculation of the American male, Travis? Present company excluded, of course."

She finished the soft drink with a rattling slupp amid the cracked ice, cheeks sucked hollow, and stood up in her sky-blue linen boat shorts, and her basque shirt, shook her hair back and smiled benignly up at me. "I counted myself in," she said in a low voice.

"How's that?"

'Since we left the river, I've felt like a bulky package you were tired of carrying around, and you were looking for a coin locker. I never knew Tush. I never met Janine. But I have a very hard nose, dear, and I don't scare, and I want to share."

"I'll give it some thought."

"You *do* that."

Four

I HAD TO give a lot of thought right then and there to getting a good quick line on Connie. Janine's parents didn't know her. But somebody who had been close to the Bannons would know who she might be. I had to dig through the fragments of old memories and piece something together. I tried walking and thinking, Puss quietly, patiently trudging along beside me.

I found a dark little cocktail lounge, and a dark table in a corner. They had one cocktail waitress, and the small

42

percentage of her that was not bare was cruelly bound and laced into the compulsory bunnyfication of tiny waist, improbable uplift and separation of breast, revelation of cleavages front and rear. She had a tired, pretty, sour little face, a listless manner. When she left with the order, Puss clamped her hand on my arm and stared after her, saying, "Santa Claus is coming to town."

They had their Christmas decoration up. It was a lush plastic spray of mistletoe, affixed exactly where the nubile legions of the Heffner Empire affix their fluffy white bunny tails. It expressed such a perfect comment on commercialized Christmas, it gave Puss a case of gasping chuckles that turned into hiccups, which were soon quelled by her big swallows from the steinkrug of dark beer on draft.

I shoved my memory back to the drinks at Tush and Janine's breakfast bar two months earlier, when we had played what happened to who. And I finally came up with Kip Schroeder, the quarterback who, after seven years of high school ball, New Jersey All-State, and five years of college ball, a couple of All-American mentions, had been held together with wire, tape and rivets. He had been obsoleted by giant strides in nutrition. He was structured like a fireplug, and every year the line he had to see over was higher and wider. But where the hell was he? He and his wife, whose name I couldn't remember, had been best man and matron of honor at the wedding of Tush and Jan. I had to have a football buff, one of those nuts who know every statistic and what happened to everybody.

I tried the bald bartender, breaking up his murmured conversation with the mistletoe lass. His frown wrinkled the naked skull almost all the way up to the crown of his head.

"I think maybe Bernie Cohn. He does the sports on WBRO-TV. It ought to be a good time to catch him there at the station. Janie, look up the number for the gennaman, and plug the phone in over there, huh?"

It was a little pink phone with a lighted dial. She had to use a lighter to find the baseboard phone connection. She started to tell me the number, then shrugged and dialed it herself and handed me the phone.

I got the switchboard and then I got Bernie, who said,

"Yes, yes, yes?" with irritable impatience until I told him my question. Then he sounded pleased. "Let me see now. Schroeder. Schroeder. I'm not drawing a blank, buddy. You can put odds on that. I'm running through the career, up to the last thing I heard. Okay. Here it is. Two years ago Kip was athletic director, Oak Valley School, and that's in . . . just a minute . . . Nutley, New Jersey. Right?"

"Sure appreciate it."

"Did I win you a bet, fella? Express your appreciation by telling all your friends to watch the Bernie Cohn show at six fifteen every weekday on your Big Voice of the Big Bay, WBRO-TV. Right?"

Listless Janie came over when I signaled her, and I ordered two more draft and asked her if I could make a credit card call on the phone. When she came back with the beers, she said, "He says okay if I stand here while you make the call. You know. On account of any long distance comes in on the bill, it's a deduct on him."

Puss reached out with a foot, hooked a chair over from the nearby table and said, "Rest your mistletoe, honey."

With her first smile, the waitress sat down, saying, "My feet are like sore teeth, honest to God. I worked waitress three years and no trouble, but in this costume the owner says high heels, and now after three months I hurt all over, honest to God."

I got through to area information on my station to station call for anyone at the phone listed in Nutley for Kip Schroeder. They didn't have one. They had a K. D. Schroeder. I tried that and got a Mrs. Schroeder, and she said yes, she was Kip's wife, Alice. Kip was out.

I said I had met her once, and she pretended politely that she remembered me perfectly. I was glad she sounded so bright. I said I was trying to locate a very good friend of Jan Bannon, named Connie.

"Connie. Connie. Can you hold on a minute while I get my Christmas card list? It's laid out even, but we haven't gotten started on it yet."

She came back and said, "I think this is who you want. Connie Alvarez. It used to be Tom and Connie, and he died. I think she was one of Jan's teachers in school. Here's the address I've got for her. To-Co Groves. That's capital To, capital Co, with a hyphen. Route Two,

Frostproof, Florida. Frostproof! And you should see the sleet coming down here today. It's worth your life to drive."

I thanked her and told her to give Kip my best, asked her how he was doing. She said he'd had two good seasons in a row and he was happy as a clam. So she asked how Tush and Jan were. What can you say? I said that the last time I'd seen the two of them, they were fine. It wasn't a lie. She said that if I saw them soon again, to tell Janine she owed her a letter and she'd write right after the holidays for sure.

I didn't want to make the next call from there, not with tired Janie listening. So I paid her, and added on top of the tip a little balm for sore feet.

Back toward the city marina, toward the drugstore, and I briefed Puss en route. "She didn't need much travel money to get there. Less than two hundred miles, I'd guess."

In the drugstore booth, on the off chance that Jan might answer, I made the call person to person to Mrs. Alvarez. I heard a maid answer the operator and say she would get Mrs. Alvarez. It was at least two minutes before Connie Alvarez answered, sounding out of breath.

"Yes?"

"Is Jan staying there with you?"

". . . I . . . I'm afraid I wouldn't be interested, thank you."

"Look, Mrs. Alvarez. This isn't Tush."

"Then, perhaps you could explain more about it, Mr. Williams."

"I get the message. She can hear your end of it. Now, listen very carefully. Please. Don't let her answer any phone calls, and keep her away from the newspapers and the radio and the television."

"I suppose there would be some reason for that."

"My name is Travis McGee. I'm going to try to get there this evening. And it might be a good idea if you could have a damned good tranquilizer handy. I'm an old friend of Tush's. I wasn't going to tell you this if you sounded bird-brained, Connie. But you sound solid. Tush is dead. And it was messy."

"In that case, Mr. Williams, I might be willing to listen. Perhaps if you could come out this evening? There's loads

45

of room here. We can put you up, and it will give us a good chance to talk business. I know a little bit about the sort of proposition you mention, I mean, the background data. I'll look forward to seeing you. By the way, we're eight miles northeast of Frostproof. Go north out of town on US Twenty-seven and turn right on State Road Six thirty, and we're about five miles from the corner on your left. I'll turn the gate lights on at dark."

And then came the fat argument with Puss Killian as we walked back to the city marina. At last she said, "Old buddy, you are leaving out one ingredient. You say she was a steady one. Great. She can cope. So maybe she is one of those who can cope with all the mechanics of a situation. A real administrator. But maybe she can't hold people. Maybe it makes her feel itchy to try to hold somebody and hug somebody and rock somebody. I have this rusty nail for a tongue, and I kick where it is going to hurt the most, but I am a warm broad, like in the puppy sense of touching and being touched. Contact with flesh. That's where the messages of the heart are, McGee. Not in words, because words are just a kind of conventional code, and they get blurred, because any word doesn't mean just the same to any two people. And I am very familiar with that old spook with the scythe and the graveyard breath. And I do *not* care to be sent back to Lauderdamndale to sit around in that sexpot houseboat and crack my knuckles. Think of me as a kind of tall poultice. Or a miracle drug. Part of your kit. And if the lady administrator can supply the same item, I will not enter a competition. I will stay the hell out of the way. But this is women's work, and two are better than one, and it is going to be ten times worse for her because she ran for cover, and there will be guilt up to here."

So I scribbled her a list of my overnight needs and sent her off to a shopping plaza winking and glittering in the distance. I checked the marina office and got the name and location of a place that could lift the *Muñequita* out and tractor it over and put it on a shelf. He phoned for me and said they had space. I ran her over and took out all the stuff I did not want to leave aboard. A boat you can check as if it were a 4,300-pound suitcase is a vast convenience for people who never know what they'll be doing tomorrow.

I watched them hose down the hull and put Little Doll tenderly on her shelf, and soon a rental sedan arrived for me, tow-barring the little three-wheeled bug that would get the delivery man back to the rental headquarters. I accomplished the red tape on car and boat, locked the gear in the trunk of the maroon two-door, and got back to the cavelike cocktail bar ten minutes before Puss came striding in with a new genuine imitation red alligator hatbox, a blue canvas zipper bag advertising an obscure airline, two suitboxes and a big shopping bag full of smaller parcels.

By five thirty we were making good time up State 710, aimed like a chalk line at the town of Okeechobee, and Puss was in the back seat, happily unwrapping packages, admiring her own good taste, and packing the items in the oversized hatbox. At last she came clambering over the back of her bucket seat, plumped herself down, latched her belt, lit her cigarette and said, "Now about a few little things aboard *The Busted Flush,* friend. Like the little ding-dong when anybody steps aboard. Like the way it is wired for sound, not the pretty music, but for tape pickup. And how about that cozy little headboard compartment with loaded weapon therein? Also, you have some very interesting areas that look as if you'd have a nice collection of purple hearts, if you got them in a war. And how about the way you go shambling mildly about, kind of sleepily relaxed, beaming at your friends and buddies, kind of slow, rawboned, awkward-like, and you were ten feet from Marilee Saturday night when she stepped on that ice cube on the sun deck and was going to pitch headfirst right off the top of that ladderway, and in some fantastic way you got there and hooked an arm around her waist and yanked her right out of the air? More? How about the lightning change of personality for the benefit of the phone man with the old-timey glasses, the way you turned into a touristy goof so completely I didn't even feel as if I knew you? How about this con you almost worked on me about being retired. How about the way I tried to pump Meyer about you, and he showed speed and footwork like you couldn't believe? How about that kind of grim professional bit with the camera and the hoist and the wire and all, so totally concentrated I could have been walking around on my

47

hands with a rose in my teeth without getting a glance from you? How about my gnawing little suspicion that you aren't going up to Frostproof to comfort this Janine, but to go pry information out of her? Enemy country, you said. Maybe for you the whole world is enemy country, McGee. But somehow it would sort of fit one lousy guess, which would be a batch of official cars screaming up and the boys in blue jumping out, and a big loudspeaker yammering for you to come out quietly or they lob in the tear gas."

"You are a warm broad. You are a warm *nosey* broad."

"So I have this eccentricity, maybe. You know, a social flaw. Some kind of insecurity reaction or something. I started sleeping with somebody and I get this terrible curiosity about them."

"So? I could have the same trouble too. But I haven't asked questions. Or tried to find out things I could find out, without much trouble, probably."

She was quiet for a long time. I glanced at her. Her hands were folded in her lap and she was biting at sucked-in lips.

"Fair is fair," she said. "When it's time to tell you, I will tell you. Not in words, but in writing, so that I get it down exactly right. Not that it is so earth-shattering or anything. But for now, for reasons I think are pretty good reasons, I want to keep it to myself. Fair being fair, if you have good reasons, okay, I ask no more."

So I told her the retirement was accurate, except I am taking it in little hunks whenever I can afford it. "It's a tricky, complex, indifferent society, Puss. It's a loophole world. And there are a lot of clever animals who know how to reach through the loopholes and pick the pockets of the unsuspecting. Carefully done, the guy who has been plucked clean has no way of getting it back. There are a thousand perfectly legal acts that can be immoral, or amoral, acts. Then the law officers have no basis of action. Attorney's can't help. The pigeon might just as well have dropped his wallet into a river full of crocodiles. He knows right where it is. And all he can do is stand on the muddy shore and wring his hands. So I'm the salvage expert. And I've known a lot of crocodiles. So I make a deal with him. I dive down, bring it up, and split it with him, fifty-fifty. When a man knows his expectation of recovery is zero, recovering half is very attractive. If I don't make it, I'm out expenses."

"Or you are a dainty dish for the crocs, man."

"So far I've been indigestible. Now Janine Bannon is a client. She doesn't know it yet. Tush would have been. A client in the classic sense of the legal squeeze. I don't understand the killing. They didn't need that. I know one thing. I have to watch myself on this one. Strangers make the best clients. Then I can play the odds and stay cold. Here I'm too emotionally hung up. I'm too angry, too sick at heart. A dirty, senseless act. So I have to watch it."

She pondered it for a time. "Just one thing that bothers me, darling. How do you find . . . enough new clients?"

I told her how I had found the last one, by combing very carefully through all the local items in the fat Sunday edition of a Miami paper. Of the items I marked that looked interesting, one was an apologetic announcement from a stamp collector's club that Mr. So-and-So, a very long and complicated Greek name, the well-known restauranteur had, at the last minute, decided to withdraw from the exhibition and not show his complete and extremely valuable collection of Greek postage stamps, which had included the famous 1857 Dusty Rose, which had brought $21,000 at a New York auction house in 1954.

I'd called an officer of the Philatelic Society who said the old gentleman was not mad at anybody, that he took a lot of pleasure in exhibiting his collection and having it admired, and that though he had sounded upset, he had not given any reason for withdrawing.

It had taken a little more research to find out what company insured the collection. An agent who said he had never met the old gentleman gave me his card. So I took his card and his name and presented myself to the old gentleman and said we wished to make a new appraisal of the collection. He stalled. The collection was in the vault at the bank. He was very busy. Some other time. So I said we had reason to believe he had disposed of some of the collection.

He broke down. He had been remounting the collection under glass for the exhibition. He had to leave his home for a doctor's appointment. He returned. Twenty-two of the most valuable stamps, including the Dusty Rose, were missing.

49

"So he was the patriarch of a big family, all very close, all sensitive to scandal, and his wife had died, and he had been remarried for two years to something of the same coloring, general impact and impressive dimension of the late Jayne Mansfield, a lassy big enough to make two of the old boy, and he was so certain she had clouted his valuable toys he'd been afraid to make a report to the cops or claim insurance. So I followed the lady to an afternoon assignation with the hotel beachboy who'd blackmailed her into heisting the stamps, and after I got through shaking him up and convincing him that the old gentleman had arranged to have her last two male chums dropped into the Florida Straits wired to old truck parts, he produced eleven stamps, including the gem of the collection, and was so eager to explain where and how he had fenced the other eleven he was letting off a fine spray of spit. I helped him pack, and put him on a bus and waved good-bye and had a nice little talk with the big blonde about how I had just barely managed to talk two tough old Greek pals of her husband's from hiring local talent to write a little warning with a hot wire across her two most obvious endowments. A cop friend shook the missing items out of the fence, and I told the old man it hadn't been his wife at all, and he had every reason to trust her. So he hopped around and sang and chuckled and we went to the bank and he gave me thirty thousand cash, a generous estimate of half the value, and he gave me a note that gives me free meals for life in the best Greek restaurants in four states, and the whole thing took five days, and I went right back to my retirement, and maybe three weeks later one Puss Killian came along and enriched it considerable."

"Pull over," she ordered. I found a place where there was room to park on the grass between the two-lane road and the canal. She unsnapped the seat belt, lunged expansively over, a big hug, a big kiss from a big girl whose eyes danced and sparkled in the fading daylight.

"Drive on," she said, snapping the belt.

I did. "Whatever it was for, it was nice."

"Well, this is a very long day, and it was partly for way way back, having that coffee-with. And it was for getting so damned scarey furious—because maybe there isn't much real anger around any more. It's for appreciating

50

mistletoe. It's mostly for being what you are, doing the nutty things you do, and letting me for once be . . . Sancho Panza."

"Please! Sancha."

"Of course."

Five

THE ENTRANCE GATE was very wide, very high, with a floodlight shining on the clean white paint and on the sign that hung from chains from the top of the arch. To-Co Groves, Inc.

It was nine fifteen. We had stopped in Okeechobee for a hasty meal of some fresh bass, fried in corn meal and bacon fat. I turned into the graveled drive and a figure stepped out of the shadows into the headlights, raising a casual hand to stop me. Ranch hat, faded blue denim work jacket and jeans. She came to my side of the car and said, "McGee? I'm Connie Alvarez."

I got out, leaving the door open, shook hands, introduced Puss. Connie leaned in and shook her hand, then straightened again. In the glow of the courtesy light I had my first good look at her. A strong-looking woman, chunky, with good shoulders, a weathered face, no makeup, very lovely dark, long-lashed eyes.

"You would have helped them if they'd hollered, McGee?"

"All I could."

"Me too. Pride. Their lousy, stiff-necked pride. How many good people has pride killed? She's up there at the house thinking the roof has fallen in on her. She doesn't know it's the roof and the chimney and the whole damn sky, and it is a lousy time to have to tell her. What happened?"

"He was on his back on the ground and about five hundred pounds of scrap iron dropped on him from ten feet in the air. Head and chest, I'd imagine. I haven't seen him, and probably wouldn't know who I was seeing if I did."

"Jesus Christ, man, you don't tiptoe around things, do you?"

51

"Do you want me to?"

"I think already you know me better than that. Are they trying to call it an accident?"

"Suicide. He's supposed to have run a wire to the ratchet stop, lay down and yanked it loose. They found it still fastened and wound around his hand. Yesterday morning."

Suddenly her brown strong fingers locked onto my wrist. "Oh my dear God! Had he gotten the note she left him?"

"No."

I heard the depth of her sigh. "That could have done it. That could have been the one thing that could have made him do it. I think I got to know him that well. I think I know how much Jan meant to that poor big sweet guy."

"Not even that, Connie. At least not that way. He was murdered. But we've got to swallow the suicide story. All of us. We've got to act as if we believed it."

"Why?"

"Why do you think?"

"I think why use amateur talent when you can hire professionals."

"Rest your mind, Mrs. A."

"We'll talk after we get this sad thing done." She leaned abruptly into the car again. "You, girl. Do you dither? Do you bleat and snuffle and carry on?"

"Go grow yourself an orange, lady."

She threw her head back and gave a single bark of humorless laughter. "Maybe you'll both do." She pulled my seat back forward and scrambled into the back seat, rustling the discarded wrapping paper. "Let's go, McGee. The gate light turns off up at the house."

I wasn't prepared for a full half mile of drive, nor for the house at the end of it, big and long and low, with upswept drama of roof lines, something by Frank Lloyd Wright out of Holiday Inns. She had me park around at the side. "I'll have my people take care of the car and bring your gear in. You people use one bedroom or two."

"Two, please," said Puss.

"Well, at least the thundering herd is sacked out by now. Her three and my two." She looked up at the stars. And we squared our shoulders and went in to drop the sky down upon Janine, to change the shape of her world and the shape of her heart forever.

It was one thirty in the morning when Puss came walking slowly into the big living room, yawning. Connie and I had been sitting for a long time in the dark leather chairs near a small crackling of fat pine in the big fireplace of coquina rock. We'd done a lot of talking.

"I think she's good until midmorning anyway," Puss said.

"But Maria better sit there by her just in case."

"She's there, Connie. If Jan wakes up, she'll wake us up. But it isn't likely."

Puss went over to the little bar in the corner, put two cubes in a squat glass, poured some brandy over them and then came over and shoved the footstool closer to me, sat on it and leaned her head against the side of my knee and yawned again. "She was trying to be so damn brave," Puss said. "She wouldn't let go, and she wouldn't let go, and then she did. And that's the best thing. Did you get the calls through, Connie?"

"I got that Sheriff and told him she knew and she was resting, and I'd call him back tomorrow and let him know what she's going to do next. I got her people and got them calmed down. She'll have to phone them tomorrow. And the boys have to be told."

"Jan said not to tell them," Puss said. "She said it's her job. She keeps asking how we can be sure he never got her note."

Connie swirled the ice in her drink and then slugged it down. "Know what I can't forget? Can't and never will? Five years and it's still so clear in my mind. Every word that was said. Oh, it was a typical brooha. Tommy and I had hundreds of them. Yell and curse, but it never really meant anything. We both had strong opinions. What we quarreled about that morning doesn't matter. After he went crashing out, I ran and yanked the door open and called after him. 'And don't be in a great big hurry to come back!' Maybe he didn't hear me. He had his jeep roaring by then. He never did come back. He didn't see the sinkhole and drove into it, and he stayed alive in the hospital two days and two nights without regaining consciousness, and he died there." She stood up, wearing a

53

crooked smile, and said, "The guilts. That's what they leave you. Tomorrow is going to be a long rough day too, people. 'Night."

I was on the downslope into sleep when the bed tipped under Puss's stealthy weight and she slipped under the sheet and blanket to pull herself long and warm against me, fragrant and gentle, with some kind of whisper-thin fabric between my hands and her flesh.

"Just hold me," she whispered. "It just seemed like such a dark, dark night to be alone." Her words were blurred, and in a very little while her breathing changed and deepened and her holding arms went slack and fell away.

The four of us arrived in Sunnydale three days later, at a little before noon on Thursday. Connie Alvarez drove the lead car, a mud-caked black Pontiac convertible of recent vintage and much engine. Janine was beside her. When the road was straight, I had all I could do to keep them in sight. Puss mumbled now and again about Daytona and Sebring.

"The whole thing sounds so nutty," she said. "Do you really think that funny-looking little old judge knows what he's doing?"

"That funny little old Judge Rufus Wellington knows what everybody is doing. And he'll have had the whole morning to pry around." I braked at the last moment, pulled the rental around a bend and peered ahead for the distant dot that would be the Pontiac. "Have you got any questions at all about your little game?"

"Hah! Can the gaudy redhead from the big city dazzle the young, earnest attorney with her promissory charms? Will Steve Besseker, the shy counselor from the piney woodlands reveal the details of local chicanery to yon glamorous wench? I might have a question at that."

"Which is . . ."

"You were a little vague about the details, McGee. Do I give all for the cause? Do I bed this bumpkin if it seems necessary, or don't you care one way or the other?"

I risked a high-speed glance at her and met the narrowed quizzical eyes of sexual challenge. I said, carefully, "I've always had the impression that if the string on the carrot was too long, and if the donkey snapped at it and got it, he'd lose his incentive and stop pulling the load."

"I resent the analogy and approve the sentiment, sir."

But challenges have to go both ways or there is no equality among the sexes. "On the other hand, I imagine that you're the best judge of your own motivations, and you would be the best judge of the appropriate stimulus and response. Such situations vary, I imagine."

"Are you trying to be a bastard?"

"Aren't we both trying?"

After a thoughtful silence she said, "Just for the hell of it, McGee, what would be your reaction if I said I'd keep the carrot on a mighty short string?"

"Killian, I would have to admit that I am just stodgy and old-fashioned enough to enjoy being the dog in your manger. I like a kind of sentimental exclusivity."

"Romantic exclusivity?"

"If you prefer."

"I prefer, thank you. So be it. I am now motivated to defend my honor. So suppose you watch yours."

The appointment had been set for twelve noon with Mr. Whitt Sanders, the President of the Shawana National Bank and Trust Company. I saw the empty Pontiac in the bank lot and parked near it and sent Puss on her way, wishing her luck. When I went into the bank, I could see Connie and Janine sitting in a glass-walled office in the rear, facing a big man across a big desk. The receptionist took me back, tapped on the door, and held it open for me.

Sanders stood up and reached across the desk and gave me a bully-boy handshake. He had tan hair and a big, sun-reddened, flakey face, a barrel of belly, a network of smile wrinkles and weather wrinkles, big red hands like ball gloves, and eyes that seemed to have the same size and expression as a pair of blueberries. "Mr. McGee!" he bellowed. "Pleasure! Sit right down and rest yourself."

I did and he said, "I was just telling the ladies that my sympathy goes out to Mrs. Bannon in this tragic time. You can rest assured, Mrs. Bannon, that the bank is doing everything in its power to liquidate the properties in question at the maximum figure obtainable. Of course certain unfortunate situations in that area have made it a difficult piece to move at this time, but we have negotiated something which I think anyone would agree is more than fair. As a matter of fact . . ."

And in came little old Judge Wellington with his cream-colored ranch hat shoved back, locks of white hair escaping in random directions, in his dusty dark suit and gold watch chain, carrying a briefcase that had perhaps first seen duty during the Lincoln-Douglas debates, his face remarkably like one of Disney's seven dwarfs, but I couldn't remember which one. "Hidey, Whitt," he said, "New paneling, eh? Purty."

"Rufus! I heard somebody say they thought they saw you over at the courthouse! *Glad* to see you."

"No. I'm not going to let you get aholt of my hand, Whitt. Not with my arthritis laying quiet for a change. So set."

Whitt Sanders looked confused. "Rufus, if you wouldn't mind waiting outside until I finish with——"

"Finish with my client? Now, even a jackass like you knows you can't keep a lawyer away from his client."

"You are representing Mrs. *Bannon!"*

"Why not? Mrs. Bannon is a dear friend of Mrs. Connie Alvarez here, and Miz Connie owns and operates To-Co Groves up to Frostproof, right in my back yard, which you may have heard of even down here in the wilderness, it being near three hundred thousand trees, prime Valencia on sour orange root stock, and she has enough legal battles going at all times with the Citrus Commission and the growers association and the concentrate plant she's got a stock interest in to keep me right busy in my declining years."

Watching the bank president, I realized it is possible for a big man to slowly come to attention while seated, and even give the impression of saluting. Connie had taken me on a tour of the groves, and I could see why Whitt Sanders reacted. For the first year after her husband had died, a management outfit had operated the groves on contract. Connie had spent every daylight hour with the crews and every evening studying, and at the end of the year she said she had been willing to take the risk of being able to do the job herself.

When we had come upon a trio of big spray trucks lumbering down the geometric lines, the nozzlemen garbed like astronauts, and I'd asked if bugs were a big problem, Connie had planted her feet, rolled her eyes skyward and chanted, "Kill off the burrowing nematode, the aphid, the rust mite, white fly, white fly fungus, Mediterranean fly, red mite, six-spot mite, rust mite, Texas mite, mealy bugs, cushion scales, black scales, soft scales, yellow scales, wax scales, snow scales, purple scales, dictyospermum, melanose, citrus scag, mealy bugs and orange-dog caterpillars, and keep killing them off, and if you don't get a hard freeze, you've got half a chance, man, of hitting today's market with a hell of a nice crop, which at today's prices costs me one dollar and sixty cents more per box to raise than I get for them." She had shrugged, scuffed at the sand. "I counted on the overproduction and set up a reserve. These prices are going to sink the half-ass operators and that'll cut production back to balance and bring back a fair price."

In the president's office the president said, "I didn't realize you were *the* Mrs. Alvarez."

"So I asked the judge if he could do anything to help my friend here, Jan Bannon."

Janine sat silent and motionless, dressed in darkness, and the blueberry eyes of Whitt Sanders seemed to slide uneasily past her.

Sanders said, at last, "I guess I don't know what you're driving at, actually. The business holdings don't fall into the estate because there was an actual foreclosure before the time of death, with all proper advertising and notifications. So title passed. It's a standard first mortgage agreement, Rufus. Title passed to the bank."

"That so?" said the Judge. "Funny. I got the impression that when I turn over to you the certified check I got here for ten thousand dollars in the name of Mrs. Bannon, that is going to cover back payments on principal, plus interest, plus fees and expenses, and leave a little over which you can apply on the next payment, and I got the impression that title is going to ease right on back to her."

"But the grace period is up! It isn't possible now!"

Judge Wellington sighed. "Bullshit," said he. Then he swept his hundred-dollar ranch hat off in courtly fashion, nodded toward Connie and Janine and said, "Begging your pardon, ladies." He dropped the hat on the floor beside his chair and said, "Whitt, I can't remember you ever being admitted to the Florida bar, so there's no point in me citing the pertinent and appropriate cases where the courts have ruled that in the cases of widows and orphans, especially where the widow was one of the parties on the mortgage, foreclosure action can be set aside provided the bank has not yet passed title on to a third party in a liquidation of the recovered assets."

"But we've accepted earnest money from——"

"One Preston LaFrance in the amount of three thousand two hundred and fifty dollars, representing ten percent of the agreed price on the foreclosed business property on the Shawana River, and the acceptance of that money did not constitute a change of ownership on the property, and here is the certified check for ten thousand, Whitt, and I request a signed receipt, with the date and the hour thereon."

"I can't accept it until I find out——"

"You take it and you make out the receipt saying you are taking it and holding it in escrow pending the decision of your legal people, or you and me are going to go around and around right here, boy. Besides, here is a situation where, by accepting the mortgage obligation and paying it up to date, Mrs. Bannon is putting that mortgage back on the books, sound and whole, in the amount originally owed and paid down to where this check puts it, and it would seem like a bank officer thinking of his stockholders—and thinking of the State Banking Commission—would snap at the chance to keep from showing a loss. Why do you seem to be holding back, Whitt?"

Sanders patted his red forehead with a handkerchief. "As you pointed out, Rufus, I'm not a lawyer. I don't know what our obligation to Mr. LaFrance might be."

"Absolutely no obligation, I can tell you, but you'll feel cozy hearing it from your own people, so we'll give you a chance to do just that. Suppose we come back at two thirty?"

"That . . . that ought to be time enough. Uh . . . Mrs. Bannon, do you intend to operate the business there yourself?"

"She's going to think about it," Judge Wellington said. "When her husband couldn't keep up on his insurance, he had the good sense to tell the company to apply the cash value to the premiums instead of drawing it out, so she has a little money to give her time to do some planning. We'll let you get on back to work, Whitt."

We left the bank and walked two blocks to the old Shawana River Hotel, and got a corner table in the dark-paneled, high-ceilinged old dining room. Janine was at my right, and the judge across from me. Connie and the judge and I ordered drinks. Jan didn't want any. There was a yellowish look to the tan of her lean, Mediterranean-boy face, and the skin of her face and hands had a papery look.

I touched her hand and said, "Okay?"

She gave me an abrupt nod, a smile that appeared for but a moment. The judge seemed lost in private thought. Finally he gave a dry little cough and said, "McGee, you seem to know what you're trying to do for this little lady, and I know Connie well enough to know she'll go along with some pretty wild ideas. But I've heard a few hints around the courthouse, and a few rumors, and I can put things together, and I wouldn't be doing right by my client not to give advice, whether it's wanted or not."

"I want your advice, Judge," Janine said.

He sipped his bourbon and licked his lips. "These little counties all got what you could call a shadow government. These folks have known each other for generations. They got to putting this land deal together, and there is a little business right in the way and doing pretty good. Expanding. So they use the county government to stunt that business and knock it down to where the price is right. It doesn't take all five county commissioners. Just a couple, plus the other three needing favors themselves sometime, with no need of anybody asking too many questions. You depended on highway trade and river trade, and giving service to local residents. Now they could have kept that road open to traffic and in pretty good shape too while fixing it, and set up a short-term contract on it. There's pollution-control ordinances on the books to keep that river in better shape. They could have denied that Tech something outfit when they petitioned to have the bridge taken out. When you didn't drop off the vine as fast as they wanted, then they put those regulatory services people onto you and really closed you down. Okay, Miz Bannon, you got squoze bad. So what I say is this. I say don't mess too fancy with these folk because in the long run you can't win. You can lay the squeeze right back onto them. I know how these folks think. You just say a hundred and twenty-five thousand, plus the buyer takes over the mortgage. No dickering. No conversations. Let them make the offers. When time starts to run out on them, somebody is going to get nervous and offer a hundred thousand, and then you by God grab it and walk away, and you'll know you've skimmed some good cream off their deal."

"That isn't enough," she said in a barely audible voice.

"But, girl, you'd be hurting them in the place that hurts the most. What are you trying to get out of this? Lord God, you can't make anybody *ashamed* of how they did you, even if they'd ever admit it wasn't just kind of a series of accidents. They just say it's dog eat dog and lots of businesses fail all the time."

"But they had Tush killed."

That little embellishment had been kept from the judge. He leaned forward, his old eyes wide. "You say killed? Now, young lady, I can understand how you could come to believe it was like that, but these folks just don't operate that way. That man of yours worked hard and long and it was all going down the drain, and sometimes a man gets to the point where he——"

"You didn't know Tush Bannon," Connie said. "I did. And Travis McGee knew him longer than either Jan or me. We're not taking any votes, Rufus. We're not talking about probably this or probably that. We're telling you he was killed."

Judge Wellington leaned back, so upset he tried to drink out of the glass he had already emptied. "Well now! Then, it must have been some fool mistake. It must have been something else that went wrong. Then, by God, the thing to do right now is put it in the hands of the State's Attorney for this Judicial District and . . ." He stopped suddenly and frowned at Connie. "By God, I must be getting old. He'd turn it over to the Assistant State Attorney for Shawana County, and the Shawana County Sheriff's Department would make the investigation, and the Shawana County Medical Examiner would do the autopsy, and all these folks are elected to office, and there'd be all the pressure to cover it over and forget it, and even if it went to a Grand Jury if it got that far, who'd get indicted? I'm getting so old I'm forgetting the facts of life. Second childhood. I'm thinking the world is like I thought it was when I was back in Stetson Law School." He scowled into his empty glass. "Maybe bring in some-body from the Attorney General's office to poke around?"

"Maybe," I said. "But first maybe we should blow some smoke down into the burrow and see what comes running out."

He though and nodded. "Now I see why you want to do what you're doing. I won't say it has much chance of working. But it'll sure stir things up." He gazed at Jan. "Miz Bannon, I know it's a great and sad and tragic loss. And doing something about it can make a person feel better somehow. But don't aim all of yourself at that one thing, of paying somebody back. Revenge. Because it can turn a person sour through and through."

"I don't care what I turn into, Judge," she said.

He met her dark gaze, then opened his menu and said, "We better get our order in."

I went alone to Ingledine's Funeral Home and arrived at quarter of two. It was on a lateral street, and was a small version of Mount Vernon, set between a Savings and Loan branch and a used car lot. I asked for Mr. Ingle-dine and the stealthy, earnest, unctuous young man told me that Mr. Ingledine had retired, and that he was Mr. Farris, Junior, and that he and his father owned and oper-ated the establishment, and how could he help me, sir.

We tiptoed past an arched doorway where, under a rose-colored spotlight, a waxy pink and white old man rested, propped up in his bronze box, with floral offerings concealing whatever the box rested upon. Two old women sat on a couch on the other side of the room, holding hands and murmuring to each other.

Mr. Farris, Junior, opened a desk drawer in a small office and took a folder out, and extracted the death cer-tificate signed by the County Medical Examiner.

"We obtained the vital statistics from available local records, sir. You might check them over for accuracy." Brantley B. Bannon, and the age looked right, and he had the next of kin right. The doctor had listed it as accidental death. I asked about it and he said that in the absence of any suicide note or any witnesses, and in view of the fact that he could have been working on the diesel engine, it would have been unfair to assume suicide.

"Would you care to . . . uh . . . view the remains, sir? I would not advise it. It's quite a . . . an extensive and nasty mutilation. There is absolutely no possibility of any reconstruction of the features. And I think it would be wise for you to discourage the widow from viewing the deceased. A memory like that would be . . . difficult to forget."

"What work have you done?"

"Well, a great deal of the blood was gone, of course. We trocared the rest of it as best we could, and the body fluids and so on, and by clamping some of the major vessels in the chest and throat area, we did manage to embalm to a certain extent. Let me see. Oh, yes, we were able to make positive identification so that we do not have to trouble anyone about that. They had at one time sold sandwiches and coffee at their marina, and the County Health Department requires a health card with a photo and thumbprint, and the Sheriff's Department verified the identity by taking a print from the body."

"You've been very efficient."

His smile was shy and pleased. "I am sorry, but I do not quite understand . . . what your function is in this, Mr. McGee?"

"Friend of the family, you could say. Here is a limited power of attorney, notarized, empowering me to make the arrangements in the name of the widow."

He looked at it with a faintly pained expression. "There'll be no services here, I would assume?"

"No. You can expect shipment instructions within the next few days." He led me back into the display room. The lids were propped open, the linings glossy, the handles burnished. They ranged from two twenty-five on up. I picked a three-hundred-dollar box. We went back into the office.

He said, "I'd recommend that we take the remains out of the storage vault and place the body in the casket and seal it, sir."

"I suggest you leave it right where it is, Mr. Farris, under refrigeration, until you get shipment instructions.

And then please don't make a permanent seal. There could be an insurance question, on an accident indemnity clause."

"Oh. I see. But you should know that storage is costing eleven thirty-three a day. That's with tax, of course."

"Of course. Now may I see your statement on this?"

He took the statement from the folder and took it into the next room. I heard the slow tapping of unskilled typing. He brought it back and handed it to me. He had added the box and two more days of vault rental. The total was seven hundred and fifty-eight dollars and thirty-eight cents.

"Mr. McGee, I am sure you will understand our position when I point out that it is our information that the deceased *was* a bankrupt, and we will have to have some assurance that . . ."

The certified check for a thousand dollars that I placed in front of him stopped him abruptly. I said, "Is this top copy mine? Just acknowledge the receipt of a thousand dollars on it, Mr. Farris, and when the body leaves here, deduct any further charges from the credit balance and mail your check to Mrs. Bannon, To-Co Groves, Route Two, Frostproof. And I see you have a photocopy of the death certificate, so you can let me have the original? Thank you."

He went with me to the front door, through the ripe smell of flowers in full bloom, through the muted organ music.

He put his pale hand out, smiled his pale smile, and said, "Please express our sympathy to the bereaved."

I stared at his hand until he pulled it back and wiped it nervously on the side of his jacket. I said, "Junior, you could make a tangible expression of your sincere sympathy."

"I don't believe I follow you."

"Before you send her the check for her credit balance, just refigure your bill. She's a young widow with three boys to raise. You padded it by at least two hundred and fifty dollars. I think it would be a nice gesture."

His face went pink. "Our rates are——"

"Ample, boy. Real ample."

Outside I took a deep breath of Shawana County air,

63

but there was something vaguely industrial in it, some faint acid that rasped the back of my throat.

We were moving in, stirring them up with a blunt stick. The old judge, with good law and good timing, was snatching the ten acres right back out of the hands of LaFrance, just when he thought he had his whole deal lined up. And soon he would know a stranger was moving into the game, buying some chips, asking for somebody to deal. When in doubt, shove a new unknown into their nice neat equations and see how they react.

Hungry men think everybody else is just as hungry. Conspiratorial men see conspiracy everywhere. I strolled through industrial stink toward the bank.

Six

WE GATHERED AGAIN in the bank president's office at two thirty. Sanders had the Bannon file on his desk, and a Mr. Lee, an attorney for the bank, sitting near his left elbow. Lee had a round, placid face and a brushcut. He could have been thirty or fifty or anything in between.

With obviously forced cordiality, Sanders said, "Well, Mrs. Bannon, the bank has decided to accept your payment and mark the mortgage account current and in good order."

Judge Wellington yawned. "You say that as if you had choice in the matter, Whitt. All right. My client is grateful. She thanks you." He opened his old briefcase and pawed in it and took out the papers that had been prepared Wednesday afternoon in the judge's law offices. He flipped them onto the desk in front of Whitt Sanders, saying, "Might as well get this taken care of too, as long as we're all foregathered here. Everything is all ready to record, but what we need is the bank's approval of the transfer of the mortgage from Mrs. Bannon to Mr. McGee here."

Mr. Lee hitched closer to the president as Sanders leafed quickly through the legal documents. He stared at Judge Wellington with a look of astonishment. "But . . . according to this, she's selling her equity in the property for fifteen thousand dollars, Rufus!"

"Wouldn't you call that a pretty good deal? Sixty thousand mortgage balance, and you were going to sell the whole kaboodle for thirty-two five and have a judgment against the estate, if any, for twenty-seven thousand five. So she pays the mortgage down to fifty thousand, then sells for fifteen thousand, which puts her five ahead instead of twenty-seven five behind. Why, this little lady is thirty-two thousand five hundred better off right this minute than she was when she walked in here. Or maybe you just look surprised she did so good. Remember, she's got a good lawyer."

"But we can't just . . . approve this transfer. We don't have enough information. Mr. McGee, we'll have to have a credit report on you, and we'll have to have a balance sheet and income statement. This would be *highly* irregular. I have a responsibility to——"

"The stockholders," the old judge said. "Whitt, you went through those papers too dang fast. Try it a little slower."

He did. He came to an abrupt stop. He stared at Connie. "You'll be the guarantor on the mortgage note, Mrs. Alvarez?!"

"That's what it says there, doesn't it?"

"If you're still nervous, Whitt," said the judge, "go look up To-Co Groves in your D. and B."

"Oh, no. I didn't mean anything like that. It was just . . ."

The judge sighed. "Could we just stop fumbling and get the red tape done so we can get this stuff recorded and set out for home?"

"Excuse me just a moment," Sanders said. He took Mr. Lee out of the office with him and over to a quiet corner of the carpeted bullpen. They held about a forty-second consultation. I hoped I knew exactly what it was about. I looked to the judge for reassurance, and got it in the form of a slow wink, an almost imperceptible nod.

Mr. Lee came back in with Sanders. He was apparently nominated by Sanders to put the matter into careful legal jargon.

"Mrs. Bannon," he said, "whether or not your sale of your interest to Mr. McGee is final at this moment, the bank feels that it is ethically obligated to inform you that shortly after two o'clock this afternoon a local attorney contacted Mr. Sanders here and asked him if the sale of

65

the foreclosed properties had been consummated. When Mr. Sanders said that it had not, this attorney then said he was representing a party whose name he could not divulge, but who had directed him to inquire of the bank if, in the event the properties had not been sold, a firm offer of eighty thousand dollars would be sufficient to acquire it."

Sanders then interrupted, making Lee look exasperated for an instant. "It isn't a firm offer," he said to Janine. "But I don't think young . . . the local attorney would make a trivial inquiry. You see, if your arrangement with Mr. McGee isn't firm, or if he would like to withdraw, this might be a lot more advantageous for you. You would get back your ten thousand, plus the overage above the sixty thousand mortgage, or another twenty thousand."

Jan had been coached in how to react, by the Judge, if Puss had been successful in conning the young attorney, Steve Besseker.

"But couldn't this mysterious party be the same Mr. Preston LaFrance you were going to sell it to?" Janine asked.

"I don't think it would be very likely that Press would——"

"But haven't you told Mr. LaFrance he wasn't going to get my property?"

"Well . . . yes," said Sanders uncomfortably.

"Then, couldn't he turn right around and make a bigger offer through a lawyer, if he wants it bad enough?" she asked.

"It might be possible. Remotely possible."

"But don't you see," she said, frowning, earnest, leaning forward, "Mr. LaFrance owns the acreage directly behind us. He's been after our property all along. He's schemed and plotted to drive us out of business, Mr. Sanders, so he could buy it, and so he's responsible for what . . . my husband . . . responsible for . . ."

She snuffled into her handkerchief and Sanders, edgy and uncomfortable, said, "Now, there. Now, now, Mrs. Bannon. We all like to have some specific thing or person to blame when . . . when things don't go right. I'm sure Press LaFrance wouldn't——"

"My husband was convinced of it, and that's enough for me," she said spiritedly. "Why, I wouldn't accept any blind offer like that if it was . . . twice as much. Three times as much! I would rather sell it to Mr. McGee for eleven cents than see that man get it!"

Whitt Sanders fussed with the documents in front of him. He looked over at Rufus Wellington. "Rufus, I'd be way out of line, as you well know, if I made any comment about . . . about the resources of anybody doing business with us. All I can say is that . . . it is remotely possible the attorney is representing Press LaFrance. But it isn't very damn probable."

"You telling me, Whitt, it's pretty much a known fact around town this LaFrance couldn't scratch up eighty thousand?"

"I didn't say that."

"Around the courthouse this morning, Whitt, talking to the County Clerk, and passing the time of day with your Assessor, I got the feeling things are a little slow lately in the land business in Shawana County. Now if this LaFrance is up to his hocks in land deals, he might be like the fella with the itch who was juggling the family china and walking a tightrope, and a bee stung him right square on . . . Sorry, ladies, we'll leave that one right there. Probably got a good-looking balance sheet, all considered, and you got some of his notes, but you won't go one more dime, and you're a little nervous about him." The judge laughed suddenly and slapped his thigh. "By God, Whitt, that explains how come you acted sorry as a skunked hound you couldn't sell off the foreclosure to this LaFrance. He must have some deal in the making that would get him free and clear. He into you a little deep, boy?"

"Now, Rufus," Sanders pleaded. "I haven't told you a thing, and I'm not about to."

"Not in words," the judge said. "But we've set in poker games together, Whitt, and I never had much trouble reading you."

So then the red tape was taken care of, and the necessary documents were recorded at the courthouse. I walked with the judge to his black air-conditioned Imperial and he stopped out of earshot of his driver, who had gotten out and opened the door for him.

"Son, we sure God rammed a crooked stick into the hornet nest and stirred it up. There'll be folk sitting up half the night trying to make sense out of it all, not knowing it doesn't make sense—not the way they're thinking. Make sure you keep back far enough from the hornets."

"I'll be careful, Judge."

"You tell that big sassy redhead she did good. That's as much woman as a man is likely to see in a long day's journey. Where are you meeting up with her?"

"Not anywhere near here," I said. "Back at Broward Beach. She said she could probably get Besseker to drive her over there, and if she couldn't, she could get there somehow."

He squinted into the late afternoon sunlight and said, "There's a gal like that so clear in my mind it's like yesterday, son. And that was nineteen twenty and six." He turned to me with a look of dismay. "And if she's alive anyplace in the world, she's somewhere in her sixties. Hard to believe. Know something? I wrote poems to that gal. First, last and onliest time in my life. You let me know how you make out with that old swamp rat, that old D. J. Carbee, will you? McGee, tell me one thing. Are you going to let the angries get in the way of pumping some cash money out of this for that widow girl and her kids?"

"The money first, Judge."

He looked at his watch and grinned. "The way Connie drives, they're probably halfway back to Frostproof by now."

It took me a long time to find anybody who could give me any kind of clear directions on how to find the Carbee place. He had no phone. He had a post office box in Sunnydale, and it was his habit to come in no oftener than once a week to pick up his mail.

In the end I had to go over the unending construction project that ran by my new property. Florida is full of long-range, unending road jobs that break the backs, pocketbooks and hearts of the roadside businesses. The primitive, inefficient, childlike Mexicans somehow manage to survey, engineer and complete eighty miles of high-speed divided highway through raw mountains and across raging torrents in six months. But the big highway contractors in Florida take a year and a half turning fifteen miles of two-lane road across absolutely flat country into four-lane divided highway.

The difference is in American know-how. It's know-how in the tax problems, and how to solve them. The State Road Department has to take the low bid, by law. So Doakes Construction says a half-year contract will cost the State ten million, and a one-year contract will cost nine, and a year-and-a-half deadline will go for eight. Then Doakes can take on three or four big jobs simultaneously, and lease the equipment from a captive corporation, and listlessly move the equipment from job to job, and spread it out to gain the biggest profit with the only signs of frantic activity can be two or three men with cement brooms, looking at first like scarecrows but, when watched carefully, can be perceived to move, much like the minute hand on a clock.

Of course if some brisk, hustling firm moved into the state and started bidding what the jobs are worth and doing them fast, it would upset the tax teacart. Some have been foolish enough to try it, and the well-established Contractor's Club has just taken round-robin turns low-bidding the interloper to death. When he has quit for lack of work, things settle down to the cozy old system whereby, through some miraculous set of coincidences, all the big boys have exactly the amount of work they need at all times.

A couple of governors ago, when too many road jobs were not up to specification, somebody ratted and there was a big hassle about the State Road Department engineers and inspectors getting envelopes with cash money therein from some of the club members. Those contractors were restrained from bidding for a little while, and the engineers and inspectors were suspended. But it died down, as it always does, and the companies were reinstated with authorization to bid on upcoming work, and the state employees were put back on the job also, with the governor explaining that men should not be judged too harshly for a "moment of weakness," even though it had been made quite clear they'd had their little moments of weakness every Friday afternoon for a long, long time.

The Shawana County project of repaving 80D was the same thing on a smaller scale. Though the workday was not over, the only sign of roadwork I saw was one bull-dozer and one scraper parked and unattended off the side of the rutted road. I stopped at my dead business property, tore off the official notices of foreclosure, and decided against busting the shiny padlocks with a tire iron. Near the far end of 80D I found the sand road I was told to look for. It wound through scrub toward the bay shore, and when I drove into the clearing at the end I saw the traditional old Florida shack of cypress and hard pine set high on pilings, so that looking under it I could see the bay water and a crooked little dock with a skiff tied up.

There was a twanging of dogs toenailing the wire of their run, and a heavy throated *Arooo, Arooo* of the indigenous hound. I was standing by the car looking at the hounds when the voice directly behind me said, "Evenin'." It gave me a violent start and when I whirled, I could see from the glint in his faded old eyes that he enjoyed the effect.

In the days before age hunched him and withered him, he could have been nearly my size. His sallow jaws were covered with long gray stubble, and his head was bald except for a sparse white tonsure. He wore torn, stained khaki pants with a narrow length of hemp line for a belt, and an old gray twill work shirt. His feet were broad and bare, and standing near him was like standing near a bear cage, but with a slight spice of kerosene amid the thickness of the odor.

I gestured toward the dog run. "Red Walkers?"

"Got some Walker in 'em. I don't sell no dogs this time of year. Got just one bitch carryin' but she got loose on me just the wrong time, so God knows what she'll drop."

"Mister Carbee, I didn't come by to look at dogs. I came on a business matter."

"Waste of time. I don't buy a thing except supplies in town and send for the rest out of the Sears."

"I'm not selling anything."

"They say that and I ask them to set, and it turns out they are after all."

"It isn't like that this time."

"Then, you come set on the stoop."

"Thank you. My name is McGee." When we had climbed the steep steps and were seated, Carbee in a rocker and me in an old kitchen chair that had several generations of different shades of paint showing, I said, "I just bought the Bannon place on the river from the widow."

"Did you, now? I seen her once and him twice. Heard he kilt himself last Sunday morning when he found he'd lost the place. Great big old boy he was. Him and that Tyler Nigra come on me one morning drifting on the bay. Year ago maybe. Heavy fog, and me out too deep to pole and the ingin deader'n King Tut. That Tyler knows ingins like he invented them. Spring thing busted on the little arm for the gas feed, and that Tyler fixed it temporary with a little piece of rubber, got it running good. That Bannon wouldn't take a thing for it. Neighborly. Couldn't been too much longer after that Tyler quit him. Heard Tyler is working at the motorsyckle place in town. Anywhere there's ingins he's got a job of work. Maybe Bannon knowed and maybe he didn't that when Tyler quit him, it was because no Nigra with sense like Tyler's got is going to stay in the middle of any white man's fussing. If you're going to run that place, Mr. McGee, the first thing you better do is get Tyler back, that is if you're peaceful with everybody."

"I'm not going to run it, Mr. Carbee. I bought it as an investment."

"Lease it off to somebody to run?"

"No. Just let it sit."

I let him ponder that one, and at last he said, "Excuse me, but it don't make good sense, unless you got it for the land value alone. The buildings are worth more than the land."

"It depends on who wants the land."

He nodded. "And how bad."

"Mr. Carbee, I've been checking land ownership at the courthouse. You own the two-hundred-acre piece that starts at my east boundary."

"Could be."

"Ever thought of selling it?"

"I've sold a little land now and again. I've got maybe seventeen, eighteen hundred acres left, scattered around the east county, and except for this hundred right here, my home place, I imagine it would all be for sale if the price was right. You thinking of making an offer? If so, you better come up with the best you can do right off,

71

because I don't dicker. Man names a price, I say Yes or I say No, and that's it."

"Best offer, eh? I better tell you, Mr. Carbee, that I would be gambling on being able to pick up other parcels too, and gambling on being able to do it while my chance of resale is still good, resale of the whole two sections. And I'll tell you right now that if everything *does* work out, I'll make a nice profit, but if it doesn't, I'll have some working capital tied up until I can find some way of getting it back out. The best I can offer on an immediate sale—provided the title is clear of course—would be five hundred an acre."

He rocked forward and slapped his big bare feet on the boards and peered at me. "One hunnerd thousand!" he whispered.

"Less your share of the closing costs."

He got up and stamped over to the railing and spat. I knew the turmoil in his mind. He had wanted to check and see if he had optioned the two hundred acres to Preston LaFrance at a good figure. Two hundred dollars an acre had seemed like a good deal until I named my price. I could assume Tush's investigation was correct, and LaFrance's option was good until April. He wouldn't dare tell me about the option, for fear I would make my deal with LaFrance. And he was afraid that if he told me the land was not for sale, opportunity might move on to some other location and then he might not even get his two hundred an acre.

It was a pretty problem, and I wondered how he would handle it. He came back and sat down. The chair creaked. "Tell you what," he said placidly. "I have to think on that. And I should talk to the man that turns in the government figures for me when I sell things and see where that would put me on taxes and so on. Let me see now. This being Thursday the twenty-third day, that would mean two weeks from today would be . . . January fourth. Then I'll know more what I should ought to do. A man can't jump at a piece of money like that right off. He has to set and taste it a time."

"I understand. But you will have to tell me Yes or No when I see you again."

"One other thing. You said you were taking a gamble.

72

What you might do is figure on maybe me taking some of the risk too, Mr. McGee."

"How so?"

"From what you said, if your deal doesn't work, then you got a hundred thousand tied up and it will take a long time to move that land at that price. But if it goes like you're hoping, you turn a good profit on it. Maybe double?"

"Maybe not."

"Let's think on it being double. One thousand dollars an acre, two hundred thousand all told. So maybe we could get a paper drawed up between us, a contract saying that you give me five thousand cash money in hand that says come next . . . oh let's say April the fifteenth . . . you got the right to buy the land from me for four hundred an acre if you're willing to buy and I'm willing to sell. And if it works out that way, then if you resell it any time inside two years or three, you agree to pay me half the difference between what you bought if for and what you get for it. So if it was for one thousand, you'd for sure clear three hundred an acre profit, and no chance getting stuck with it. Of course if I want to sell on April the fifteenth and you don't want to buy, I keep your five thousand. But if you want to buy and I've decided not to sell, you get it all back."

He looked at me, benign and gentle and O so eager to be agreeable and fair to all. Way up the coast from us were the little nests of the hideaway mansions of the international bankers, and to the south of us was all the trickery and duplicity of hotel and resort syndicate financing. He had the precise look of a man betting into a pair of kings showing, and him with a three in the hole and a pair of threes up, and a perfect recollection of having seen the other two kings dealt to hands that had folded, one of them a hole card inadvertently exposed when the hand was tossed in.

"Mr. Carbee," I said. "I think we'll get along fine. You might even sell me an undivided half interest for two hundred an acre, and we could make it a joint venture."

"It'll be a pleasure to do business with you, Mister."

It seemed to me that old Mr. D. J. Carbee could have floated very nicely in the tricky currents of Hobe Sound or Collins Avenue, and I had a sudden respect for the guile of Preston LaFrance. But I did not envy him the little talk he was going to have to have with the old man just as soon as the old man could catch up to him. There was a shaggy old high-sided International Harvester station wagon parked over near the dog run, and it seemed probable that D.J. would be going into Sunnydale either this evening or early in the morning.

It was full dark when I drove into the city of Broward Beach. The stores were open, because tomorrow was Christmas Eve. Hefty Salvation Army lassies in their wagon-train bonnets dingle-dangled spare change into their kettles, and fat foam Santas were affixed to the palm boles and light standards, high enough to keep the kids from yanking their foam feet off. "Adeste Fidelis" was coming from somewhere, possibly a downtown church, electronic chimes that could rattle fillings in teeth, and overpowered the retail sound tracks of sprightlier seasonal music. I went through town and out to the beach and parked in the lot of the place I had told her to be, an expansive, glossy, improbable motel called Dune-Away, with a place pasted to it called The Annex, where food and drink was worth the prices they charge, even in the off season, and where if an attractive lassie wishes to be picked up, the hard-nose management will smooth the way, and if she doesn't, those same professionals can chill the random Lothario quickly, quietly and completely.

I looked at the lounge from the doorway and saw her alone at a banquette against the far wall. As I headed across toward her I was aware of a wary waiter also moving on an interception course. But he and I saw her quick recognition and saw her face light up in greeting. So he held the table out for me to sit beside her, and went off with our order.

"You missed our boy by ten minutes," she said. "He was very dear. Not my type. One of those narrow-boned dark ones, a bit stuffy. He wants to be with it, but he laughs a little too soon or a little too late, and he seems to sit and steer his car instead of drive it. Let me see. He's thirty-one and he's been married to Linda for five years, and they have two kids and she is a fantastic golfer, and her father owns the Buick Agency in Sunnydale, and he is worried about her drinking. He kept giving me a certain business with the eyebrows that maybe he learned in front of his mirror, and I made his hands clammy when we sat close. He didn't have the guts to take a hack at me right out of the clear blue. He'd have to be encouraged so that then he could tell himself he hadn't started it, and he's only human, isn't he? He's very nervous about the impression he makes, and he's steeped in all that radical right wing hoke about conspiracies and a bankrupt America and Chinese bombs, and it was a drag to listen big-eyed to that tired gunk and say Oh and Ahh and Imagine that! He does a lot of civic stuff and joins everything, and thinks of himself as being the fearless attorney, standing up for right and purity. As the dear judge would say—Bullshit. He tried to help Tush Bannon, and then when it got a little sticky, he dropped him. Know how he explained it to me? This is precious!"

She paused for the waiter to serve the drinks, then went into an imitation of Steve Besseker: "So long as we are operating under the Capitalistic System, Puss, and remember it is the best the world has yet devised, men will take business risks and some will win and some will lose. I won't deny there were certain pressures on Bannon, but he got so he thought everything was some kind of a plot. He started whining and stopped fighting. That's when I lost my respect for him and washed my hands of him."

"Yes," I said. "That is precious. That is very dear."

"I never met your friend Tush, Travis. But I don't think he ever whined."

"He wouldn't know how. Congratulations. You snowed him very nicely. Have any trouble with it?"

"None! I hitched my chair closer and closer to his and I kept my voice very low and full of secrets, and I kept my eyes wide and I put my fingertips on his arm. I told him that I was employed by Gary Santo and we had investigated him and it was Mr. Santo's decision that he could be trusted with certain delicate and private negotiations involving one of Mr. Santo's operations in this area, and could be trusted not to reveal the name of his client. I explained that it was so hush-hush that if he was foolish enough to even try to reach Mr. Santo by phone or in person, he would ruin everything for himself. But if things went well, then he could think in terms of a retainer of five figures annually. You know, when he began to swallow it, his eyes looked glazed and his mouth hung open. I almost started laughing. So he phoned the query about the eighty thousand to the bank like a good little fellow, and he was *so* upset when he met me later and told me that Mrs. Bannon had regained title and then sold it to some mysterious stranger named McGee from Fort Lauderdale. I thought he would cry. I told him I was sure that Mr. Santo would be convinced that he had done all he could. I told him he would get his instructions from me by phone or in person. I asked him if he would be willing to meet me sometimes, if it was necessary. In Miami, or even Havana or New York. All expenses paid, of course."

"Who told you to say that?"

"I made it up. It seemed like a good idea. I mean it makes him think more about me and not so much about it being a pretty funny way for a man like Santo to do business. Was I wrong?"

"No. I like it. And the final little hook? Did you remember to get that in?"

"Yes, but very casual, and not until he came in here to have a drink with me. I just said that I know the way Mr. Santo's mind works, and he would certainly wonder if there was any connection between a Mr. Preston La-France and Mr. McGee, any business connection, and if he could find out in advance of my phoning him about it, it might make a good impression on Mr. Gary Santo."

"Reaction?"

"Nothing in particular. He said he'd try to find out." She shrugged. "He's just a trivial little man, honey, really. And this is the first little whiff he's had of something big and important and kind of glamorous, and he can't hardly stand it. Feed me, please. I'm sitting here aching and gnawing, and I keep looking at that door where the waiters go by with those steaks."

She ate with a savage and elegant precision, and an occasional little sound of contentment. I told her that as a reward for special sly services and for being a persuasive liar, I would stake us to the most elaborate accommodations the Dune-Away could provide.

"And go back in the boat in the morning?" she asked. "Would it be vulgar, dear, if I asked a special favor?

76

So much has happened and I am so pooped, really, that all I can think about is that gigantic, fantastic, marvelous bed aboard the *Flush,* and it would be a nice place to wake up on the morning before Christmas, and I want to get to that bed faster than your pretty little boat can get me there. Possible?"

"Race you to the car, Red."

She was asleep by the time I hit the first stoplight, and slept all the way back, and groused about being shaken awake to walk from the car to the houseboat. I made her stand on the dock while I went aboard and, before unlocking the door, checked the little bulbs behind the sliding panel in the outside port bulkhead of the lounge. The bulbs were out, so I turned the knife switch below the bulb, turning off the little Radar Sentry that monitored the below-decks areas of the *Flush* while I was away from her. Had anyone broken in, their mass and movement would have closed the circuit that lighted the two hidden bulbs, or lighted one of them if by any chance the other had burned out. The gadget can be rigged if anyone wants, to turn on floodlights or sound a siren or even phone the cops. But I didn't want an alarm system that would spook the intruder. I just wanted to know if I'd had visitors, and then I could take the necessary steps to make them welcome if they happened to be still there.

I beckoned her aboard, and she came inside, stumbling and yawning. We shared a shower, and then we shared a lazy, easeful, gentled quarter hour of love, wherein she murmured she didn't think she could but don't go to any special trouble, darling, it doesn't matter that much, and then she murmured that if it wasn't too late for a lady to change her mind, sir, and it was just barely not too late to be able to wait just long enough, and so she rose, and caught, sighed long, and fell away purring. She called me back from my edge of sleep by gently thumbing my left eye open and saying, "Are you there? Listen, for making all these days and nights so full, the lady thanks you. Thanks for letting me come along for more than just the ride, McGee. Thanks for helping me cram three bushels of living into a one peck basket. Are you there?"

"You are O so welcome, lady."

Seven

MEYER CAME OVER on Christmas morning with a cumbersome vat of eggnog and three battered pewter mugs. We had a nice driving rain out of the northwest and a wind that made the *Flush* shift and groan and thump. I put on Christmas tapes because it was no day to trust FM programming. Sooner or later daddy would see mommy kissing Rudolph. Meyer and I played chess. Puss Killian, in yellow terry coveralls, sat and wrote letters. She never said who they were to, and I had never asked.

He won with one of those pawn-pressure games, the massive and ponderous advance that irritates me into doing the usual stupid thing, like a sacrifice that favors him, just to get elbow room on the board.

As we finished, Puss came over, shoving her letter into her pocket and said, "Should we call Jan and say merry merry? Which is worse, I guess, to call her or not call her?"

"There's one of Meyer's laws that covers it. Tell her, Meyer."

He beamed up at her. "Of course. In all emotional conflicts, dear girl, the thing you find the hardest to do is the thing you should do. So I guess you call."

"Thanks a lot. Trav? Will you do it? Please? Then you can turn it over to me. Okay?"

So I placed the call. Connie sounded too hearty. I guess it wasn't such a great day at the groves. Janine imitated the requirements of friendship and holiday. But there was deadness under her tone of voice. I knew she would not break up, not with that weight of the deadness holding her down. After all the things to say I could think of, most of them so trite I felt like both Bob *and* Ray, I gave the phone over to Puss. She sat at the desk and talked for a long time with Janine, in low tones. Then she said Connie wanted to talk to me again. She said Janine had gone to her room, so she could talk freely. She asked me when the body would be picked up. I said I'd made arrangements and they would come and get it tomorrow. The holidays had caused a delay.

"Any communication from sunny Sunnydale, Connie?"

"Nothing at all. Nothing yet."

As I hung up I turned and saw Puss leaving the lounge, almost at a gallop, and heard her give a big harsh sob.

I looked at Meyer and he shrugged and said, "The tears started to drip, and then she started to snuffle and then she took off."

I filled our mugs and brought him up to date on my financial affairs in Shawana County.

He pondered the situation and said, "It's pretty flexible. There's a lot of ways it could go."

"That's the general idea. To keep my skirts clean I have to have a legitimate sale of my legitimate ownership in that marina and motel. I think that's where I pick LaFrance clean. If he could offer thirty-two five, I'll settle for forty thousand, *and* he assumes the mortgage. He'll have to go for it because that's the only way he'll have a package he can provide Santo—his own fifty acres, my ten, and the option on old Carbee's two hundred. Now this LaFrance is a greedy and larcenous bastard. He was trying to make the deal as sweet as possible for himself by driving Tush into the ground and getting those ten acres cheap. I think he will continue to be a greedy and larcenous bastard, and I think that if I can offer him a little extra edge, for cash under the table, he'll get the cash somehow, and I hope it will be from that brother-in-law of his on the County Commission." I went and checked the name in my notebook. "P. K. Hazzard. Known as Monk. He—meaning Preston LaFrance—is going to be very jumpy, so you and I are going to work a little variation on the old pigeon drop."

His big bushy brows climbed his Neanderthal forehead. "We are?"

"Meyer, I think you'd make a nice plant location expert, somebody with the authority to make firm recommendations to a nice big fat rich company."

"It is an exact science, my good fellow," he said. "We take all the factors—labor supply, area schools and recreation facilities, transportation costs, construction costs, distance from primary markets, and by adjusting these by formula before programming the computer, we can arrive at a valid conclusion as . . . Travis, what is a pigeon drop?"

"Unlike what might first come to mind, Meyer, this is something one drops *onto* a pigeon."

"You couldn't have made it more clear. One thing. Aren't you on a little dangerous ground on this body-snatching thing?"

"Body-snatching! Me? Meyer! A perfectly legitimate funeral home in Miami is going to pick up that body in a licensed hearse and bring it back to Miami and air-ship it from there to Milwaukee."

"And the place is run by a man who owes you a big favor, and that hearse is going to make a stop at a very well equipped and staffed pathology lab during the off hours, where two more of your strange friends are going to determine if there was some cause of death besides dropping an engine block on him."

"Meyer, please! It's just normal curiosity. Jan gave her permission. Is there an ordinance against it?"

"What about concealing evidence of a crime?"

"If you're nervous about evidence we don't even have yet, you don't have to help me play games with LaFrance."

"So who's nervous?"

"I am. A little."

We sat in silence. The tape had run out and turned off. I wondered if I should go in and give Puss a little comforting pat to cure the Noel blues. Too many pasts crowd in on you at mistletoe time. It's the good ones that hurt.

"Meyer?"

"At your service."

"On the sale of the marina thing to LaFrance, Jan will end up with thirty thousand, net. If we can work that pigeon drop, she'll get maybe fifty, maybe a hundred on top of that. Money won't buy what she's lost, but it would be nice to get her a really good big chunk. If I could find out that Gary Santo knew about what was being done to the Bannons, knew about it and didn't give a damn because he was pressuring LaFrance into assembling the adjoining parcels so he could buy them for resale, then it would be nice to take a slice of his bread too."

"Now *wait* a minute! This is not somebody that goes for your pigeon drop. This man operates very big, my friend. He has lawyers and accountants double-checking every move."

"I was thinking of something legitimate. Something in your line. Like some kind of an investment where you would know it was going to go sour and he wouldn't. Then couldn't there be some way of . . . funneling money out of the same proposition into Janine's pocket? Hell, Santo is a plunger. With all the protection, he's still a plunger. Some kind of a listed stock, maybe, like those they were rigging on the American Exchange you were telling me about one time."

"So why should Gary Santo listen to Meyer?"

"Because first we build you a track record. You dig into those charts of yours and make some of those field trips and surveys and come up with some very very hot growth items. And I think I've got just the pipeline, once I develop it a little, to feed them to him. The pipeline is named Mary Smith. She has brown straight glossy hair. She is small, and stacked, and she looks sullen and hungry."

"So if the great Gary Santo knew nothing about your friend Bannon?"

"I know Tush tried to get to him and couldn't get past the girl-curtain. He didn't think Santo was the kind of man who'd want the little guy crushed under his wheels. Somehow Santo squeezed LaFrance and LaFrance squeezed various folk, which happened to include Tush. If Santo knew—and let the roof fall on Tush—for a lousy little crumb of the acreage he needs up there, then I would like to have him get it where it stings. And, if so, can you work up something?"

Meyer got up and plodded back and forth, all hair and simian concentration, and scowling little bright blue eyes. He stopped and sighed. "McGee, I don't know. I just don't know. The problem divides itself into two interdependent parts. First I would have to get a line on a dirty situation like Westec before it leaks out. Those people falsified their earnings statements to keep the stock at a high level so they could pick up smaller companies on favorable merger terms. Then one executive put in for eight million worth of the stock, traded on the American Exchange, and he couldn't come up with the money to pay for the stock and that's when trading was suspended. Now *if* I could smell out something like that, heading for disaster, and then if I can pick a few legitimate winners to make him feel as if I—"

"Or as if you *had* picked some winners, Meyer."

He looked startled for just a moment, and then came that broad Meyer smile that turns one of the ugliest faces of the Western World into what one of the articulate lassies among the Meyer Irregulars one season called "a beautiful proof that someday, somehow, the human race is going to make it."

"Dated, official, machine-printed confirmations of stock purchases on official forms from a reputable brokerage house! Hindsight! Perfect! One day, maybe two, in New York, and I can come back with proof I'm such a genius I bought——"

"You had *me* buy . . ."

"Yes. I see. I had you buy highfliers right at the point where they were taking off, and I don't have to go back far, less than a year in every case. Gulton, Xtra, Leasco Data, Texas Gulf Sulphur, Goldfield Mohawk Data. Fantastic performers! Listen, I won't make it too good. If every buy was at the bottom, there'd be suspicion. Like instead of Gulton at fifty dollars a share, you get on at sixty-five."

"Where is it now?"

"It went up to nearly a hundred and ten, split two for one, and the last time I looked it's maybe sixty dollars." He sat down and emptied the nog mug again. "Travis, how rich do you want to be? I can use an old and dear friend who will be delighted to help, so I can get you monthly margin account statements showing the security position, the debit and so on."

"Say I started a year ago with a hundred thousand."

"Congratulations! You are now worth a quarter of a million."

"Success hasn't spoiled me, Meyer. Have you noticed?"

"All I notice are your criminal instincts, my dear Travis, and how rash you are with your queen, which lets me whip you at chess, and how right now you are too tightened up over this Tush business. You are too close to this one. Be careful. I don't want to lose you. Some terrible people might take over Slip F-18. Nondrinkers, going around saying shush."

Puss Killian came drifting back into the lounge, looking

wan. Her face was puffed, her eyes red. She snuffled and then honked into a Kleenex, and said, "Give me that Meyer's Law again, please? The exact words."

"In all emotional conflicts the thing you find hardest to do is the thing you should do."

"I was afraid that was what you said, Meyer. What we all do is make excuses why we shouldn't do the hard things. Like apologize. Like visit the dying. Like spend a little time with bores."

"Stop short of masochism, dear girl," Meyer said.

"I always have. Too far short, maybe. Gad! I feel as if I'd been pressed flat and dried out, like an old flower in a bad book. *Do* something, gentlemen!"

And so we did. Meyer and I went off in opposite directions, head-hunting. He had a quota of five—three female and two male. I went after two couples. It is an old contest. They can be friends, or acquaintances, or absolute strangers. After the festivities, we rate them on a scale of ten, the measurement being whether or not you'd be willing to spend a month on a small boat with them. We made a good Christmas bag, because there was a compulsion to have a good time. We unfastened all the umbilical devices affixing the *Flush* to her mooring space, and, with eighteen yuletide souls aboard, chugged down into the breadths of Biscayne Bay under clearing skies, edged the old girl as close as I could get her to good beach with good protection near Southwest Point, stayed the night in drink, argumentation, minimal sleep, beach walks, a touch of skinnydipping for those brave hearts who can stand the December waters, and came trundling back up to home base the next day.

Sometimes it doesn't work at all, but this time it had jelled. There had been some good minds, outrageous opinions, furious squabbles, laugh-till-you-cry incidents, games and contests, confessions and accusations, tears and broad smiles. But no sloppy drunks, no broken crockery, or teeth. We aimed homeward tired and content and, for the most part, friends. Waterborne group therapy, Meyer calls it. It restored Puss Killian. Late on Tuesday afternoon as we were scoring our recent boatmates, with Puss as arbiter when we disagreed, she said, "Does anyone else have the feeling that little jaunt lasted at least a week?"

"When they don't seem to," said Meyer, "they haven't

worked." Which could be another one of Meyer's Laws, but he says it is too close to aphorism to be significant.

Eight

WEDNESDAY, DECEMBER 27TH, before Puss and Janine and I had to catch the flight out of Miami to Milwaukee for Tush's funeral the next day, I had a chance to talk with Dr. Mike Guardina at the lab. I left the gals with the car and told them I wouldn't be long, so not to wander too far.

Mike took me into a small office and closed the door, and took a folder out of the locked file. He is thin, intent, strung on taut wires, totally intent on finding out why people die. He is qualified in about all the kinds of pathology they have.

"Trav, the first impression was of too much damage. Way too much to go with the way it was supposed to happen, from what we found on your roll of film once we made prints. So much damage that actually trying to locate any specific tissue damage or bone damage not likely to have been caused by the impact of that weight dropping on him would have been pretty iffy. About all we can say for certain is that there is a good chance he wasn't shot in the head first, nor much of a chance that there was any blow that struck him from behind. Now you *did* want a cause of death to a reasonable medical certainty, but I gathered from your conversation over the phone with me that you want suicide ruled out if possible."

"But if you can't——"

"This is another approach. Take a look at these." He put three 8 x 10 glossies on the desk top. He pointed with the eraser end of a yellow pencil. "This is a blowup of the central portion of one of your pictures, Trav, where you had that block cranked high and you aimed up at it. See these rusty hexagonal nuts along here, toward what we will call the rear end of the block? Look at this one in particular. Somebody apparently tried to knock it off with a cold chisel, and knocked off a third of it before they gave up. Now this next print is full frame, of the chest area of the subject. Note these three marks circled with a grease pencil, and marked A, B and C. This third print is actually a triptych, an enlargement of A, B and C. The area marked A shows a clear imprint or incised impression of that damaged nut. The encircled B area shows the same imprint exactly, and it is about four inches from the point marked A, in a lateral direction across the crushed chest, from right to left. Imprint C is, as you can see from the print of the whole chest area, another inch and a quarter or inch and a half further, going from right to left, from imprint B. But here, as it struck, or would seem to have struck a previously damaged area, we do not have as obvious an identical match. However, if you want me to project the thirty-five millimeter color slides we took of points A, B and C, I think you will see that it is reasonable to suppose that impact area C represents the same deformed nut."

"In simple lousy English," I said, "you are certain that the engine block was dropped onto him twice, and you can make a case that it could have been dropped, cranked up, dropped again, cranked up, and dropped the third time."

"Yes," said Mike. "It wouldn't be consistent with suicide."

Long ago and far away I could see Tush Bannon under the needle spray in the long shower room that smelled of old socks, soap and disinfectant, rubbing up a suds on that barrel chest and bawling, off-key, ". . . and this is my storrrreeee, as you can plainly see. Never let a sailor put his hand above your kneeeeeeee."

"Spare me the slides, Mike. Can I have dupes of these?"

"Got them right here for you. Smaller. Five by sevens. Okay?"

"Fine. And what about a grand jury? Will it make you nervous if we don't do a thing?"

"What could you do with it? Somebody got clumsy. They found him crushed under that thing and so they cranked it up and it slipped and fell on him again and they cranked it up again and locked it. He was obviously dead, so why make a big statement about the crank slipping? We can't prove the third drop, even though I feel certain it happened. You understand what I'm saying, Trav. In a court of law any neophyte defense attorney could set up an

85

area of reasonable doubt you could take a truck convoy through."

"But if there ever comes a time for affidavits?"

"Me and Harry Bayder, and the tape going as we worked, and a resident in pathology taking notes. Time and place, and an accurate identification of the body, and signed statements in the file from all three of us. Just in case. If and when you ever get something else to go with it."

"You are a good man, Guardina."

"Beyond compare, surely. Keep in touch, hombre."

All I could tell Janine, or wanted to tell Janine, was that any last faint possibility of suicide was long long gone. I told her on the way out to the airport. She didn't say a thing. I had my hands on the wheel at ten of and ten after. She reached up and put her long fingers on the ten after wrist. At the chapel in Milwaukee, when we bowed our heads in prayer, I looked down at the underside of my right wrist and saw the four dark-blue half moon marks where her nails had bitten deep. Her parents thought she should have brought her three young sons to the services. They thought Tush should have been shipped sooner and buried earlier. They thought she should come home with the boys and stay. They thought her tailored navy-blue suit was not proper attire for a widow. They thought it odd she had brought along this McGee person and this Killian woman when there were so many old friends who were—or should have been—so much closer in a time of need. They resented not knowing Connie Alvarez. They had remembered that she had been at Janine's wedding, but they let it be known she had struck them as a rather coarse and peculiar person, not at all the ladylike type their daughter should cultivate. They made it clear that it was an affront to them that poor Janine should go back immediately to Florida with these . . . these *strangers*.

On the flight back we had three side by side. Janine was in the middle. She said, turning her face from Puss to me and back, "I'm sorry. They just . . . they aren't . . ."

Puss hugged her and said, "Honey, if you put the knock on them you'll feel like a traitor. Everybody has people, and their people don't want to let them go or admit they're

86

gone when they're gone. They love you. That's good enough. Right?"

"Should I have brought the boys? That's what I keep wondering."

"Ask each one of them when he gets to be twenty-one, dear. Ask them if they felt as if they had been left out of anything," Puss said.

So they sat, holding hands, and Jan fell asleep. Puss gave me a sleepy wink and then she was gone too. I looked out of the jet at December gray, at cloud towers reaching up toward us. Tush was gone, and too many others were gone, and I sought chill comfort in an analogy of death that has been with me for years. It doesn't explain or justify. It just seems to remind me how things are.

Picture a very swift torrent, a river rushing down between rocky walls. There is a long, shallow bar of sand and gravel that runs right down the middle of the river. It is under water. You are born and you have to stand on that narrow, submerged bar, where everyone stands. The ones born before you, the ones older than you, are upriver from you. The younger ones stand braced on the bar downriver. And the whole long bar is slowly moving down that river of time, washing away at the upstream end and building up downstream.

Your time, the time of all your contemporaries, schoolmates, your loves and your adversaries, is that part of the shifting bar on which you stand. And it is crowded at first. You can see the way it thins out, upstream from you. The old ones are washed away and their bodies go swiftly by, like logs in the current. Downstream where the younger ones stand thick, you can see them flounder, lose footing, wash away. Always there is more room where you stand, but always the swift water grows deeper, and you feel the shift of the sand and the gravel under your feet as the river wears it away. Someone looking for a safer place can nudge you off balance, and you are gone. Someone who has stood beside you for a long time gives a forlorn cry and you reach to catch their hand, but the fingertips slide away and they are gone. There are the sounds in the rocky gorge, the roar of the water, the shifting, gritty sound of sand and gravel underfoot, the forlorn cries of despair as the nearby ones, and the ones upstream, are taken by the current. Some old ones who stand on a good place, well braced, understanding currents and balance, last a long time. A Churchill, fat cigar atilt, sourly amused at his own endurance and, in the end, indifferent to rivers and the rage of waters. Far downstream from you are the thin, startled cries of the ones who never got planted, never got set, never quite understood the message of the torrent.

Tush was gone, and our part of the bar was emptier, and the jet raced from the sunset behind us to the night ahead, and beside me slept the two women, hand in hand, their lashes laying against the high flesh of their cheeks with a heartbreaking precision, a childish surrender, an inexpressible vulnerability.

By Saturday, the next to the last day of the year, I was beginning to feel surly and uneasy. I held a slack line. I felt that I had deftly pulled the barbed hook through the underlip of one Preston LaFrance, and that boating him was inevitable. He had to come aboard the *Flush,* flapping, gills working. The name McGee had suddenly cropped up at too many points in his life. McGee at the bank with the widow. McGee at Ingledine's, making the arrangements about the body. McGee out at the old shack, souring his deal with old D. J. Carbee. McGee, the new owner of the property he wanted.

But the line lay slack on the water, without the slightest twitch or tension. Puss and I drove up to Broward Beach early Saturday morning, turned the car in, and came back down the Waterway in the *Muñequita.* I made a fast run, thinking I might find LaFrance when I got back to *The Busted Flush.* Nothing. Puss was withdrawn, remote, and did not help my mood by telling me she was going away Monday morning for a little while. A few days. No clue as to where or why. And be damned if I'd ask. As she packed a bag it seemed a gratuitous affront that she should hum to herself. What was she so cheery about?

And why didn't Meyer phone from New York? Too busy having a fine time with old stockbroker buddies, probably.

At ten minutes after four the slack line twitched. I tested the tension cautiously. It was still through the underlip. I shooed Puss into the master stateroom and invited Preston LaFrance into the lounge. He came in, grinning, hesitant. A gaunt and ugly and sandy one. Maybe the young Sinclair Lewis, if the old photographs are accurate. Fifty percent hick. Fifty percent con artist. Cowlick. Long lumpy face. Lantern jaw. Nervous cough. Ploughboy hands. Brash sports jacket with the wrong button buttoned. A gangly diffidence overlaying a flavor of confidence. When he looked around the lounge, his expression vague, I had the feeling he saw everything that had any bearing on his own aims and motives, and could price the whole layout within plus or minus three percent.

His big hand was warm, dry and utterly slack. "Mr. McGee, we seem to be aiming in kind of the same direction on a little matter, and what I thought, I thought it might be time to see if we can eat out of the same dish or spill the dinner."

"I guess that depends on how hungry we are, LaFrance. Sit down. Get you a drink?"

"Mostly I'm called Press. Short for Preston. Thank you kindly, and if you would have such a thing as a glass of milk, that would be fine. I had an ulcer and got over it, and they tell me sipping milk instead of kitchen whisky will keep me from having the next one. And I guess you've upped my milk bill by maybe half, Mr. McGee."

"Mostly I'm called Trav. Short for Travis. And we stock milk, because there is very little damn else you can put on cornflakes."

"You are so *right!*"

I brought him his glass of milk, and a beer for me. He sat on the long yellow couch. I pulled a chair a little too close, turned the back toward him and straddled it, forearm along the back of the chair, chin on the forearm, expression politely expectant and benign. It put my face two feet from his, and six inches higher, with the brightest window right behind me. Closeness is a tactical weapon. We do not like our little envelope of anticipated separation and privacy penetrated. It is a variable distance, depending on the needs and necessities of the moment. We endure the inadvertent pressure of the flank of the office worker in the crowded down-elevator at five o'clock. If we are alone with the office worker, if it is male—without overtones of fag—then it is insolent challenge, demanding action. Being jostled in a crowded airport is acceptable; on a wide and empty sidewalk it is not. A fixed stare is a form of penetration of the envelope, carrying different messages according to the sort-out of sex, station, race, ages and environment.

Always we want some separation, some tiny measure of distance regardless of how clumsily our culture mechanizes an inadvertent togetherness. The only exception time is when sex is good in all dimensions, so that even in the deepest joining there is the awareness of that final barrier, an apartness measured by only the dimension of a membrane, and part of the surge of it is a struggle to overcome even that much apartness.

The lounge aboard the *Flush* is a sizeable enclosure, and I positioned myself well inside the area of logical separation. Once you learn the expectations of distances, small and great, you can use them in tactical ways, watching for reaction, for a pulling back, a pained stiffness of expression, an awkwardness. Or position yourself beyond the plausible distance and watch for the forward lean, the advance, the slight what-is-wrong-with-me agitation. It is a kind of language without words, a communication, and incites a reversion to the primitive compulsion of the pecking order, the barnyard messages—You get too close so I peck you back to where you belong.

Press LaFrance sipped his milk, looking down into the glass. He looked to the side and reached and put the half glass on the end table. He then hiked one limber Ichabod leg up, heel on the edge of the couch cushion, long fingers of both hands laced around his ankle, slouching just enough to interpose the knee between us so that he looked at me over the top of it. With that interposition he increased the subjective distance between us.

"Fifty mortgage plus fifteen cash equals sixty-five thousand," said he. "And that is better than twice what any licensed appraiser would put on it."

"For the same use Bannon put it to. A man with his house on fire and a man dying of thirst would put a different value on a glass of water."

"Hard to put a value on 'if,' Trav. Link three or four ifs together and it comes out long odds, so you can't go very high."

"There are some men, Press, who get a little confused between greed and shrewdness. Maybe they are a little bit shrewd, and then they want to buy at the lowest dollar and sell at the highest, and finally it comes out as if they weren't shrewd at all. They end up doing the very same thing as if they were stupid to begin with."

The knobbly face colored a little and the mouth stiffened then relaxed as the color faded. "A fella could have made an offer way back, through a third party, and a fair offer, all considered, but somebody could have been too bullheaded to listen."

"Fair offer?"

"We aren't talking marina, McGee. We aren't talking motel. You know that and I know it. We are talking ten acres."

"Ten acres in the middle of the deal, smack in the middle of it, like a June bug in the birthday cake."

"So I was coming up with thirty-two hundred and fifty an acre for those ten acres."

"Which gives you sixty acres, if you'd gotten it. What did the fifty behind Bannon's place cost you?"

"A fair price."

"One thousand dollars in nineteen fifty-one, according to the tax stamps on the deed as recorded in the Shawana County Courthouse, which comes out to twenty dollars an acre. That was probably a fair price in nineteen fifty-one. We can do a little arithmetic, Press. When you pay me forty thousand for clear title to the Bannon place, and assume the mortgage, then you have a ninety-one-thousand cost figure on the sixty acres, or just about fifteen hundred an acre. That will turn you a profit of five hundred an acre on resale, or thirty thousand, and because you are a reasonable man and because you are in a bind, you are going to be sensible and take it."

He was absolutely immobile for long seconds. I think he even stopped breathing. He dropped the knee, swiveled and got up and peered down at me. "Man, you lost your cotton-pickin' mind for sure! That would be two thousand an acre on resale! The deal with my buyer is for nine hundred. I couldn't pay you any forty thousand and take over a fifty-thousand mortgage! I'd come up with a loss of six hundred an acre. Where do you get this crazy two-thousand figure?"

"Why, Press! You'd make out just fine on nine hundred an acre! You've got old D. J. Carbee screwed. You pay him two hundred an acre, or forty thousand, and you resell it to Gary Santo for nine hundred, which comes to a hundred and eighty thousand. So deduct that thirty-six thousand you'll lose on that sixty acres, and there you are, fat and sassy, and a hundred and forty-four thousand ahead."

He picked up the glass and drained the milk, wiped a chin-drip on the back of his wrist. "D.J. told me he didn't tell you a thing about that option. So by God, you knew about it when you went and offered him five hundred an acre. You upset that old man something pitiful."

"Maybe I was trying to upset you, Press."

He sat down on the far end of the yellow couch. He shook his head like a sad hound. "What in the world are you after, McGee?"

"Money. Just like you, Press."

"You knew I had to show up here. You left a trail and you left loose ends. But you didn't do all this just to charge me forty thousand for something that cost you fifteen."

"That isn't much profit, come to think of it. What do you think I ought to charge you? Sixty? A hundred?"

"Oh, come *on!*" he wailed.

"You can't come up with much. You've got the shorts, haven't you? Overextended?"

"Don't you worry about *me!*"

"But I *do!* I'll tell you what I'll do for you, LaFrance. I'll pay you fifty thousand dollars in cash for your fifty acres *and* the option you've got on the Carbee acreage. Then you're out of the whole thing with a nice profit."

He stiffened. "Hell *no!* Then you got the whole two hundred and sixty acres Santo wants to buy."

"But I wouldn't sell it to him. The price isn't right."

"But you can't move it, McGee, unless you move Santo's parcel at the same time! Calitron has to have the whole four hundred and eighty acres. You know the rest of it, so you have to know that much."

"I know the Calitron Corporation will go as high as seventeen hundred an acre to Gary Santo." It was nice to have the name of the corporate buyer.

Preston LaFrance brooded about it. "He never did let on what he expects to get. But there's not a damn thing anybody can do about that. Hell, Santo can just let his land sit there for ten years. He doesn't have to sweat these things out."

"In a smaller sense, Press, that's my policy too."

He looked startled, and then alarmed. "Now, you wouldn't squirrel up the whole deal by setting on that little ten acres forever, would you. Jesus, man, Calitron will go somewhere else if they get held up! Then where are we?"

"Maybe I've got a buyer who doesn't need that much room. I'm thinking of your health, Press. Fifty thousand and no more worries, and your ulcer will feel fine. You can pay off some of the notes at the bank and make Whitt Sanders happy."

His jaw firmed up. "I'll play it like a Mexican standoff, mister. I'll squat on my fifty and you squat on your ten."

"It's like what you said when you came in. Do we learn to eat out of the same dish or do we spill the dinner? Know what the difference is, Press? I'm not hungry and you are."

He cracked the knuckles of both hands, methodically, one at a time. "Now you said something about being shrewd and being greedy both and how it turns out stupid, Trav. I've been working on this thing one way or another for a year and a half, about. The way things are, I have to make it big, and that's the truth. Not big the way Santo thinks about money, but big for me. I'm leveling with you. I've got to come out of this six figures ahead anyway, or with the present timing I'm going to end up way the hell back where I started in forty-six when I got out of the service, and I don't want for that to happen. I had it within an inch of being home free, and you slipped in out of nowhere and bollixed it all up for me. Okay, it was smart business and you're pretty cute. So right now I think it's up to you to find some way to fix it so we get to eat out of the same dish, each to his need. I've got my good option out of old Carbee, even if he is thinking about shooting me since you went to see him. And I got the fifty acres behind your place."

"As long as you're leveling, you can settle one thing that bothers me a little. Back when you found out Bannon

93

wouldn't sell and wouldn't budge, and if you had the shorts so you couldn't offer him enough, why didn't you turn the problem over to Gary Santo. With what he'd stand to make, he could have paid Bannon twenty cents for every dime he had in that business, and bought him a new location."

"I told Santo about that! I had that same idea. It took me a whole month to get to talk to him face to face, and then I had to chase him up to Atlanta, where they were opening up a hotel he's got money in, where he's got a penthouse thing he keeps for himself. I was up there drinking and waiting around maybe an hour and then he was ready to talk and we went back into one of the bedrooms and I told him these Bannons were a nice little family, working hard and doing pretty good, and if he could make them a good offer, which I wasn't in any shape to do, then we were all ready to move. So he said don't bother me with the details, LaFrance. He said that if he had to take care of all my problems, why should I have a slice of the cake. He said that come next May first he'd pay the full two hundred and thirty-four thousand for a clean, clear title to the two hundred and sixty acres to the east of his holdings, or I could forget the whole thing. And that was what I couldn't do, McGee—forget the whole thing."

"So you broke them. You busted them down to a price you could afford. You didn't have any other choice."

"No other choice in the world, excepting to go broke myself. I swear, if it had been my own brother running that place, it would have had to be just the same. But let me tell you, I never did count on Bannon killing himself. That never entered my head one minute. We were having a late Sunday breakfast in the kitchen when I got a phone call telling me what he'd done, and after I hung up and thought about it, I went right in the bathroom and threw up. I swear, it made me sick. I was in bed most of the day. Suzy wanted to call the Doc, but I told her it was just probably something I ate at the hotel Saturday night, at the testimonial dinner for old Ben Linder, retiring from the law, looking like a little old gray ghost the way the cancer is eating him up." He sighed. "You know, having you come out of noplace and snatch those ten acres away from me is like punishment for what

94

Bannon did to himself. It's like getting the word that nothing ever is going to work out right anymore for me, and things used to go so good there for a while."

"Maybe Bannon didn't kill himself."

His sagging head snapped up. "What are you trying to do now? What kind of new game are you playing?"

"Just a thought. I suppose it was pretty well known who was putting the pressure on Bannon and why. Maybe somebody wanted you and Monk Hazzard to be appreciative. Maybe they roughed Bannon up just to prove a lot of real diligence and cooperation and went a little too far. And if Bannon just happened to die on them, it would be a pretty good way of fixing it so that nobody would ever be able to find out that Bannon took a bad beating."

He chewed a crumb of skin off the corner of his thumb. "Suzy said if it was sure going to crush a man's head anyway, he might as well be face down so he couldn't see it falling . . ." He straightened and shook his head. "No. There's nobody around who'd do a man that way. Nobody I know. Nobody Monk knows."

I looked at my watch. "I'll tell you exactly what you do, Press. I'll be up there on Thursday the fourth. I'll have somebody with me who can tell you something you might find interesting. But the only way you can get to talk to them is to have that forty thousand in cash or certified check all ready and waiting, and I'll have a deed and closing statement and so on. Show me the money and then you can talk to the man I'll bring along. Then you can decide whether you want to buy the Bannon place. Because that's the only way you're going to have any dish to eat out of."

He stood up. "Otherwise?"

"Otherwise I just wait you out, and I wait until the Calitron deal is dead, and then I make my own deal with Carbee, because he certainly isn't going to renew that option with you, and then I see if my buyer can get along without your land and without the Santo land, and I think it's quite possible that two hundred and ten acres might be enough."

"You wouldn't be running a bluff?"

"Prove you have forty thousand to get into the table stakes game, and we'll give you a little peek at the hole card. Believe me, it's the last and only chance you've got."

From the dock he looked back toward me, standing on the afterdeck. He shook his head and said, "You know, damn it, McGee, it's almost easier dealing with that son of a bitch Santo. At least you know more about what the hell is going on."

I went back in and hollered to Puss that she could come out. I took a yellow cushion off the couch and lifted the little Sony 800 out of its nest and took it over to the desk. We'd used up two-thirds of the five-inch reel of half-mil tape at three and three quarters ips. I unplugged the mike and plugged in the line cord to save the battery drain and rewound it to the beginning. I stretched out on the couch and Puss sat cross-legged on the floor and we listened to it all the way through. I got up just once and held the rewind key down a few moments, and replayed the account of the talk with Santo in Atlanta, and let it continue on from there.

At the end, Puss got up and punched it off and came over and hip-thumped herself a little room on the edge of the couch. "Is that what we've got for a villain, dear? That weak, scared, sly, sorry man? Just scrambling and hustling and trying to keep his stupid head above water? So his stomach hurts all the time, and he threw up."

"Settle for Santo?"

"Maybe indifference *is* the greatest sin, darling. I'll settle for Santo, until a new one comes along. McGee, tomorrow is New Year's Eve."

"So it is. So it is indeed."

"How would you feel about no throngs, dear?"

"I was thinking about trying to prove two is a throng."

"I think two people could purely lang the hell out of auld zyne if they put their minds to it. Is it zyne, or syne or what?"

"It is old acquaintance ne'er forgot."

"New acquaintance ne'er forgot. What happens to people who start on Black Velvets and taper off on champagne?"

"They seldom remember their own names."

"Let's try for that."

A slow gray rain came down all day long on the last day of the year. We kept the *Flush* buttoned up, the phone off, ignored the bing-bong of the regulars who

96

were drifting from boat to boat. It was a private world, and she provided a throng of girls therein. Never had she released all that mad and wonderful vitality for so long. She had come all the way out of the shell she had been keeping herself in for the last few days. We peaked at that point where the wine held us in an unreal place, neither drunk nor sober, neither sane nor crazy, where the funny things were thrice funny, where all the games were inexhaustible, where tears were part of laughter or sadness, and every taste was sharpened, every odor pungent, every nerve branch incomparably sensitized. The ones who are half alive can reach that place, perhaps, with their trips and their acids and their freaking, but reality truly felt, awareness made totally aware, is a magic they can't carry around in powdered form. She was a throng of girls and she filled the houseboat and filled the day and filled the long evening. Some of the girls were ten, and some were fifteen, and some were ten thousand years old. And, like Alice, I had to run as fast as I could to stay in the same place. HAPP-eee New Year, my love . . .

I awakened on Monday with the impression that I might have to get up and bang my head against the wall to get my heart started. The bedside clock was at seven after eleven. No hangover. Just that leaden heavy contentment of an expenditure so total the account was seriously overdrawn. I plodded my way into the vast shower stall, soaped and then stood swaying, eyes closed under the steaming roar, like a horse sleeping in the rain. Finally out of a sense of duty and character I fixed the heads to needle spray and switched it to cold. As I hopped and gasped, I thought dourly of how inaccurate are all the bridegroom jokes about window shades. A long and private holiday with a sizable, sturdy, vital, demanding and inventive lass leaves you with the impression that you had merely rowed a couple of tons of block across a lake, then ran them up to the top of a mountain with a dozen or so trips with a wheelbarrow, then rolled back down the mountain into the lake and drowned.

As with sad and reminiscent smile I was reaching for my toothbrush, I noticed that hers was gone. Okay. So she had packed early. But while brushing, I reached my free hand up and opened the other cupboard. It was bare.

She had taken everything of hers, for the first time in all these months.

I rinsed and spat and wrapped the big damp towel around my waist and went in search of her. Of course there was nothing of hers left aboard. She was gone. She had scotch-taped a note to the side of the coffeepot. It was in her freehand printing, using a red ballpoint.

And so, my scruffy darling, cometh an end to all good things. Endeth with a flourish, what? You are the best that could have happened to me. It isn't Killian and it wasn't Seattle, so don't waste time and money. And nothing you said or did. Your saying and your doing are a memorable perfection. I am just not a very constant type, love. For once I wanted to quit when I was ahead. Think kindly of the girl. Because she did love you, does love you, will love you from here on in. Cross my heart. (Say my good-byes to all the good ones.)

Instead of a signature she had drawn a circle with two little almond shapes for eyes, and a great big curved line for a smile. Three tears were dripping down out of each eye.

But, damn it, I wasn't *ready* yet.

Those were the words in my mind. I read them back and suddenly understood them, and I sat down in the booth suddenly full of self-understanding and self-loathing.

Sure, Puss-baby. We just hadn't reached the cutoff point where McGee would make the break on *his* terms. Which would have kept you from quitting while you were ahead. The key word is 'Yet.' So all that's hurt is pride, you sorry son of a bitch.

I could have done without that kind of self-revelation. I felt like a very trivial and tiresome animal, a sluggish animal sitting slumped in its tired slack hide—hide that bore the small and involuntary marks of fang and claw of the otherwise gentle she-thing now gone for good. Who is the user, Trav baby, and who is the used? And have you ever given anybody anything worth the having.

I clamped my jaw until my teeth squeaked and my ears buzzed. Why such a big hang-up over another promiscuous broad? Town was full of them. Go whistle up another one. Be the jolly old lover-boy, and be glad the

98

redhead left before she turned into a drag, before she started bugging you about making it something legal and forever, and a-crawl with kids.

I like last year's McGee better.

Nine

MEYER WAS BACK on the second day of the new year, back on Tuesday at ten in the morning, and came over in his New York garments after leaving his suitcase off on his boat, so eager was he to display the fruits of his efforts.

There were two thin sheafs of brokerage house forms, paperclipped together. He sat across from me in the galley booth and said, "That batch is the monthly margin account statements."

The forms were printed in pale blue ink on a thin off-white paper. The name of the firm was but vaguely familiar. Shutts, Gaylor, Stith and Company. 44 Wall Street. New York 10004. Established 1902.

"And these are the confirmations of purchases and sales. The prices are correct for the date of sale. The monthly statement of account checks against the confirmations, of course. The monthly statements cover eleven months, including last month. I put in several where you bought at such and such a figure and then sold after they'd gone up just a few points. They went up further and then dropped like stones. I gave you two small losses, short term, on the same basis. In effect in eleven months you built a hundred thousand into almost two hundred and ninety thousand, so that according to the summary, right now you could sell two hundred thousand worth, pay a twenty-five percent long-term gain, and pocket a hundred and fifty thousand, leaving almost your original investment in the securities you'd still be holding."

"What about anybody checking it out?"

"Your account number . . . that number there . . . oh-three-nine-seven-one-one-oh, that's in legitimate sequence. Somebody started an account eleven months ago, then canceled out. It's a small, conservative, reputable house. I can tell you that there is not one other person in the world they would do this for. I had to make so many solemn oaths I've forgotten half of them. If anybody checks back to the margin clerk, he will say it is all legitimate. If anybody tries to go further, they will come upon either Emmet Stith or Whitsett Gaylor, who'll confirm."

"So how did I make payment to them?"

"Always by check on the Bank of Nova Scotia in Nassau."

It was beautiful. There is no way that even a Gary Santo could pry information out of the bank of Nova Scotia. It is a system some call Zurich West.

I leafed through the sheets. I had bought at the right time. I'd done very well.

"So what is wrong with you?" Meyer asked.

"I'm just great. Nifty peachy."

"You are stimulating. Like a dirge. Where's Puss?"

"Gone for good."

"So!"

"So?"

"So I don't think you drove that one off. So it was her choice. So she isn't the kind who says it is for good and then come back all of a sudden. With her, gone is gone. So if I were you, I would be just as bad off as you look. Or worse. So if I were you and one like that was gone for good, I'd miss hell out of her and wonder if maybe I'd handled things a little differently somehow, I could have kept her around permanently."

"That's enough about 'so.' "

He got out of the booth. "When you want to be civilized, I live over there on a boat. *The John Maynard Keynes*. Fourteen hundred and forty a year, special annual rate, less a discount for paying the year in advance. Ask for Meyer."

"Okay, okay. These sheets are perfect. You did a hell of a job up there. You are intelligent, crafty, loyal, persuasive and diligent. Puss or no Puss, the job goes on. LaFrance showed. I'll play you the tape. It's interesting. He spilled the name of the company. Calitron. Mean anything?"

"A name only. Listed on the big board. A growth issue, going at thirty times earnings. Volatile. I'll check it out. Play the tape and I'll go away and let you sit and chew your hands and moan a little."

"I'm glad I depend on you for sympathy, Meyer."

"What sympathy should you get? A little arrangement, wasn't it? A sea urchin arranged the meeting. The urchin didn't wash up, she didn't step on it, what have you lost? Don't answer! Your disposition you've lost. Play the tape before I start to cry."

I put it on. I stretched out on the yellow couch. I closed my eyes. If I opened them quick enough, turned my head quick enough, I would see Puss sitting cross-legged on the floor, scowling as she listened to Preston LaFrance.

When it was through, I turned it off. Meyer sighed. He said, "I think he will have the forty thousand. Even knowing I was hearing nonsense, I could believe you a little. Forty thousand is better than getting poked in the eye with a stick."

"You left something out. Did you find the kind of a company Gary Santo should invest in?"

After the first five sentences I was totally lost. I stopped him and told him to start over again, and give it to me in baby talk.

He sighed; pondered. "Try this. A company has only so many shares of stock issued. The number of shares is called the 'float.' When there aren't many shares, it is called a 'thin float.' Somebody buys ten thousand shares of General Motors, he might move it up an eighth of a point—twelve and a half cents a share—just by the effect of his demand on the floating supply. But if he put in an order for ten thousand shares of Peewee Incorporated, the demand might shove it right through the roof. It might boost it four or five dollars a share. Are you with me?"

"So far."

"Every day in every newspaper it shows you, with the two zeros left off the end, how many shares of every listed stock were bought and sold. People watch like hawks. Two kinds of people. One guy wants capital gains. He wants to buy something for twenty dollars a share, hold it for six months and a day, sell it for forty a share, pay Uncle twenty-five percent of the profit in capital gains tax, or five dollars, and put fifteen in his pocket. Other characters are traders. They sit in brokerage offices and watch the tape. They want to buy a stock for twenty a share, sell it next week at twenty-five, when it drops down from twenty-six, buy it back at twenty-seven, sell at thirty, buy back at twenty-eight, sell at thirty-five and so on. They pay straight income tax on their net gain. Gary Santo is the first type, the capital gain guy, because all his income is being taxed at the maximum rate already."

"Still with you, Professor."

"Splendid! Now when something good is going to happen to a little company, the number of shares sold and bought every day goes up. It becomes more active. The price of the stock goes up. So it gets noticed. So more people want to get in the act and make a buck. That creates more demand. The demand pushes the price higher. In every trade, Travis, nobody can buy unless somebody is willing to sell. The more people who want to hand on, the fewer shares floating around, and the higher it goes, because the price has to go up to the point where somebody will say: Okay, I've made enough off this stock, so I'll sell it. I'll put in my order to sell it at two-dollars a share higher than it is right now. It is a big snowball rolling *up* the hill. Okay?"

"One thing. What keeps Santo from making a lot of money too?"

"Nothing, if he gets out in time. But look at the credentials I fixed you up with. All spendid values back at the time you bought them, at the time you apparently bought them. Stock prices go up because the company is *making* money, and has the look of making *more* money than before when they make their next earnings report. So the stock I found, Santo will think it has the same beautiful future like these you made the capital gains out of. They are still all hanging up there pretty good. So why should he be nervous? I tell you, he would be nervous if he knows what a terrible lousy stock I found."

"What is it?"

"A dog called Fletcher Industries. I read maybe two hundred balance sheets and operating statements. I started with two hundred and weeded down and down and down, hunting for something that looks okay fine on the surface but is rotten underneath. It could win a prize for the worst stock. It has a thin float. It shows sales and profits going up every year. It has a nice profit margin, nice book value, big words in the annual financial report about a glowing future and so on."

"So what's wrong with it?"

"This I shouldn't even try to explain. Listen, there are maybe eight perfectly ethical and legitimate choices a C.P.A. has when he is figuring profit per share. Each choice makes the profit higher or lower, accordingly. You could find some old conservative companies that make the eight choices so they show the lowest per share profit. Most companies make one choice one way, another, another way, so in general it cancels out. But this little Fletcher outfit, they use every chance they have to make profits look bigger. I reworked their statements. The stock sells right now for fifteen a share. Over the last twelve months the earnings reports say they made ninety-six cents a share. This was up from seventy-seven cents the previous year. Use the most conservative methods and you know what it is? It is a lousy eleven cents the previous year, and it is a four-cent loss this year. Such a statement they publish! The book value is all puffed up. The profit margin is nonsense. Even the cash flow is jiggered up."

"Book value? Cash flow?"

"Forget it. You don't have to know. All you have to know is that no matter how careful Santo is, the published trading volume will go up, the stock will go up, a lot of careless people will jump on the wagon and push it higher. They'll think a big increase in earnings is going on. Or a merger, or a new product. Like with the ones you are supposed to have bought. But this one has no substance. It will go up like penny rockets and when it starts down, it should maybe end up a two-dollar stock where it belongs."

"So we con him into buying it, Meyer. So it goes up and up and he makes a lot of paper profit, and then when it goes down, he sells out and keeps the profit."

"With everybody selling, with everybody trying to save out some profit, who will buy it? No buyers and they'll suspend trading, investigate the heavy speculation, and when it opens again, it will open in the cellar. Santo should lose most or all of his bundle."

"So how does Janine make the money you were talking about?"

"With the forty thousand from LaFrance we start her off, pick up three thousand shares. As it moves, I use the increased market value to pick up more for her. I watch it like an eagle, and then I start pulling her out of it very, very gently, and putting her into a nice solid little sleeper I happened to find when I was looking for this Fletcher dog. It should give her a hundred-percent gain in a year, along with a nice dividend yield."

"How much can you make for her if things work out right?"

"If? Did I hear you say if? You get Santo to bite at it, and I'll do the rest. End of the year? Oh, say the original stake plus a quarter million."

"Come *on*, Meyer!"

"Oh, that's before short-term gains tax on Fletcher. You see, that's what'll lock Santo into it. He'll be hoping to ride the profit for six months. Say a fifty to sixty thousand tax she'll pay."

"You kill me, Meyer,"

"Make sure nobody else kills you. It would be boring around here."

For the first time since I knew Puss would never come back, I felt a faint and reluctant little tremor of excitement and anticipation.

Meyer, frowning, said, "You are going to see LaFrance the day after tomorrow? Does that give us time to do everything we have to do?"

"I was just making him sweaty, Meyer. I'll phone him Thursday night and say we'll have to change the arrangement. Don't call us. We'll call you. And I can get a pretty good indication of whether he has the forty all ready."

"You know, you look more like yourself, Travis."

"It's the sympathy that does it, every time."

"An obligation of friendship. What do you do first?"

"Find that little pipeline."

After a long conference Wednesday morning with Meyer about strategy and tactics, and the documentation he ought to have, I went down to Miami. The offices of Santo Enterprises were in an unimpressive six-story office building on North East 26th Terrace, a half block east of Biscayne. Reception was on the sixth floor. A wide corridor, glass doors at the end, and beyond them a paneled room, thick blue rug, and elegant blonde desk-table on a raised dais and, behind it with a look of polite and chilly query, a slender princess with white dynel hair, glowing in the drama-light of a little ceiling spot, who asked me in the beautiful clarity of the English upper class if she might be of service.

When I said I would like to see Mr. Santo, she looked remotely amused. "Soddy, sir, but he is out of the citeh. Possibleh someone else could help you?"

"I'm inclined to doubt it."

"Praps if you might tell me the nature of your business, sir?"

"I'd rather not."

"Ektually, then, there isn't much that can be done, sir. Mr. Santo only sees one by appointment, and he would certainly not relish having his secretry make an appointment . . . blind, as it were. You see the problem, do you not?"

"Why don't I talk to his secretary, then?"

"But you see, sir, I would have to know the nature of your business to know *which* secretry you should speak with."

"Does he have a super-special personal private one?"

"Oh yes, of course. But, sir, one must have an appointment to speak with her. And to make the appointment I should have to——"

"Know the nature of my business."

"Quite."

"Miss, we're both in trouble."

"I wouldn't really say *both* of us, sir."

"If you don't help me a little bit, and when I do get to Gary Santo, which I most certainly will, he is going to wonder what took me so long, and I am going to tell him that I just couldn't get past that limey wench with the white hair under the spotlight."

"But, sir! Really, I have——"

"Your orders."

"Quite!"

"Do I look like a con artist? Do I look like a sales-man? Do I look like a pest? Dear girl, aren't you supposed to exercise *some* instinct and judgment about people?"

"Sir, one might possibly say . . . pest, should this go on

105

too much longer. Oh! My word! Are you a pilot? Is it about that . . . currency matter?"

"I am not a pilot. But some currency might enter into it. I just remembered something. Somebody said at one point that to get to Santo with a certain suggestion, they had to clear through Mary Smith. Is that a person or some kind of a code name for something?"

"Mary Smith would be a person, sir."

"A special personal private secretary, maybe?"

"Praps just private secretry, sir, might be suitable."

"Now, please don't tell me I need an appointment with her."

She studied me for a moment, tilted her head, looked slightly quizzical and inwardly—and possibly bitterly—amused. The appraisal was like unto that given a side of beef when the US Grade stamp is not easy to read.

"You could give me your name, sir?"

"McGee. T. McGee."

"This is teddibly irregular. Just a chawnce, y'know."

"Tell her I do card tricks, have never been completely domesticated, and show signs of having been struck sharply in the face in years gone by."

"At least you are amusing," she said.

"Quite!" said I.

"Please have a seat. I'll find out what she says, Mr. McGee."

I sat cautiously in a chair that looked like the slope-end of a blue bathtub resting on a white pedestal, and found it more comfortable than it looked. Windowless rooms always give me the feeling of having been tricked. Now they've got you, boy, and they're going to come through all the doors at once. I opened a mint copy of *Fortune* and a grizzled fellow looked out at me with alert and friendly squint of eye, advertising my chummy neighborhood power company. I think I could remember having seen him on somebody's television set shilling an adenoidal housewife into squealing in ecstasy about suds.

The limey maiden murmured into the oversized mouth-piece of one of those privacy telephones. In a little while she hung up and said with a certain air of accomplishment and mild surprise, "She will be out in a few moments, sir."

A flush door, bone-white, off to the left of the recep-

106

tionist opened, and little Miss Mary Smith came through and toward me without a glance at the receptionist. I put *Fortune* aside and stood up. She marched to within four feet of me and stopped and looked up into my face. At least it was not a name they handed around the office. She was the one I had seen with Tush Bannon in the bar lounge atop the International Hotel. The dark and rich brown-auburn hair fell in a straight gloss. I had misread, across the room the last time, the expression on her face. It was not petulance, not discontent. It was a total and almost lifeless indifference, a completely negative response. In a special way it was a challenge. It said, "Prove I should relate to you, buddy." Her eyes were the improbable emerald of expensive contact lenses, made more improbable by just enough eye makeup to make them look bigger than they were. And they were generous to start with. Her skin texture was a new grainless DuPont plastic. The small mouth did not really pout. It was just that both upper and under lip were so heavy it was the only choice it had. They were artfully covered with pink frost. White blouse, navy skirt—that nunnery flavor of offices and hospital wards.

She looked up at me, motionless as department store wax, with two millimeters of query in one eyebrow.

"The eyebrow," I said, "is the exact same shade of those wooly bear caterpillars I remember from my childhood. You'd look for them in the fall to see if they were heading north or south. It was supposed to predict what kind of a winter we'd have."

"So you've verified Elizabeth's claim you're mildly amusing. This is a busy office."

"And I just happened to come bumbling in off the street to bother all you busy, dedicated people."

She took a step back, a quarter turn. "Then, if that's all."

"I want to see Santo. What do I have to say to you? A magic word?"

"Try good bye."

"My God, you *are* a silly, pretentious little bitch!"

"That doesn't work either, Mr. McGee. The only thing that *does* work is to state your business. If Mr. Santo did not employ people of some judgment to screen out the

107

clowns, his time would be taken up with clowns . . . and eccentrics, and clumsy con men. Do you want him to finance a flying saucer?" She rested a finger against her small chin and tilted her head. "No, you have that deep-water look. A bit salty? This is probably more of that treasure-map nonsense. Spanish galleons, Mr. McGee? And you have some genuine gold coins minted in the New World? I would say we average eight or ten of you people a month. So either you tell me or you don't tell anyone here at any time. Is that quite clear?"

"All right. I will tell you. I will tell you enough so that you will open the door for me to see Santo."

"May we call him Mr. Santo?"

"But I am not going to talk standing here like the last guests at a cocktail party. I want to sit at a desk or a table and you can sit on the other side of it and listen to as much as I care to tell you."

"Or as much as I care to listen to." She turned to the receptionist and said, "I shall be in Conference D, Elizabeth."

"Thank you, Miss Smith," said the humble limey.

I pushed the glass door open for little Miss Mary Smith and followed her down the corridor. Her walk was engaging, as it seemed to involve a conscious effort to inhibit any swing and flourish of her solid little rear end, and was successful to but a limited degree.

Conference D was a ten by twelve cubicle. But the end wall opposite the door was all window, looking out across Biscayne Bay to the improbable architectural confectionary of Miami Beach, with a sunlit glitter and shimmer of traffic across the Julia Tuttle Causeway a little to the north, and the residential islands off the Venetian Causeway about the same distance south. It was a gray room with gray armchairs, six of them, around a Chinese red conference table. On one wall was a shallow gray case, glass-fronted, wherein a very diversified collection of white nylon gears and cogs and rods and bushings of various sizes had been arranged against a Chinese red background in simulation of some of the art forms of Louise Nevelson.

I could be reasonably certain that as we had walked down the corridor, Elizabeth had, as common practice, turned on whatever bug system was used in Conference D. After all, Elizabeth could look through the glass doors and see which door we had entered.

I had learned the right terms from Meyer. She sat across from me, radiating skepticism.

"I am a speculator, Mary Smith. I'm not a trader. My specialty is in the maximized capital gains area. There is enough income from certain other sources so that the Fed hasn't, and won't, class me as a professional and cut it all back to straight income. Is this over your head."

"Hardly! In fact, you've almost run out of time, Mr. McGee."

"I do *not* want to sell Santo a hot item. I do *not* want him in any syndicate operation. I do *not* want any piece of his action, or even any knowledge of the details just so long as he *does* move in on it. This is not nickel and dime. It's a listed security. Now, usually I operate in a sort of informal syndicate deal. Every man for himself, but we make the same move at the same time. But we've done so well we've got some security leaks. I dug this one out and it's too damned good to get the edge taken off of it by too many leaks. I could probably establish a position in it and then arrange a show of interest on the part of one of the aggressive funds. But they work out in the open, and the blocks they buy are too big."

I looked at her questioningly. "You haven't lost me. And your time hasn't run out," she said.

"So I have the word here and there that Santo will swing when something looks good. And I think he is smart enough to ease his way into it, because if he comes in too hard and fast, it is going to go up the ladder so fast I'm not going to have a chance to use the buying power on the margin account to keep doubling on the way up. He'll have to set it up to work through several accounts, and be willing to sell off blocks of it to kill the momentum if it starts to go too fast."

"You said something about it not being nickel and dime."

"So it would depend entirely on how far he wants to go with it. If he goes in, it will take a million to create the pressure it needs. I would say he could come in anywhere from one million on up to a tops of four. Over four and it would put it too far out of balance and attract too much attention in the long run. Frankly, I'd be hitch-hiking, using his buying pressure to get on for the ride up, and taking the chance he can keep the climb controlled. I could assemble syndicate money because the track record is good, but the leaks would hurt. If I had the million, I wouldn't be here. Let's say he can count on three hundred percent long-term gains, if he doesn't plumber it. This is the kind of thing that comes along every three to five years, where all the factors fit like a beautiful watch."

"Mr. Santo has very little tendency to plumber anything."

"That was my evaluation. And when the ride is over, I should be where I won't have to fool with syndicates and Santo. I'll be where I can make my own markets."

"A listed security?"

"And a company in a potentially dynamic growth area."

For the first time I saw the suggestion of a smile on that heavy little-girl mouth. "And absolutely no point at all in asking you the name of it, of course. But I can ask you for . . . bank references?"

"That's a silly question. If he wants to dig around and check me out, lots of luck. He could find worms in the apple. All he'll be interested in is the track record." I took the envelope out of my inside jacket pocket and took out the brokerage account forms and flipped them over to her. "Take a look, if you can read them and interpret them, and then you can give Santo a nice verbal reference."

She went through the margin account monthly summary forms first, sheet by sheet. Midway through she gave me a sudden green glance of reappraisal. On the last one, the December one, I had penciled beside each stock listed in the security position the January second market value. She checked those values against the purchase confirmations—not all of them, just a random few.

"May I hold these for a few days?" she asked.

"No."

"Can I have them Xeroxed? It would take just a few minutes."

I hesitated. "On one basis, and I can't enforce it. You see them and Santo sees them, and that's it."

"That would be up to him."

"So relay my humble request to the great man, sweetie."

"Do you have to be so sarcastic?"

"Am I supposed to be impressed by Gary Santo? He happens to be my number one on a list of three possibles. Whoever it turns out to be will make a bundle on their terms while they help me make a bundle on my terms. I didn't come to beg, sweetie."

"You *do* make that clear. I'll be right back."

"If you ever stoop to manual labor around this shop, I think it would be nice if you did the Xeroxing yourself."

"I shall, sweetie. And you just made a nice brownie point. Cautious is as cautious does. We treasure that around here."

She was back in under ten minutes. She did not sit again. I stowed the account forms in the envelope and in my pocket.

I said, "You see, Miss, there's all those chests of gold coin busted open and spilled out right across the white sand bottom next to Hustler Reef."

"That was clumsy, wasn't it? I must stop typecasting. Of course you realize I have no idea whether or not this will appeal to Mr. Santo. The idea, I mean. If it does, he will have to know the security you're talking about, and he will want to have it checked."

"Quietly, I hope."

"Of course."

"When do I get to see him?"

"How can I reach you?"

"I'm going to be on the move. Suppose I phone you tomorrow afternoon."

She shook her head. "Friday. Say at four in the afternoon. Ask for me by name and give my extension number or you won't be put through. Sixty-six."

"Just what *is* your job around here, Mary Smith?"

"You might call me a buffer zone."

"Have I gotten past you?"

"On Friday we'll both know, won't we?"

Ten

ON THURSDAY EVENING I reached Preston LaFrance by phone at his home in Sunnydale. I taped it so that Meyer and I could study the playback.

"McGee? Trav? I've been wondering all day——"

"Too much has been happening, Press. I might say that things are shaping up a little better than I'd hoped. I might have some good news for you when I'm able to get up there."

"I need some good news, and you can believe it. When are you coming up."

"I'll have to let you know. That money we talked about. Have you got it set aside?"

"Let me get one thing straight. I get to know about what's going on before I have to go ahead and buy that damned thing for three or four times what it's worth, don't I? I mean I get a chance to make a decision based on what you tell me?"

"Naturally. But as you must realize, I'm not in this thing for *that* kind of a profit."

"I can figure that out for myself all right. Okay, I've got that money set aside, in case I want to go along."

"You will. I'll have the papers all drawn and bring them along. But one thing has come up which worries me a little, Press."

His voice tightened up. "What? What?"

"Have you had any recent contact with Santo?"

"No. No reason to. Why?"

"I think it would be a very good thing if you make certain he never hears about any kind of deal between you and me."

"I don't understand what you——"

"Did you hear anything about somebody topping your offer that same day title reverted to Mrs. Bannon, and I bought it from her?"

"I sure did, and it puzzled the hell out of me. It come through Steve Besseker here, and he won't say who made it."

"I have it on pretty good authority that Besseker was representing Gary Santo."

"What! The hell you say! Steve?"

"Santo sent some woman up to give him his orders, apparently. A tall redhead."

"By God, somebody was kidding Steve about seeing him over in Broward Beach with a big good-looking redhead sometime just before Christmas."

"It was probably the same day I bought the Bannon property. And it strikes me that the way things are going, Santo would want to know if there is any present or pending agreement between you and me, and he might have asked Besseker to find out."

I could hear him breathing, and then he said softly, "Well, I'll be a son of a bitch! The very next day he asked me if I knew you, and if maybe you were acting for me because, like Whitt Sanders said, that Bannon woman certainly wouldn't have sold to me no matter what I offered her. What's going *on*, McGee?"

"I'm afraid he's gotten wind of the deal I'm trying to pull off, and it would sting him a little. I suppose Besseker will keep him posted on every move you make. Well, we may have to move a little faster than I planned. Santo will hear about you buying the Bannon place from me as soon as the sale is recorded. Until then, keep your mouth shut because I wouldn't want to have it turn out that you end up with no share in either his deal or mine."

"Listen, I can't risk anything like that happen——"

"Sit tight, Press. Hang on. Keep the faith."

As he started to speak again I hung up on him.

About an hour later I played it for Meyer. He listened and then shook his head. "What's the point, Travis? Why are you confounding that dull boy with all this business of wheels within wheels?"

"For the variation of the pigeon drop, my friend. If suddenly the whole world seems more conspiratorial than he ever believed it was, then he'll be in a better mood to stand still for the sleight of hand. Confused people are less skeptical. I was going to use Besseker another way, but it had to be through Puss, and she doesn't seem to be around any more, so I salvaged a piece of the situation anyway."

"But one thing puzzles me," Meyer said. "Here you

are worming your way into one kind of thing, directly with Santo. And up there you have your thumb in another kind of pie, but that is Santo's too, but not so direct. Up there you are Travis McGee, this address. And down there in Santo Enterprises, you are Travis McGee, this address. There is the chance that by some accident Santo or one of his people finds out you are into both things. That would immediately alert a man like Santo. He could find the relationship between you and Bannon, and he would smell mice."

"So?"

"Maybe I should have been the one to set up the investment thing."

"It would take the joy out of it. He might never make the connection. I need the chance to look him in the eye, laugh at his jokes, share some booze with him, and then sting him where it hurts. Then he can find out why it happened to him. I'll tell him, given the chance. For the rest of his life, the name Bannon is going to make him feel sick."

"Maybe he has some people who will make you feel sick in other ways."

"And sometimes they almost make it."

"This time they could."

"You always worry. It's nice. If you stopped, *I'd* worry."

He sighed. "Okay. So look at my expert, specialist, impressive kit. Meyer, the big industrialist."

He had the aerials of the Shawana River area, and the series of overlays marked as planned. He had soil surveys, water table data, labor supply data. He had business cards on expensive buff stock, engraved, turning him into G. Ludweg Meyer, Ph. D., Executive Vice President of Barker, Epstein and Wilks, Inc. Management Engineering Services.

"Let us sincerely pray," he said, "that one of these cards never finds its way back to that very sound and good firm."

"It might be therapeutic. It might stir them up. Let me see the correspondence file."

The letterhead startled me. It looked totally authentic. One of the giant corporations that have become household words in these days of electronic fantasy. I stared at him and he beamed at me and said, "It was a bit of luck. So wonder about it. Note that it is from the office of the President of the corporation. That is his name, truly. Note that it is marked confidential. Note the very impressive carbon ribbon type face. See the secretarial initials at the bottom. Those are the initials of his actual private secretary. The signature is not great. I copied it from a copy of their annual report. The top letters are background. The key letter is about the fourth one down. There. That's the one. Is it what you had in mind?"

The president called him *My dear Ludweg:* The first paragraph acknowledged the receipt of reports and recommendations, and then the letter went on to say, *I tend to agree with your appraisal of the competitive implications and possible danger to our industry position in that particular manufacturing division should Calitron establish a branch facility in such close proximity to Tech-Tex Applications, Inc. Though the branch facility we now have in the final planning stage is smaller, one could logically assume that proximity to TTA would benefit profit margin to the same extent percentagewise.*

In view of the necessity of moving quickly, and the favorable report our people brought back, you are authorized to make a firm commitment in the name of the Corporation for from 200 acres minimum or 260 maximum either in general area A, or general area B. A separate letter of authorization is appended hereto. In view of the other interest in these industrial lands, you are authorized to bid up to $2 thousand per acre, or a maximum of between $400 thousand and $520 thousand, at your discretion.

"Very nice," I said.

"What should my approach be up there? How should I act?"

"Self-important, influential, crooked, and careful of being caught at it. Great letters, Meyer. You are showing more and more talent every time you get into one of these things."

"And getting more and more scared. Isn't this a conspiracy to defraud?"

"Let's say to highjack. Now let me tell you how it is supposed to work."

He buried his face in his hands and said, "I can hardly

wait to hear." After I explained it, it took him a long time to smile.

When I phoned Mary Smith at four on Friday, she said, "Mr. McGee, would it be possible for you to have a drink with Mr. Santo this evening at seven at the Sultana Hotel on Miami Beach?"

"I can arrange it."

"The Out-Island Room, then, at seven. Just ask for Mr. Santo's table."

I arrived at the arched doorway a few minutes after seven. A lackey with a face like a Rumanian werewolf slunk out of the gloom and looked at me with total disdain, as if Central Casting had sent the wrong type with the wrong clothes. It was a cold day, and I had put on the Irish jacket. After five or six years, twigs still occasionally fall out of the dark, coarse weave.

"Mr. Santo's table, please."

"And your name?"

"McGee!"

He lit up with joy at beholding me. He popped his fingers and a waiter trotted over, bowed several times, and led me back through the labyrinths of partitions and alcoves to a deep corner, to a semicircular banquette big enough for six, and a semicircular table to fit. He pulled the table out, bowed me in, put it back and bowed and asked for my drink order.

At ten after he came on the run and pulled the table out again as the Santo party arrived. Gary Santo, Mary Smith, Colonel Burns, Mrs. Von Kroeder. I measured Santo as we shook hands. He was not as tall as he looked in his pictures, but with all the shoulders and chest so frequently mentioned in his publicity. He was shading fifty, but fighting it and winning the same way those more directly in show business win it, with the facials, the luxuriant hairpiece touched just enough with gray, the laborious hours in the home gym, and the sessions on the rubbing table, and the hefty shots of vitamins and hormones, and a hell of a good dentist. He came on all virility, white teeth, wrestler's handshake, and the knack of looking you squarely in the eye and crinkling his eyes as if you and he shared a joke on the rest of the world.

116

In resonant boyish baritone he told me I knew Mary Smith, of course, and presented me to Halda Von Kroeder, who had as much thin, pale, graceful neck as I have ever seen, a small, pert head, a tall, slat-thin body, a cascade of emeralds, and a set of breasts so awe-inspiring she gave the impresssion of leaning slightly backward to keep herself in balance. "So bleezed," she said in a Germanic rasp, then hiccuped.

Colonel Dud Burns had the look of eagles . . . defeathered, earthbound, and worried about cirrhosis. Gary Santo arranged the group with himself in the middle and, at his left, first Mary Smith and then me at the end, and with Halda and Burns in that order at his right.

Mary Smith was at that daring outer limit where style becomes comedy. There was more eye makeup, and the mouth more frosted. She wore a gray sweater with a great deal of complex stitchery and welts and seams. It came down to within six inches of her knees. Showing under the sweater was two inches of blue tweed skirt. Below the skirt were sheer blue stockings that were a perfect match for shoes with stubby heels and high, stiff tongues. On her head was a wide-brimmed hat shaped much like the hats the novilleros wear in the bullring. It was of a stiff eggshell fabric in a coarse weave. She had it perched aslant on the gloss of the brown-auburn spill of hair, with a white thong under her chin, a blue wooden thong bead at the corner of her little jaw. The sweater sleeves came midway down her forearms. Her gloves and purse matched the eggshell hat. When she pulled her gloves off, she uncovered nails painted a thick, pearly, opalescent white.

She sat bolt upright like a bright and obedient child and smiled at me with wide eyes and careful mouth, and told Santo she would have the regular, which turned out to be a straight shot of Wild Turkey with water, no ice, on the side. When she got it, she went at it with frequent little sippings. each of which must have been three or four drops by volume.

Santo turned finally, after some in-group jokes and conversation I couldn't follow, and faced me across Mary Smith, his back squarely toward the kraut lady.

"Our little Poo Bear here gives you a good mark, McGee."

"Poo Bear Smith?" I asked.

"It's an office thing," she said. "I have this instinct or something. He says what about this one and I say Poo. And that one, and I say Poo. Then the next one I say okay for brownie points."

"She's got a nose for it. Questions, McGee. If I go for it, if I like the flavor of it, how much do you have to know?"

"The day you start and how much you are going to spring for all together."

"Have you taken a position in it?"

"About the same way porcupines make love, but I'm nowhere near as far in as I want to be. It's been moving in a narrow range and I've been buying on the downs."

"Will you need to know my orders?"

"No. I'll have a man tape-watching it."

"There's one place where we have to be coordinated on it, and that's getting off it."

"As carefully as we get on, I hope."

"And the last thing, of course, is the name of it."

"Right here?"

"The other two can't hear, and Mary is the best you've ever seen at keeping her mouth shut. About anything."

"Fletcher Industries. American Exchange."

"Want to brief me a little?"

"Why should I? It's a duplication of effort. If your people can't see why it's as good as it is, you need new people."

"You have your full complete share of mouth, McGee."

"Have you gotten too accustomed to total humility on all sides, Santo?"

"Hush, now!" said Mary Smith. "You both hush. You're both right. Don't you two go all ballsy and wicked when you're going to be helping each other."

Santo threw his head back and laughed his boyish laugh. "Her biggest trouble is making sense. By Wednesday . . . that will be . . ."

"The tenth," said Mary Smith.

" . . . phone her and she'll have the Yes or No on it, and give you a probable figure."

"Will do," I said.

He smiled down into her face. He said to her, "I think I like your new friend, Mary. I think he's maybe brought

118

us another winner." He took out his bill clip, slipped some bills out of it, and put them quickly into her purse. "I'm so sure, here's an advance on your bonus. Use it to take him to where the steaks are."

She looked at her watch. "Yes, you'd better start moving it, Gary. Ben will be out there with your luggage. Kiss Bonnie Bea for me."

He made the smallest of gestures and people came on the run to pull the table away, hand him the check for signature, bow the three of them out and away.

We went up the beach in her little red car to what she called one of "her" places, a little bar dark as pockets. Once we were sitting across a very low and narrow little table from each other, so that we had to hunch over it in intimate arrangement, she figuratively rolled up her sleeves and went to work. She had awaited the pass, and for once there hadn't been one.

She had put the strange hat aside. She shook out her gleaming hair. A stray pattern of light rested on a long diagonal across her face, from eyes to lips.

She dipped into her shot like a moth, put it down, picked up the stray lip-drop with tongue tip. "Want to know, Travis? Want the crazy message?" It was half whisper, her voice dragging.

"Message by special delivery. Sure, Mary Smith."

She made her eyes very wide and solemn. Her lips parted. She reached and took my hand in both of hers and pulled it slowly to her side of the table. She turned my slack fist over, then put the nails of her right hand high on the inside of my wrist, and slowly drew her nails along my wrist and over my palm, uncurling my slack fingers as she did so. Holding my fingers down, she dipped her head suddenly, pressed the mouth moist against my palm, lifted her head very quickly and stared at me, her face both sly and fake-frightened.

"Is there more?" I asked.

She turned my hand over and formed it into a fist and, holding it in both her hands, lifted it, held it, her elbows braced on the table. She bumped her chin into the knuckles, closed her eyes.

"Pow," she whispered. "Like right off, the first minute. Pow. I'm *never* like that."

119

"Comes a time," I said.

"There does indeed, Mr. Travis McGee." She tilted my fist slightly for a better angle, and went across the knuckle ridge with her warm little mouth, taking a gentle little bite at each knuckle and kissing the space between each knuckle. With each kiss, her tongue tip flicked at the closed space between fingers.

"When it's going to be what it's going to be, there's that message, don't you think? An old-timey thing, way deep, that's been waiting for it special. So very rough crazy everlasting special. And you know it too. Don't you? Don't you?"

She sat back there someplace behind those swarming eyes, listening to herself pant, in such a soft little wondrous way. She watched herself work herself up, no doubt measuring the bra-tickle of the nipples becoming erectile, sensing the new softness of thigh and belly. This was one of the new breed who assist the manipulators. Gary Santo, being a manipulator in a large way could be expected to have one who would know her business backward and forward and upside down. He might have two, three or a dozen in the retinue. He would keep them loyal not only with money, but with the feeling of being part of an operating team and performing a function for the team.

Sex with a particularly skilled and desirable woman who could convince you that you were the greatest thing since fried rice was a marvelous gadget for one of the manipulators. The bedazzled male is incautious, mazed, thunderstruck. In that condition he can provide the maximum benefit to the manipulator and the least problem. He will come trundling along in the entourage just to be near his brand-new love-light. He will tell her all he knows and all he hopes, and in a frenzy of team spirit and accomplishment, she will bang him out of his mind and drop him right back where she found him when the manipulator has the last crumb of information he can use. But while he's getting the treatment, he tags along with the team, with the group but not really a part of the group, aware that the team knows the basis for the attraction, aware of a team attitude of kindly contempt for him but so enthralled in his doggy, lolling, bitch-trailing way he will endure the little humiliations to keep getting what becomes more instead of less necessary to him the more he gets of it.

The role requires a woman exceptionally confident and decorative, a woman of a hearty and insistent sexuality, a woman who understands that serving the manipulator in this way is part of the price of the ticket on all the best flights to the best places, and if you want to be coy, or choosy or chicken, you can drop right back to the posture chair and the old electric and the girl's room scuttlebutt about who might get promoted to what. It takes special gals to travel with the team, so dig in and enjoy the special assignments, because between the romps the guy will talk and you tote the crumbs back to Gary and he fits them together.

The manipulators are the brash gamblers putting little corporations together to make big ones, and they are the talent packagers who stick a half dozen special abilities together and end up with the percentage off the top of the network serial show, and they are the showboaters who take on the tax cases of the mighty and fight the Fed to a draw—or a cheap compromise—and they are the inventive money men who direct the conversion of hoodlum funds into legitimate enterprise, and they are the whiz kids who tear down the honest old buildings and stick up the glittery new boxes on the lease-back, write-off, tax shelter kick, and they are the ones that boost the market price of a stock up and unload and then kick it back down and buy back.

They buzz around the country and the world in little groups, where everybody is always laughing, and at the resorts and airports and executive dining rooms, at the padded bars and the swinging casinos, in the groups there are always the Mary Smiths, pert, tidy, high-style, voracious and completely with it, eyes a-dance, freed by The Pill to happily pull down the game the manipulator fingers for her, the new Gal Friday who has become the Gal Friday Night.

It is a new breed that did not exist a few years back, but cultures seem to have an uncanny way of spawning creatures to fill any need. So situation ethics, plus profitable manipulation, brought this merry regiment out of the wings, as if they had been waiting there all along. It would be pointless to conjecture about immorality or

121

amorality, or make analogies about whoredom, that word with the ring of biblical accusation. A Mary Smith would not even be upset, merely puzzled.

In the diagonal of light she rested her chin against my fist, her two warm and shapely little hands holding it there, elbow-braced, and made her eyes huge, then dipped and turned her head first one way and then the other, to slowly drag first one sheaf of the dense and fragrant hair across the back of my hand and then the other.

I remembered the shaggy and ancient joke of the young man in the strange city who had arrived with the phone number of a hundred-dollar girl. He called her up and was invited up to her luxurious apartment, where she cooked him a gourmet meal, recited French poetry, played the piano for him and sang with professional skill. She mentioned that she spoke six languages, had a master's degree in psychology, and had designed and made the gown she wore on her lovely body. At last as she led him in toward the canopied bed he had to ask. And so he said, "Please would you tell me how a girl like you got into . . . a business like this?"

She twinkled up at him and sighed and said, "Just lucky, I guess."

Mary Smith took a deep and shivering breath and said, "There is a steak, darling, and it is not frozen and never has been, and it is in the meat-keeper thing in my apartment, which is, God help us, a con-do-min-i-um, which will never cease to sound like a dirty word, and the apartment is twelve and a half minutes away, give or take ten seconds, and the steak will keep for us, darling, until three A.M., or until twelve noon tomorrow for a Texan's breakfast for us because I don't have to tend the store until Monday morning, and that twelve and a half minutes might just be the longest twelve and a half minutes in my life up till now."

The temptation was to accept the whole con. But there is an immense perversity in the male animal at the most unexpected times. And why *didn't* you climb Mount Everest, Sir Hillary? Because it was there, fellow. And I could see her in memory in another bar, by daylight, teeth set in that meaty little underlip, eyes half closed, listening to Tush, and turning her head slowly from side to side in a

122

denial as definite as the slam of a door and clack of the lock. She would be exquisite in all detail, from earlobes to cute little toes to the dimples at the base of the spine. She would be fragrant, immaculate, prehensile and totally skilled, and she would ring all the changes, and pace herself beautifully, and draw me to her pace, and inflate my ego with her breathless astonishment at how it had been the most fantastic and lasting that had ever happened to her and how she had thought it could never even be equaled again, but lo and behold, when it had happened again, it was even more so, and if it ever got to be any more than that, she just couldn't stand it at all; it would blow her out of her mind, and how did we get to be so great, darling, so that really and truly it is as if it was the very first time ever with anybody.

The temptation was to take the man's Ferrari around the track a few times, just to prove to yourself you couldn't get hooked on a great piece of machinery or on the whole speed competition bit.

But it was right there and it was buzzing with it, and how do you sidestep without creating some unhappy suspicions about the whole approach? It would have to be some fancy footwork, and it would have to be on her terms, something she could comprehend immediately.

I slipped into my elk-hide ring-shoes just in time, just as her eyes narrowed and she said, "You're not exactly overwhelming the girl with enthusiasm, old buddy."

"Decisions, decisions, decisions," I said. "I seem to have this hex lately."

She let my hand go. "What's to decide?"

"There is this very pigheaded man sitting in a hotel suite and looking at the phone and getting madder and madder by the minute. I have been trying to unload this and that for cash money so I can get the maximum out of our little gem of opportunity. And he flew down from Chicago because this particular item happens to be worth about twenty thousand more to him than to anybody else in the world, for reasons I will not go into at the moment. So I told him I had to delay our meet because of something that came up, and I would try to get there by eight. And right now it is quarter to nine, and he is the type who feels unsure of who he is right down in the gut where it matters most, the type who to prove he is who he thinks he is might wait about one minute more and cut off his nose to spite his face, or he may have cut it off already and be on his way to the airport. I have been looking at you and trying to get a little controlled piece of amnesia about him, but it doesn't seem to work so good."

She sat taller and gave a little shake like a toy poodle who has just been lifted out of her doggy-bath, and gave her hair a few pats, and gave a hitch at her complicated sweater and said, "Darling, you are an absolute idiot! Why didn't you *say* something? Didn't you think I'd understand? I'm all grown up and everything."

"Let's say I was enjoying myself. I was listening to the message of the Poo Bear Smith."

She reached and patted my arm and with a crooked little smile and a bawdy wink said, "Let's put it this way. The twenty grand won't keep. You hustle and phone him. There's a phone at the end of that hallway over there that goes to the biff."

I went to the phone and lit a match and looked up a random number and dialed it and asked a nasal woman if I could speak to Mr. Bannon. She told me I had a wrong number and hung up, and so I talked for a while over the empty wire to Tush and told him the news of the moment, with a few comments on the weather. He didn't have a thing to say.

I went back to the table and told the chicklet that my man was very frosty, very frosty indeed, but still available for negotiation. She said, "Darling, if you'd lost him on account of me, I was sitting here deciding I was going to make one hell of a try at being worth the whole twenty big ones, but no broad in the world carries a tag like that. I might have choked up and blown the whole match."

"I like a practical woman."

"Can I drop you at his hotel?"

"Thanks, but I gave myself time to go pick up my car at the Sultana, if you want to drop me there."

"And wait for you, I hope, I hope?"

"I guess you better wait at your place, because I am not exactly together on price with this clown yet."

She lifted her purse onto her lap, opened it and dug around inside and took out a little flashlight. She gave it to me and I held it for her while she took out a little golden notebook with a snap fastener. She opened it and slipped the little gold pencil out of the little gold loop and said, "I just realized I'm absolutely starving, dear, so let's say it'll be ten before I get home. This is the unlisted number. And this is the address, on Indian Creek Drive, on the west side going north. Look for a raspberry-colored thing with a white canopy and white awnings and white balconies. Call me first, love, because I want the delicious feeling you're on your way to me."

Again she drove the little red car. She whirred into the Sultana parking area, cutting off her lights as she did so to keep the front boys from noticing us and whistling her up to the entrance. She unstrung her bead, put her hat on the shelf in back, said, "Um" and splayed her little fingers on the nape of my neck and impacted a kiss with sufficient know-how to leave my knees feeling loose and fragile as I strode to my rental car after she had driven away.

At twenty to midnight, aboard *The Busted Flush,* after I had washed up after my plate of scrambled eggs and onion, I got the little sheet she had torn out of her notebook. It was oyster-colored parchment, thin and stiff, with tear-out perforations down the left side. And in the bottom right-hand corner was imprinted, in the plainest imaginable type face, in gold: Love, Mary Smith.

I direct-dialed her number.

It rang five times, and then her muffled, silky voice said, "Mmmmm?"

"T. McGee, ma'am."

I heard a small yowly yawn. "W'time zit, sweetie?"

"Quarter to Cinderella, almost."

"Mmm. I was having the most interesting dream about you. And I have on this interesting little yellow night garment I bought in Tokyo. And I dumped this and that in the big hot tub, and so I smell interesting, sort of like between sandalwood and old rose petals, and something else mixed in. Some kind of spicy smell that makes me think of Mexico. Do you like Mexico as much as I do? How soon will you be here, my darling?"

"That's a very good question."

"I don't like the sound of that, somehow."

"That makes two of us."

"You sound so depressed. Troubles?"

"Out of the blue. Now we've ordered up some food and we're waiting for a third party, and by dawn's early light my guess is that we'll be a hundred miles from here looking at the property in question, on the Tamiami Trail, just this side of Naples."

"Oh poo!"

"I think I'd use a word with a little more bite to it."

She gave a long sigh. "Well," she said, "down, girl. Bear me in mind, will you?"

"Get all the rest you need. And I will phone you precisely at twelve noon tomorrow and we'll get out the old starting blocks again."

"The old track shoes. Bang. They're off. Anyway, as long as you might have some faint idea what you're missing, dear, drive a very hard bargain. You should be motivated, God knows."

After I hung up, I packed a pipe and took it topsides and stretched out on a dew-damp sunpad, down out of the bite of the breeze, and looked at the cold stars.

Where is the committee, I thought. They certainly should have made their choice by now. They are going to come aboard and make their speeches and I'm going to blush and scuff and say, "Shucks, fellas." The National Annual Award for Purity, Character, and Incomprehensible Sexual Continence in the face of an Ultimate Temptation. Heavens to Betsy, any American Boy living in the Age of Heffner would plunge at the chance to bounce that little pumpkin because she fitted the ultimate playmate formula, which is maximized pleasure with minimized responsibility. With a nice build, Charlie. With a lot of class, Charlie, you know what I mean. A broad that really goes for it, and she had a real hang-up on me, Charlie. You never seen any chick so ready, Charlie buddy, to scramble out of her classy clothes and hop into the sack. Tell you what I did, pal. I walked away. How about that?

There had to be a nice medal to go with the National Annual Award. With the insignia of the society. A shield with a discarded bunny tail, and an empty bed, and a buttock rampant of a field of cobwebs, with the Latin inscription, *"Non Futchus."*

A nice pink and white old gentleman would pin the medal to the bare hide of the chest, as recommended by Joe Heller, while a violin would play, "Just Friendship, Friendship."

The ceremonial kiss on the stalwart, manly, unsullied cheek and . . .

A huff of wind came and flipped the point of my collar against my throat. It ruffled the canvas laced to the sundeck rail. The collar was the tickle of the brisk red hair of Puss, and the canvas sound was her chuckle, and without warning I had such an aching longing for her it was like long knives in my bowels, and my eyes stung.

You never do anything for no reason at all, and you never refrain from doing something for no reason at all. Sometimes it just takes a little longer for the reason to get unstuck from the bottom of the brew and float to the top where you can see it.

I rapped the pipe out and went below. So it wasn't righteous denial at all. Or a lofty, supercilious disapproval. It was the monogamous compulsion based on the ancient wisdom of the heart. Puss had made of all of herself an abundant gift, not just the giving of the body or the sating of a physical want. And no matter how skilled the erotic talents of a Mary Smith, sensation would not balance out that privacy of self that she could not give, nor would want to, nor perhaps could ever give even if she wanted to.

And I knew just how it would have been with Mary Smith, because Puss was all too recent and all too sadly missed. All the secret elegancies of Mary Smith would merely have told me of wrong shapes, wrong sizes, wrong textures, wrong sounds from her throat, wrong ways of holding, wrong tempos and tryings and wrong oils of a wrong pungency. So it would have become with her a faked act of memory and mourning, to end in an after-love depression that would make the touch of her, the nearness of her, hugely irritating.

Puss was too recent.

After I was in bed, I went back and forth across the same old paradox: Then if Puss gave of herself so totally, opening up all the girl-cupboards in the back of heart and mind, how could she leave? Why did she leave?

There was a little chill that drifted across the back of my mind and was gone, as before, still unidentified.

There had been one cupboard unopened, all those months.

But at least I could now stop making wistful fantasies about the little garden of delights in its yellow garment from Tokyo.

Hogamus, Higamus. Mary's polygamous.
Higamus, Hogamus. Trav is monogamous.

For a while. It won't be any good until big Red wears off more. It will be a drag. And when it seems time to begin to expect something of it, and the opportunity comes along, don't risk it with a Mary Smith, whose involvement would be about on the same order as all other kinds of occupational therapy.

Eleven

ON SATURDAY before noon I looked through the stowage areas for fifteen minutes before I found my gadget. It is called the McGee Electric Alibi. The two D cells had expired, so I replaced them with fresh ones and tested it. Once upon a time it was a doorbell, but I removed the bell and replaced it with a piece of hardwood that has exactly the right timbre and resonance.

I direct-dialed my love and hunched over the desk top so I could listen to the earpiece and hold the mouthpiece at the pretested and precalculated distance from the mouthpiece. It only rang twice before she picked up the phone, but twice was enough to give me the duration and interval of the rings.

"Darling?" she said. It was exactly noon, as promised.

I pressed the button, transmitting the raucous clatter of a phone that keeps trying to ring after you've picked it up.

Between the first two imitation rings I heard her say, " . . . dammit to . . . " and in the next gap, ". . . stinking thing . . . ." I heard the clicking as she rattled the bar. ". . . n of a bitch . . ." I gave it eight fake rings and that made ten in all, as they instruct you in the yellow pages, and hung up.

Poor guy calls up all steamed up, right on time, and she isn't even home. Fine thing. So he thinks maybe her clock is wrong and she ran out for a paper or a loaf of bread or something. Five minutes later I tried again, and she answered, and I rattled her eager, frustrated, infuriated, helpless little eardrum and this time heard her cry over and above the racket, "Goddamn it to hell!"

So on the off chance, the guy would call the office, so I phoned at once before she would decide I might, and a subdued voice said, "Three one two one."

"Is Mary Smith there, please? Extension sixty-six."

"Miss Smith is not in today, sir."

"Well . . . if she should come in or phone in, would you tell her that Mr. McGee has been trying to reach her, and he'll phone her at home again at three o'clock."

"Is there a number where she can reach you, sir?"

"No. I don't expect to be here much longer, thanks."

She would know I had the right number, as I had reached her before. I had the bell on my phone switched off. I could make outgoing calls, however. So I tried her at twelve thirty. She hung up on the second rasp. At one her line was busy when I tried it. I had been hoping for that. It would be a help. A few minutes later it wasn't busy. She caught it on the first ring. "Hello?" Raaaasp. Cry of pure despair. Clunk as she hung up.

Snoopy the dog wears a guilty and evil grin from time to time. I couldn't work one up.

Meyer and I were in the lounge going over final details when I suddenly realized it was exactly three. I had no time to prepare him for the Electric Alibi. I heard a distinct sob before she hung up.

He stared at me as I came back to the chair. "Sometimes you worry me, Travis. It's something about the way your mind works."

"I often find it depressing." I stood up again. "Hell, we're all set. I'm going to drive up and see Janine and Connie. I'll stay over, and drive down to Sunnydale early Monday. You get there about noon and get a motel room somewhere, and go to the hotel I told you about for lunch. I'll show up with our pigeon. I think that sometime about maybe five or six o'clock Miss Mary Smith will show up and beat on the doors. I think I've described her well enough. Keep an eye out for her and intercept her

129

and tell her you think I'm on the Alabama Tiger's cruiser and point the way."

"Consolation prize?"

"Who for?"

He gave up and sighed and left. I phoned To-Co Groves and Connie's cry of pleasure at my coming was convincing enough. I buttoned up, switched the Sentry on, and put my gear in the car. Then I walked to the Tiger's permanent floating houseparty. Even with the boat closed up, the Afro-Cuban beat was loud. When I opened the door to the big main cabin area the sound nearly drove me backward. The big Ampex system was blasting, and the regulars were all around the perimeter because Junebug had herself a new challenger. She is a rubbery brown solid chunk of twenty-something-year-old girl, a sturdy mix of Irish, Gypsy and Cherokee. She wore a pink fuzzy bikini, and she was a go-going dervish, black short hair snapping, face and eyes a blur, body flexing and pumping to the beat, which Styles was sharpening with a blur of hands on the battered old bongos. The challenger was one of the king-sized beach bunnies, one of the big young straight-haired blondes about nineteen who look so much alike lately they should wear numbers on the side like stock cars. The money was in three piles on the deck by the Tiger's big bare feet. The big bunny was beginning to lag and flounder, miss the beat and catch up. Her mouth hung open. Her hip action in her zebra bikini was getting ratchety. The Tiger sat in a high glaze, swaying on the stool, smiling to himself, glass in hand. Muggsie Odell gave me her big smile, and I pointed at my watch and raised an eyebrow. She checked her watch, then flashed me seven sets of ten fingers plus four. Except for being so sweaty her body looked oiled, the Junebug looked absolutely fresh after seventy-four minutes of it. Maybe the challengers can go all day long to the beat they're used to, but they don't realize the additional demand on stamina of the Afro-Cuban tempo. One of them is reputed to have lasted over two hours before hitting the deck, but the Junebug wasn't even close to her own limit.

I crooked a finger at Muggsie. She nodded and followed me out and closed the hatch against the noise.

We sat on the wide transom and Muggsie said, "She's

good for five more minutes, if that. I just as soon not be in there. They're waiting for her to fall down, and she's a stubborn kid and she'll keep going until she does drop. I just don't like to see them fall down like dead."

"A favor?"

"Depends. Probably yes, McGee."

"I'm going away for a couple of days. A very very nice little package is going to come right here looking for me. I'm having her steered here. The name is Mary Smith."

"No kidding!"

"Tell her I was here with the group but I went away and you think I said I was going to come back, so it would be best for her to wait. Meanwhile, has Hero been around?"

I was interrupted by a yell from the group. The door burst open and somebody stopped the tape. The Junebug came out, yelling Ya HAA, Ya HAAA, and jumping into the air with every third stride. Through the open door I could see the bunny face-down on the deck trying to push herself up, with people reaching to help her. June-bug gave a great leap to the dock, spun the valve on the dock hose and held the nozzle aimed right at the crown of her head. After it had streamed down her face and across her smile and pasted her dark hair flat, she stuck the nozzle under her bikini top for a few moments and then under the elastic of the bikini bottoms and, with an ecstatic smile, worked it slowly all the way around to the back and around the other side of that muscular body to the front again.

"Anybody else?" she yelled. "Any new pigeon, step up and put your bread on the deck! The old Junebug is ready."

"I'd watch *her* fall," Muggsie said grimly. "I'd watch her fall and hope for a couple of good bounces. What's this with Hero? What are you asking about Hero?"

"Has he been around?"

"Who can stop him? You know Hero. Every hour, cruising in and seeing if there's any new stuff he hasn't seen before. With him it's a dedication. Are you saying aim Hero at this Mary Smith? What's the matter? You hate the girl?"

"Let's say they deserve each other. As soon as he starts

131

trying to snow her, Muggsie, you go back to her and say you just heard that I came here in a bad mood and there was girl who wanted to cheer me up and we went off together, so maybe there's no point in waiting."

"Why don't I just chunk her on the head and help Hero carry her back to his pad?"

"Because it is entirely possible she'll chunk him on the head and take him back to hers."

"Oh. One of those. Anyway, Hero certainly is a handsome guy, and he certainly has enough charm for a whole charm school, and he certainly has given an awful lot of lady tourists a vacation they'll never forget. I was saying just the other day, I could really go for that guy, if only he just wasn't a real rotten person through and through."

"You mean if you didn't know him."

"That's what I must mean. Wherever you're going, have fun, Trav. I'll unite the happy couple and get her off your hands for good."

As I left I walked by Junebug on the dock, toweling herself dry. "Hey you, McGee," she said, with the big white mocking grin. "Hey, you never tole me when we're gonna start to go steady. How about it?"

I looked at all that brown rubbery, arrogant vitality. "I told you, Junebug, the very next time I get a death wish, I'll look you up."

"Some coward!"

"You can believe it."

"Aww. Poor fella. I wouldn't kill you. Just cripple you up pretty good, hah?"

"I think your trouble is that you're too shy. You lack self-confidence. Get out and meet people."

When I was a long way away I could still hear Junebug cawing with laughter.

I made good time and got to the Groves an hour after nightfall. We had drinks by the fire of fat pine, and a good dinner, and good talk. Janine got up and came over to me, hesitated, then leaned and touched her lips to the side of my face, and went off to bed.

Connie asked me what I thought of how Jan looked and acted.

"Listless. Thinner. More bones in her face."

"She's not eating well or sleeping well. She'll start to

132

read or sew and end up staring into space. I hear her wandering around the house in the middle of the night. She's not coming out of it the way she should. I don't know what to do to snap her out of it. She's a damned fine girl, Trav. She's turning into a ghost."

"It's good of you to have her and the kids here."

"Don't be a jackass! I told her she can stay forever and I mean it. Those are three good kids. Five kids make a good kind of noise to have in the house. It's been quiet around here too damned long."

She asked about my redhead, and why I hadn't brought her along. When I said we'd called it off, she was suddenly furious, saying she thought I had more sense than that. I had to explain that it wasn't my idea and I'd been given no chance to make her change her mind. Then she was merely puzzled, saying it didn't make any sense at all.

On Sunday the three of us went fifty miles in Connie's Pontiac at her customary Indianapolis pace up to Rufus Wellington's law office. He had had his elderly secretary come in, and she was just finishing the typing of the deed and other documents pertinent to my sale of the Bannon property to Preston LaFrance. I had the power of attorney with me that Meyer had given me, which, when signed by Janine and witnessed, would authorize him to buy and sell securities in her name in the margin account he was establishing for her at the brokerage firm he used in Lauderdale.

Rufus eyed me and said, "You sure LaFrance will pay forty for an equity that isn't even there? Young man, do me the favor of not telling me what kind of persuasion you're fixing to use on him. I don't think I would like to know. I don't even want to know who this Meyer is, thank you. Any member of the bar is an officer of the court."

"If I have any trouble with the bank approving of the transfer of the mortgage to LaFrance, can you help?"

"I can phone Whitt Sanders and remind him of something that would make him approve transferring it to a little red hen. But I don't want to use it less I have to, just like I didn't have to when Connie went on the note with you. I have the feeling LaFrance is going to have trouble making those payments on the mortgage."

"If you don't want me to tell you anything, Judge, why do you make leading statements and then wait for me to explain?"

"Because I guess I figure you're not likely to tell me, son. But I do have a couple of clients here. You, Connie, and you, Miz Janine, and it would rest my mind to feel sure that nothing would come back on these ladies from anything too cute you are figuring on working on some of those folks down there in Sunnydale."

"Rest your mind, Judge," I said.

He leaned back, looked beyond us into the misty places of memory and said, "When I was a rough, wild young man, which seems like it was all in a different world than this one, I ended up down in Mexico one time, near Victoria, on a horse ranch. You had to prove you were all man. There was a thing they did, called the *paseo de muerte*. Maybe I don't have the lingo just right, but it's close. It was just riding full out, a full hard run over rocky land on half-broke horses, and the one who wants to test you, he comes up on you on one side, and he grins and you grin back and kick your feet free of the stirrups and you change horses right there, risking the way the footing is, and spooking one of the horses, or losing ahold. Once you'd show them you were ready to do it anytime, then they'd leave you be, because they weren't any more anxious deep inside to keep doing it than you were. Any fool could see that every time a man did it, his odds got shorter." He shook his head and smiled. "Long hours and short money, and one day out of no-place I could imagine came the idea I could start reading for the law. Why did I start all this? There was some point I was going to make. Oh. You keep in mind, Travis McGee, that the money game is one wild horse, and the vengeance for murder is another wild horse, and you try riding them both, you can fall between and get your skull stamped with an iron shoe. Bannon was your friend, and Connie's friend, and he was your husband, Miz Janine, daddy of your boys. Murder can come in when the money game goes bad. But don't think of it as being black dirty evil, but more of it being sick and sad, of some stumbling jackass that didn't mean it to come out that way, and he wakes up in the night and thinks on it and he gets sweaty and he hears his heart going like mad.

134

Well, you folks have refused my kind offer to come on home with me for kitchen whisky and side meat and fancy conversation, so you will forgive me if I tell you all to be careful, and speed you on your way."

I phoned Press LaFrance in the late afternoon and arranged to meet him in Sunnydale the next morning. He sounded cautious and nervous and he gave me the impression of a certain evasiveness. He assured me the forty was still waiting, and he was anxious to listen, but I had the uneasy feeling that something had changed.

I went out to the sheds and sat on the truck dock, feeling dispirited. I finally admitted to myself that I felt guilty about Mary Smith. I could rationalize it as an adroit defensive maneuver. Gary Santo had aimed her at me. Maybe the little code word had been "steak." He had evaluated me and decided there was enough chance of additional useful information to turn her loose. So I had sidestepped her and aimed her at Hero.

But, after all, she knew her way around. She was about as gullible, innocent and vulnerable as those limey lassies who had starred in the Profumo affair. It was a good chance that she would case Hero in about forty seconds and turn him off, because he could certainly never be a business assignment.

I wished, however, that one little comment about Hero had not lodged itself so firmly in my memory. He looked like the big, gentle, slow-moving, kindly star of a hundred Westerns, and he had the charm to make a woman feel admired, protected and cherished, until he could ease her back to his pad, or back to her place, or any nearby nest he could beg, borrow or rent.

And there he would tirelessly demonstrate that degree of satyriasis that stopped short of landing him in various kinds of corrective institutions. He cruised the festive areas and cut his quarry out of merry packs with easy skill and monomaniacal determination. The comment that lingered in my mind came from a weary man who came aboard Meyer's boat one hot Sunday afternoon and said, "Knowing Hero this long, I sure God should have had the good sense never to let him bring a woman aboard my ketch last evening, but with Myra and the kids off visiting her folks, and the forward cabin empty, and me a little

135

smashed, I said okay and what he had was some young schoolteacher he'd found right over at the *Yankee Clipper* in a big batch of schoolteachers having a party before going on a five-day cruise to the Islands out of Everglades. The ship left this morning and she sure God isn't going to make that cruise. Giggly woman, kind of mousy and trying to get along without her glasses, and built real good, especially up front. His angle was showing her a Bahama-built ketch on account of she was going to the Bahamas. I left them aboard and that was nine or ten o'clock and I came back at midnight or later thinking they'd be gone. Honest to God, I'm dead for sleep, men. It would get quieted down and I'd be drifting off and it would start up again. With all that whinnying and squeaking and thrashing around, the nearest thing it sounds like, and it's still going on from time to time, is like somebody beating carpets with a shoat. One day Hero is going to nail him one with heart trouble and she just isn't going to last it out. I should have had more sense last night. Meyer, what would you say to me going below and getting a little nap?"

So maybe, I thought, Hero never came back to the Tiger's, or maybe Mary Smith never drove up from Miami to try to find me, and if she did, maybe Meyer missed her. Or little Muggsie could have decided she deserved better.

Janine came walking slowly from the house, hands deep in the pockets of a borrowed gray cardigan worn over white ranch jeans. She hadn't seen me, and when I called to her, she turned and came over.

"Have a good nap?"

"I slept a little." She sat on an upended cement block and reached and picked up a piece of lath and started drawing lines in the dirt with the sharp end. She tilted her head and stared up at me, squinting against the brightness of the sky.

"Trav," she said, "I keep wondering about one thing. It keeps bothering me. I keep trying to figure out what happened, but I can't seem to think of anything logical. It's sort of strange."

"Like?"

"How did Tush get out there? I had the car. He was going to come into Sunnydale by bus and phone me to come get him. Did somebody give him a ride, or what?"

"I never thought about that."

"Then, whoever gave him the ride could tell when he got there. They . . . found him at what time was it?"

"A sheriff's deputy found him at nine o'clock, approximately. The medical examiner estimated he had been dead from one to four hours at the time he was found."

"From five thirty to eight thirty, then. In there somewhere, somebody . . . killed him. But he was so strong, Trav. You know how powerful he was. He wouldn't just stretch out and let somebody . . . He was dead when they put him there. Maybe whoever drove him out there saw somebody hanging around."

"We're going to get to all that, Jan. Believe me, we're going to do our best to find out. But first we've got to do some salvage work for you."

She made a bitter mouth and looked down and drew a dollar sign. She reached a foot out and slowly scuffed it out. "Money. It got to mean so damned much, you know. Getting pinched worse and worse, and snapping at each other about it, and being so scared we were going to lose the whole thing we started with. And now it doesn't mean anything. Nothing at all."

"With those three kids to bring up? Shoes and dentists and school and presents?"

"Oh, I suppose it will be something I'll have to think about. But right now I'm just . . . nowhere. You're sure you can fix it so I'll end up with thirty thousand clear, and you seem so sure you can make me a lot more out of that stock stuff I don't understand at all. I ought to sound grateful and pleased and delighted and so on."

"Not for my sake. Or Meyer's."

"Everybody is doing things for me. But I ran. Everybody knows that. I'm a lousy person. I don't like myself. Trav, I used to like myself well enough."

I slid off the dock and took her hand and pulled her up. "Let's walk for a while." We walked and I gave her some dreary little sermons about how never quite matching up to what you want of yourself is the basic of the human condition. She heard, but I don't know if she believed. I was trying hard to believe my own hard sell, because I kept thinking of carpets and shoats and wide

137

wide emerald eyes and a delicately provocative little pressure of teeth against the knuckles of my stupid right hand.

Twelve

I ARRIVED in downtown Sunnydale at nine o'clock on Monday morning and parked in the bank lot, and walked toward the Shawana River Hotel, where I had arranged to meet LaFrance in the coffee shop.

When I went into the lobby, two men in green twill uniforms moved in from either side to position themselves with an unhurried competence between me and the glass double doors. A cricket-sized man of about sixty planted himself spread-legged in front of me and said, "Nice and easy, now. You just lay both hands atop your head. You're a big one, all right. Freddy?"

One of the others came in from behind and reached around me and patted all the appropriate pockets and places. I had recognized the sheriff's voice from having heard it over the phone. He wore a businessman's hat wadded onto the back of his head. Straight gray hair stuck out in Will Rogers style. He wore an unpressed dark suit with a small gold star in the lapel. The suit coat hung open, exposing a holstered belly gun small enough to be an Airweight. Small enough to look toylike, but in no sense a toy.

The legal papers, billfold and keys were handed to Sheriff Bunny Burgoon. From his voice I had thought he would be all belly, with porcine features. He opened the wallet, flipped through the pliofilm envelopes. He stopped at the driver's license and studied it.

"Your name Travis McGee? You can put your hands down, boy."

"That's my name."

"Now we're going on over to my office and talk some."

"Can I ask why?"

"It's my duty to tell you that you got no obligation to answer any questions I or any of my officers may ask you without the presence of any attorney of your choice, and you are in your rights to request the Court appoint an attorney to represent your interests in this matter, and

138

anything you say in response to interrogation, with or without the presence of your legal representative, may be held in evidence against you."

He had run all the words together, like a court clerk swearing a witness.

"Is there a charge?"

"Not up to this minute, boy. You're being taken in for interrogation in connection with a felony committed in the county jurisdiction."

"If I'm being taken in, Sheriff, then it is an arrest, isn't it?"

"Boy, aren't you coming along willingly and voluntarily like is the duty of any citizen to assist law officers in the pursuit of their duty?"

"Why certainly, Sheriff! Willingly and voluntarily, and not in the cage in the back of a county sedan, and with my keys and papers and wallet in my pockets. Otherwise it's an arrest, and if so, my personal attorney is Judge Rufus Wellington and you better get him on the horn and get him down here."

"Read his name in the paper, boy?"

"Instead of bothering the judge, why don't you just ask Whitt Sanders if the judge represents me?"

I was watching for a shift of uncertainty in his eyes and saw it. Apparently he had not anticipated any connection with the local power structure. He motioned one of the two deputies close, stood tall, and without taking his eyes off me, murmured into the younger man's ear. The deputy walked out. Burgoon asked me to come over and sit on a couch in the lobby. The deputy was back in five minutes and the sheriff went over and talked quietly with him, then came over and gave me back my possessions. With one of the deputies ten paces behind us, we walked through the morning sunshine to the Shawana County Courthouse and around to the side and into the entrance labeled COUNTY SHERIFF.

I was aware of a particularly avid curiosity on the part of the desk personnel and the communication clerk as he led me back into his office. The slats of the blinds were almost closed. He turned on the ceiling fluorescence and his desk lamp. He had me sit in a straight chair facing his desk and six feet from it. The sheriff looked at the papers on his blotter, put them aside and sat in his big black chair. A portly man in deputy uniform came in and sighed and sat in a chair back against the wall. "Willie will be bringing it along, Sherf."

Burgoon nodded. There was silence. I looked at the framed testimonials on the walls, and the framed pictures of Burgoon taken with various political notables, past and present. Some file drawers were partially open. The contents looked untidy, with documents sticking up out of the file folders.

"Make that deal with Harry?" Burgoon asked.

The portly one said, "He give me an estimate of over seventeen hundred. And it was supposed to be a twenty-year roof. I told Cathy we could buy a lot of buckets to set under the leaks for seventeen hundred."

"Harry does nice work."

"Wisht I'd used him when I was building."

Burgoon looked at me. "You made up your mind about a lawyer yet, mister?" I had been promoted from boy.

"Sheriff, I think it would be easier for me to make that decision if I had more information about what you think I did. It could be something we might be able to straighten out without bothering anybody."

"Maybe. Maybe not."

"When and where did the alleged crime take place? That might give me something to go on."

"It took place, mister, on the morning of December seventeenth last, and it took place at a marina on the Shawana River just about eleven miles east of here."

"That was a Sunday morning?"

"Yes it was."

"Would you be trying to make a capital case, Sheriff?"

"Murder first."

I remembered that Sunday with no trouble. Puss, Barni Baker, Mick Coseen, Meyer, Marilee, in fact a lot more people than we had needed or wanted aboard, and a dozen ways to refresh their memories that it was that exact day.

"Just one more question and I can give you an answer. Am I supposed to be connected with it in some way, or are you trying to say I was there at that time?"

"There at that time and did commit an act of violence which resulted in the death of one Brantley B. Bannon."

"Then, I don't think I need a lawyer to straighten things out."

It seemed to startle Burgoon. He said irritably, "Tom, what the hell is holding up that damn Willie?"

"Right here, Sheriff. Right here," said a thin young man who came in carrying a tape recorder. He put it on the corner of the sheriff's desk, knelt on the rug and plugged it in. "Sheriff, you just push——"

"I know, I know! Get on back to work and close the door." When the door was closed, Burgoon said, "We took this with the court reporter and on tape at the same time, and there hasn't been time to transcribe it yet. You get to hear it on account of now we've got that damn new law on full disclosure, and the defense would get a certified copy of the transcript anyways, and the State's Attorney said it was all right I should do it this way. You listen, and then you answer questions and make a statement, and then we hold you and this goes to a special meeting of the Grand Jury for the indictment so you can be arraigned proper."

He punched it on and leaned back and closed his eyes and rested his fingertips together. The tape had a lot of hiss. Apparently nobody ever bothered to clean or demagnetize the heads. But the questions and answers were clear enough.

I recognized the flat, insipid, dreary little-girl voice before she even gave her name, saying that she was Mrs. Roger Denn, Arlene Denn, and that she had been living with her husband at the Banyan Cottages, Cottage number 12 ever since the tenth of December, that she was twenty-two years old and that she was self-employed, as was her husband, making and selling art objects to gift shops. Prior to that time they had lived aboard a houseboat the Bannons had rented them, tied up at the Bannon Boatel on the river, and had lived there eight months.

"What were the circumstances of your leaving?"

"Well, they had to come and take the houseboats back. They owed on them and some men came and towed them off, I don't know where. That was . . . early in December, I don't know exactly what day."

"What happened then?"

"We put all our things in the two end units of the motel just for a while, until we could find something, because Mr. Bannon said it looked like he might lose the place. We went looking and we found a place at the Banyan Cottages and moved in on the tenth, and we were making trips in the station wagon to bring our supplies and so on back to the cottages."

As she spoke on the tape, through the hiss, I could picture her clearly, pallid and sloppy and doughy, with dirty blonde hair and a mouth that hung open, and meaningless blue eyes.

"What was the occasion of your last visit to Bannon's motel."

"It was because of missing some silver wire. We use it in the jewelry. On Saturday, that was the sixteenth, we looked all over for it and it was just gone. We knew then that the place was foreclosed out there, but we still had a key to the end units on account of Roger forgot to leave it off when we made the last trip. I kept thinking that maybe what could have happened to it, we had a lot of supplies piled on the beds and maybe the wire slipped down and caught somehow like at the headboard or the footboard, because I had crawled around looking to see if we'd left anything on the floor the last trip we took. Roger kept saying to forget it because it was real trouble going into a place sealed off by the court, and maybe they'd changed the locks. But it was twenty dollars' worth of wire and maybe seventeen left on the roll, and we don't do so good we can just throw away seventeen dollars. So we sort of had a fight about it, and I said I was going to go out there whether he was or not, so I went out when it was just getting to be daylight the next day, which was Sunday. I drove right on by, slow, to see if anybody was there and I didn't see anybody, so I went a ways up the road and put the station wagon in a little kind of overgrown place that used to be a cleared road once. I backed it in. You know, kind of hiding it, and I went back with the key and when I was pretty sure nobody was around, I tried the key and it worked and I let myself in and started hunting for that wire."

"What happened next?"

"I guess I was hunting for maybe ten minutes or fifteen minutes. I don't know just what time it was. Maybe sometime between seven and seven thirty and I heard a car coming, so I squatted down so nobody could look in and see me when they went by. One of the windows, those awning kind of window things, was open three or four inches. So I heard the car drive in and it stopped and then I heard a car door slam and then I heard another car door slam and I heard men's voices."

"Could you hear what was said?"

"No sir. They were loudest near the car and then kind of faded when they were walking toward the marina. I couldn't hear words but I had the feeling they were mad at each other, almost shouting. I think one word that was shouted was Jan. That was Mrs. Bannon's name. Janine. But I couldn't be sure."

"What happened next?"

"I didn't know what to do. I was afraid to leave. I tried to peek out the windows and see where they went to, to see if it was safe for me to sneak out."

"Could you see the car?"

"No sir. But I knew I would hear it if it started up."

"Then what happened?"

"Somebody shouted a lot louder, and further away, and I knew they were real mad. It sounded to me like Mr. Bannon. Then it was quiet. Then maybe five minutes later I looked out the back window that looks toward the river, and I saw a man dragging Mr. Bannon across the ground. He had his arms wrapped around Mr. Bannon's ankles and he was leaning forward and pulling hard and pulling Mr. Bannon along. I was kneeling and looking out a corner of the window, like with one eye. He dragged him right to that old hoist thing and then kind of rolled and shoved and pushed him under the motor. Mr. Bannon was real limp, like unconscious or dead. The man stood up and looked at him and then he looked all around. I ducked down and when I got up enough nerve to look again, he was walking toward the hoist thing again from the marina and he was carrying something small, some wire and something. I watched him and he kneeled down and did something to Mr. Bannon I couldn't see, and then he worked some more at the hoist thing. Then he turned the crank and the motor went up real slow. I could hear the clickety sound it made. Then he stood near the gear part and bent over and did something and . . . the motor fell down onto Mr. Bannon. There was a rackety sound when it came down and the wire ropes slapped around and hit those poles and made a ringing sound."

"And then?"

"He cranked it up halfway and looked at Mr. Bannon close, and cranked it up the rest of the way and let it fall on him again. When he cranked it up again, Mr. Bannon looked . . . kind of flattened out. He didn't put it all the way up again. He just let it fall from there and he left it there and picked up something off the ground and then kind of stopped and dropped it and then picked it up and wiped it on some kind of a rag and dropped it again. He was nearly running when he left. And then I heard one car door slam and after a little while the car started up. I stayed way down until it was gone."

"Which way did it go?"

"Back this way, toward Sunnydale."

"Did you get a good look at the man?"

"Yes sir, I did."

"Had you ever seen him before?"

"Yes sir."

"Would you recognize him if you saw him again?"

"Yes sir."

"Do you know him by name?"

"Yes sir."

"What is his name?"

"His name is Mr. McGee."

"Under what circumstances did you first see Mr. McGee?"

"I only saw him two times before that, both on the same day. It was back in October. I don't know the exact day. He was a friend of theirs and he came in a nice boat to visit them. He took them over to Broward Beach in the boat that night for dinner and I sat with the little boys. So I met him when I came over to sit, and then I saw him again when they came back."

"Did they seem friendly, McGee and the Bannons?"

"I . . . guess so."

"You seem hesitant. Why?"

"I had the feeling it was Mrs. Bannon he came to see."

"What gave you that feeling?"

"Well, actually I saw him three times that day. It was an awful hot day. Mr. Bannon and Mr. McGee had fixed Mr. Bannon's car. Then Mr. Bannon went off to get the boys from school. I saw Mrs. Bannon taking a pitcher of iced tea to one of the units. I wanted to ask her about something she was going to bring me from town, to save a trip. I needed it in my work and I went down there to where she took the iced tea, thinking she would come right out. When she didn't, I sort of looked in the window. I didn't know his name then, not until later. But I saw Mr. McGee and Mrs. Bannon laying on the bed, kissing."

"Did you notice anything else that day in October that seemed odd or unusual to you?"

"No sir. Nothing else at all, sir."

"What did you do after McGee drove away?"

"Well, I thought I better wait a little while in case he forgot something and came back. So I looked for the wire some more and I found it. I left and made sure the door was locked and then I ran all the way to our car. I threw the key in the bushes when I was getting into the car, the room key."

"Why did you do that?"

"I was very frightened, I guess. I didn't want anybody to know I'd been in the motel."

"I show you a motel room key. Is this that same key you threw away?"

"I think so. Yes sir. That's the key."

"Did you relate all this to your husband?"

"No sir. I didn't tell him anything."

"Why not?"

"Because he said I shouldn't go out there, and even though I did find the silver wire, he was still right about that. I wish I hadn't gone out there that Sunday morning."

"Will you tell us why you finally came forward, Mrs. Denn?"

"I thought they would catch Mr. McGee. But they didn't. I worried and worried about it and the other night I told my husband the whole thing and he said I had to come and see you. I begged him not to make me do it but he said I had to. That's why I'm here."

Sheriff Burgoon turned it off. "There's more. But it covers the same ground. It doesn't bring up anything new. It's an eyeball witness, boy, with nothing to gain or lose.

We took her out there and she showed us the window and you get a real good view from there."

He had demoted me back to boy, heartened by his evidence.

"I think she saw almost exactly what she says she saw, sheriff."

"Want to change your mind about a lawyer?"

"Motive, opportunity, weapon, and an eyewitness. Sheriff, don't you think it's all wrapped up just a little too neatly?"

"A man can be damn unlucky."

"How true. I wonder just who he is."

"Suppose you make a little sense."

"Okay. Here is something that the unlucky man, whoever he is, had to take a chance on. He had to take a chance on there being some probability or possibility of my being in this area at that time, and my having no way to prove I wasn't."

"It's going to take a pretty good piece of proof."

"I can place myself aboard my houseboat where I live, *The Busted Flush,* Slip F-18, Bahia Mar, Fort Lauderdale, at nine o'clock that Sunday morning. Does the rest of the tape establish her best guess as to the time I'm supposed to have left after the murder?"

"Maybe eight thirty, give or take fifteen minutes," he said. "But let's get to just how you place yourself there and how come you'd remember it so good."

"Because I arrived at Bannon's place the following afternoon and found out he was dead. I found out he had died the previous morning. Somehow you remember what you were doing at the time a good friend died."

"And just what were you doing?"

"Socializing, Sheriff Burgoon. Being a jolly host, right out in front of everybody. I think that I could probably come up with the names of at least twenty people who saw me and talked to me between nine and ten o'clock that morning. Some of them are totally unreliable. I don't pick them for social standing and credit rating, and I wouldn't ask you or anyone to believe them if they swore on every Bible in Shawana County. But there are a half dozen well worth believing. Suppose you write down the names and addresses and pick a couple of names off the list and question them by phone right now any way you feel like. Try any trick or trap you can think up."

"What did you mean saying she saw almost exactly what she says she saw, mister?"

"She saw everything except me doing it. She saw somebody else do it, and that changes your theory about nothing to gain or lose."

"How do you mean?"

"Somebody prepped her pretty good, Sheriff. I might even have thought that she saw somebody she sincerely mistook for me. But the iced tea sequence was a little too much."

"Didn't happen?"

"I got hot and sweaty helping Tush fix the spring shackle on his car. I showered in the motel unit they loaned me. I had just finished dressing when Jan brought the pitcher of tea and two glasses. We talked about the problems they were having. Maybe fat-girl even looked in the window. But no bed and no kisses. Nothing like that between us. Not even any thought of it on either side. At the moment I happen to own the Bannon place, Sheriff. I bought it from Jan Bannon. Why in hell would I do that?"

"*You* are the one bought it!"

"I'm here today to try to resell it to Press LaFrance."

Burgoon looked very thoughtful. "He's surely been wanting it so bad he could taste it. Trying to put some kind of parcel together for resale. Don't he own a patch out there, Tom?"

"Fifty acres right behind."

Burgoon nodded. "Probably could move it if he had river frontage to go with it."

Tom scrubbed his snow-white brush cut and coughed and said, "Bunny, that Bannon woman didn't seem to me to be that kind of woman when I had to go out there and roust her and the kids out and seal it up. That's one part of this job I surely hate. We tried to make it easy as we could, but there isn't any good way to make it easy. She was one upset woman and you can believe it."

The sheriff asked me for the names of my witnesses and wrote them down.

I thought of something else. How come they had been waiting for me at the hotel? And did that have anything

147

to do with LaFrance's evasiveness when I had phoned him?

"Who told you I was coming to the hotel, Sheriff?"

"Wasn't it Freddy dug that up, Tom?" Burgoon asked. When Tom nodded, Burgoon said, "Didn't you say you were coming here to see Press LaFrance? Then, that answers it, sure enough. Freddy Hazzard is Press's nephew, his sister's eldest boy. He's my youngest deputy, mister. You saw him at the hotel, the lanky one."

"Is he the son of one of your County Commissioners?"

"Sure is. Monk's boy. But that's got no bearing on me taking him on. Freddy came out of service with a good record in the M.P. and he earns his pay right down the line."

"Didn't somebody say that it was somebody named Freddy who found the body?"

"That's right. On a routine patrol at nine thirty. You see, I had a note for Bannon from his missus, and she'd left a suitcase here for him, and I didn't know but what Bannon might hitch a ride to his place or come by boat or something. She'd said he was planning to be back Friday or Saturday, so I had the boys keeping an eye on it out there off and on." He peered at me. "You getting at something?"

"I don't know, Sheriff. I'm going to check out all right. You have a hunch I will, and you hate to admit it to yourself because it's such a nice neat painless little case."

He slapped his hand on the desk top. "But why would some other damned fool, if somebody else besides you did it, why would they want to pick *you* for it? They should know there was a chance you'd be in the clear. Why not some description to fit somebody we'd look for and never find?"

"Suppose this person heard, second hand, that I had a theory somebody had done too good a job of working Tush Bannon over and killed him, then dropped the engine on him to hide the traces, and fixed the wire to make it look like suicide?"

"If you can prove you said that to anybody at any time, mister, it might be more help than this list of folks I wrote down."

"I told that same person that maybe it was somebody who was trying to do him a favor and do Monk Hazzard

148

a favor, by trying to take some of the spunk out of Bannon so he would leave quietly. Because the person I was talking to has been trying to get that land."

"LaFrance?" Burgoon said, almost whispering it. "Tom, you think Press ought to come in for a little talk?"

"Can I make a suggestion, Sheriff?" I asked.

"You mean you've got another way to make things worse than they are right now?"

"Isn't the weakest place the fat girl? She lied and she'll know who made her lie. Don't you think she could be brought in to make a positive identification?"

"You ever been in this line of work?"

"Not directly."

"You got a record, mister?"

"Four arrests. No convictions, Sheriff. Nothing ever even came to trial."

"Now, just what would those arrests have been for, mister?"

"Assault, which turned out to be self-defense. Breaking and entering, and it turned out I had the owner's permission. Conspiracy, and somebody decided to withdraw the charges. Piracy on the high seas, dismissed for lack of evidence."

"You're not exactly in any rut, are you? Tom, send somebody after that Arlene Denn."

After he left, I said to the Sheriff, "When did she make that statement?"

"Saturday, starting about . . . maybe eleven in the morning."

"Did you try to have me picked up in Lauderdale?"

"Sure did."

"And Deputy Hazzard found out yesterday in the late afternoon that I would be at the hotel this morning?"

"He got the tip last night and phoned me at home."

"Did he have any objections to the way you set it up to take me?"

"Well . . . he did say maybe if I stationed him across there, like on the roof of the service station with a carbine, it would be good insurance if you smelled something and decided not to go into the hotel at all." He shook his head. "Freddy is a good boy. It doesn't fit the way you want me to think it fits."

"I'm not trying to sell you anything."

In twenty minutes Tom brought her in. She stopped abruptly just inside the door and gave me a single glassy blue look and looked away. She wore a paint-spattered man's T-shirt hanging outside her bulging jeans, and apparently nothing under the T-shirt.

"Move over near Tom and let her set in that chair," he said to me. She sat and stared at Burgoon, her face so vapid she looked dimwitted.

"Now then, Arlie," said Burgoon, "we had a nice talk day before yesterday and you helped us a lot and we appreciate it. Now, don't you be nervous. There's another part of it you've got to do. Do you know that man setting over there by Tom."

" . . . Yes sir."

"What's his name, Arlie?"

"The one I told you about. Mr. McGee."

"Now, you turn and look at him and be sure and if you are sure it's the man you saw dropping that engine onto Mr. Bannon, you point your finger at him and you say, 'That's the same man.' "

She turned and she looked at the wall about a foot over my head and stabbed a finger at me and said, "That's the same man."

"You had a clear view of him on the morning of December seventeenth? No chance of a mistake?"

"No sir."

"Now, don't be nervous. You're doing just fine. We've got another little problem you can help us with. It turns out Mr. McGee was way down in Fort Lauderdale that same identical morning at the same time you think you saw him, and he was on a boat with some very important people. A federal judge and a state senator and a famous surgeon, and they say he was right there at that same time. Now, Arlie, just how in the wide world are we going to get around that?"

She stared fixedly at him, her mouth sagging open.

"Arlie, are those big people lying and are you the one telling the truth, so help you God?"

"I saw what I saw."

"Who told you to make up these lies, Arlie?"

"I told you what I saw."

"Now, Arlie, you recall what I said before, about you having the right to be represented by a lawyer and so on?"

"So?"

"I'm telling you again, girl. You don't have to answer any questions. Because I think I'm going to hold you and book you."

She shrugged plump shoulders. "Do what you feel like."

Crickety little Burgoon glanced over at Tom and then looked at the fat girl again. "Girl, I don't think you rightly know just how much trouble you're asking for. You see, I *know* you're lying."

Tom, responding to his signal, came in on cue. "Bunny, why in God's name you being so kindly to this fat dumb slut? Let me run her on out to the stockade and turn her over to Miss Mary. Leave her out there three or four days and Miss Mary would purely enjoy sweatin' off fifteen pounds of slop and teaching her some manners. She'd have a nice attitude when you have her brought back in."

Arlene Denn turned and stared at Tom. She bit her lip and swallowed and looked back at Burgoon, who said, "Now, if we have to come to that, Tom, we'll come to that. But this isn't any ninety-day county case. And this isn't any one to five up to the state women's prison. What the law of the State of Florida says is that giving false testimony in a capital case, or withholding evidence in a capital case is punishable by a maximum sentence of imprisonment for the rest of her natural life."

She stiffened as much as her figure permitted, sat up straight and said, "You've got to be kidding, Sheriff!"

"You know how to read, girl?"

"Of course I know how to read!"

He dug a battered manual out of a desk drawer, licked his thumb and found the right page. He handed it across to her. "Second paragraph down. That there is sort of a short form of everything against the law. It's what new deputies have to study up on and pass a test."

She read it and handed the manual back. She looked over at me. The look of vacuous stupidity was gone, and I realized it was the mask she wore for the world she was in.

"Now, without me saying I *would* change my story, Sheriff, let's suppose I did. What would happen to me?"

"Would the new story be the exact truth, Arlie?"

"Let's say it would be."

"Would it have you out there seeing anything at all?"

"Let's say it would have me seeing somebody else instead of Mr. McGee. Let's say that when I looked in the window, Mr. McGee and Mrs. Bannon were just talking."

Burgoon said, "What do you think, Tom?"

"I think she ought to do some laundry work for Miss Mary for thirty days."

"Maybe. Maybe not. I'd say it's going to depend on *why* she showed up with those lies."

"Regardless," said Arlie, "would you bust me for any more than thirty days?"

"Only if it turns out you're telling more lies. We are going to check this new one out every way there is, girl."

"Okay, then, here is the way it really was . . ."

The sheriff told her to wait a moment. He spoke into his intercom and got hold of Willie and told him to bring in some fresh tape, and told him the Denn girl was changing her story, and stop the transcript on the old story. Willie groaned audibly. He came in with the fresh tape, took the old one off the machine and set it for record.

"It's mostly all still good what I said before," Arlene said. "I just have to change some parts. I mean it would save doing the whole question bit right from the start, wouldn't it?"

"Then, save that tape, Willie," said Bunny Burgoon, "and close the door on the way out."

He started the tape rolling, and established time and place and the identity of the witness.

"Now, Mrs. Denn, you have told us that you wish to change portions of your previous statement."

"Just two . . . no, three parts."

"What would be the first change?"

"I didn't hear anybody say anything that sounded like Jan. The two men were mad at each other, but I didn't hear any word like that."

"And what is the second change you wish to make?"

"What if you decide to protect your own and throw me to the dogs, Sheriff?"

"What is the second change you wish to make?"

"Well . . . it wasn't Mr. McGee I saw. The man I saw did everything in the other statement the way I told it. But it was Deputy Sheriff Freddy Hazzard."

"Oh, God *damn* it!" said Tom.

"Hush up," said Bunny. "And the third change?"

"I looked in the window back in October but they were just talking. Drinking tea. That was all."

"Now, hold it a minute, girl. Tom, you go tell Walker and Englert to pick Freddy up and bring him back here and . . . Damn it, tell them to take his weapon and put him in the interrogation room and hold him until I can get around to him. When does he come on duty, Tom?"

"I think tonight he's on the eight to eight again. But you know Freddy."

"Sheriff?" the girl said as Tom left the office. "You weren't having me on, were you? About how big I could get busted for telling something that didn't happen?"

"I never said a truer thing in my life, Mrs. Denn."

"Why box me?" I asked her.

The vacant blue look she gave me was a total indifference. "Every straight one looks exactly alike to me."

Tom came back in looking distressed. "Damn it all, Bunny, he was out there checking the skip list when you came over the box telling Willie this girl was changing her story. And he walked right out and took off. He's in uniform, driving number three. Terry is trying to raise him on the horn but no answer. All points?"

Burgoon closed his eyes and rattled his fingers on the desk top. "No. If he's running, there's eighty-five back ways out of this county and he knows every one of them. Let's see what more we've got here." He leaned wearily and put the recorder back on.

"Who induced you to lie about what you saw that Sunday morning, Arlie?"

"Deputy Hazzard."

"What inducement did he offer you?"

"Not to get busted for possession, and some other things he said he could bust us for."

"Possession? Do you mean narcotics, girl?"

"That's your word. That's the fuzz word. But all we had was acid and grass. Booze is a lot worse for you."

"Arlie, are you and your husband addicts?"

"What does that mean? We're affiliates with the group up in Jax. And we get up there now and then. We take trips sometimes here, but it's a group thing. You couldn't comprehend, Sheriff. We all have our own thing. We don't bug the straights, and why shouldn't they leave us alone?"

"How did Deputy Hazzard learn you'd been a witness?"

"Like an accident. Last Thursday night out at the Banyan Cottages there was a complaint from somebody, and I guess it would be on your records here someplace. I didn't even know Hazzard's name. But he was the one who came there. Five of the kids had come down from Jax, three of them gals, in an old camper truck in the afternoon, from the Blossom Group in Jacksonville, and they had some new short acid from the Coast that never gives you a down trip and blows your mind for an hour only. We had almost two lids of Acapulco Gold, and we just started a lot of turn-ons there in the cottage, relating to each other, that's all. At night, sometime, I don't know what time, maybe the music got too loud. An Indian record. East Indian, and the player repeats and repeats. Maybe it was the strobes. We've got one and they brought two, and each one had a different recycle time, so there was a kind of pattern changing all the time. I guess you have to know the way it was when Hazzard came busting in. We had the mattresses and the blankets on the floor, and one of the gals was a cute little teeny-bopper and I'd painted her all over eyes."

"Ice?" said the sheriff.

"Eyes," she said impatiently. "Like eyeballs and eyelashes. All colors. And one boy and girl were wearing just little bells and rattles. You do whatever. Who are you hurting? It was blossom-time. A love-in, sort of, and our own business. Just with the strobe lights and the samisen music and he came breaking in because maybe we didn't hear him. Him and his gun and his black leather evil thing for hitting and hurting. You can't turn off a high like in a second. So he found the lights and ordered things in a big voice and nobody did what he said or cared. So he starts yelling and chunking people. The teeny-bopper wanted to tune him in and turn him on I guess and she started throwing flowers at him and he chunked her too. Of the seven of us he chunked the four that were turned on to the biggest high, chunked them cold, and he chunked the record player, busted it all to hell and got the other three of us finally sitting in a row on the cold bare bed springs holding onto the backs of our necks. Not scared or angry or anything. Just sorry there's no way of ever getting through to that kind of a straight. All he thinks of is busting people and busting things. And he chunked all the three strobes and broke them up. They're expensive and hard to find ones that don't overheat and burn out when you keep them cycling a long time. In my high I understood all about him. He was breaking things and hitting heads because he hated himself, and I had seen him mushing Mr. Bannon with that heavy motor, and I knew that was why he hated himself. He collected up all the grass and the three little vials of powdered acid, and he picked up all the color polaroids laying around that a boy had taken earlier to take back to Jax to the group on account of the girl painted all over eyes was a big turn-on for him."

"Lord Jesus God Almighty," said the sheriff in a hushed voice.

"He was going to radio for help and take everybody in and bust them, and I just felt sorry for him being so empty of love and so I said to him that he hated himself for what he did to Mr. Bannon. He looked at me and he picked up a blanket and wrapped it around me and took me out in the night. He shoved me up against his car and I told him the whole thing, just the way I saw it. I told him he could trade in his hate for love, and we could show him the way. I could feel myself beginning to come off the high, because I began to think about it being a lot of bad trouble, and it was a poor time to get busted because of orders Roger and I had to fill. He kept wanting to know who I'd told about it, and while I was coming off the trip I got smart enough to say maybe I had and maybe I hadn't. So he said he was going to keep the evidence and think about what he was going to do, and we should cool it and he would come talk to me the next day.

"So in the morning the kids headed on away in the camper truck and the first thing I did was tell Roger the whole thing. That was Friday, and Hazzard came out in the afternoon and sent Roger out of the place and talked to me. He said he'd put the evidence away in a safe place, and in the pictures he had proof on both Roger and me on the teeny-bopper on corrupting a minor, and lewd and lascivious conduct. Then he questioned me over and over on what I saw that Sunday. Then he brought up if I knew a friend of Bannon's named McGee. I told him about just that one day, and he made me remember every little part of it. So he walked back and forth and then he told me I was going to come in and make a statement and what I was going to say. I asked him why I should do anything he said, because if he left us alone, I wouldn't say anything about him. He said if I didn't do it, he would bust us both good, and he had enough proof and enough charges to get us both five to ten anyway. And I said if he tried to bust us that way, when he took us in, I'd tell what I saw him do. And he said then it would be pretty clear to everybody that I was making it up just to try to get him in trouble for doing his job and nobody would believe it because nobody ever believes an acid head about anything, and those pictures would make a hog sick. He said if I did my part, then after McGee was convicted, he'd give back everything he took. Then he gave me a chance to talk it over alone with Roger and for a while we thought maybe we ought to just take off and go merge into a colony someplace, but we went that road for a while and we relate better like plastics."

"What? What?" asked the sheriff.

"Take the group thing now and then, and have a square thing we do for bread. We take off and we lose the trade we've built up that comes to maybe a hundred and fifty a week on average, and then maybe that Hazzard could get us brought back anyhow." She combed the fingers of both hands back through the dark blonde stiffness of her long hair, shook it back and said, "So we decided okay, only what we didn't know is how I could get busted a lot bigger for the statement than for what he's got on us, and I didn't know McGee would be in the clear, because he said maybe McGee might not even get to answer any questions at all. So where are we?"

"Where are you?" the sheriff asked. "Honest to God, I don't even know *what* you are, girl."

I looked at my watch. It was just eleven o'clock. The sheriff told Arlie he'd like to hold her and her husband in protective custody on a voluntary basis, and she agreed. I knew that part of the case against Freddy Hazzard would be Press LaFrance's testimony about whatever conversation he'd had with his nephew, triggered by my comment to LaFrance about the possible reason why Tush had been killed. But had I reminded Burgoon of that point, he was going to mess up my timing, which was already two hours off. So I wondered out loud if Tush could have come in by bus early Sunday morning and if Hazzard, cruising around, had picked him up near the bus station and driven him out there.

Arlie had been taken off to the female detention tank. Tom, the chief deputy, said that if anybody could place Hazzard and Bannon together in town at dawn on Sunday, it would lock it up tighter.

"Tighter than the way he run?" Burgoon asked. "He was a *good* boy. He worked harder than any two others I got. Just a little bit too handy with that mail-order pacifier sometimes. But you take a county where you got some hard cases back in the piney woods, a little head-knocking keeps things leveled off. He lived clean and straight. It must have shook that boy when he checked out that complaint, walking in on that. Like looking into a bucket of mealy grubs. What's going wrong with folks lately, McGee?"

I had neared the ultimate promotion, to Mr. McGee.

"It's a mass movement against head-knocking, Sheriff."

"What kind of a joke is that?"

"All kinds of head-knocking. Commercial, artistic and religious. They're trying to say people should love people. It's never been a very popular product. Get too persistent, and they nail you up on the timbers on a hill."

He stared at me with indignation. "Are *you* one of *them?*"

"I recognize the problem. That's all. But the hippies solve it by stopping the world and getting off. No solution, Sheriff. I don't seek solutions. That takes group effort. And every group effort in the world requiring more than two people is a foul-up, inevitably. So I just stand back of the foul line and when something happens that doesn't get called by the referees, I sometimes get into the game for a couple of minutes."

"Around here today," he said sadly, "it's beginning to seem to me like in my sleep last night I must have forgot half the English language."

"Can I go take care of my business matter?"

He looked at Tom, got some signal in reply, and said, "Stay in the area, Mr. McGee."

Thirteen

I saw Preston LaFrance sitting at his desk inside his little real estate office in a converted store on Central Street. He had his head in his hands, and he was alone.

When he heard the door open, he looked up with the beginnings of the affable show-you-a-fine-parcel smile, and it froze there partially developed. He jumped and boggled and said, "McGee! You . . . you're alone? But I saw you with . . . you were . . . "

"Sorry I couldn't keep the coffee date, Press. I had to go answer some fool questions the sheriff wanted to ask me."

"Bunny . . . let you go?"

"What's the matter with you? Are you disappointed?"

"No! Hell, no! Sit down! Sit down, Trav! Cigar? Take that chair. It's more comfortable."

I sat down. "Did you have the same weird idea Burgoon had? Did you think I killed Bannon?"

"But Freddy said an eyewitness had turned up, and they were going to grab you down there in Lauderdale and he was going to go down and bring you back."

"It would have been an exciting trip."

"What happened? What about the eyewitness?"

"Burgoon satisfied himself that she was lying and I wasn't."

"Freddy said everything fitted together."

"It did."

"What? What do you mean?"

"It worried you a little, Press, when I told you that maybe somebody was trying to give you and Monk Hazzard a lot of cooperation in rousting Bannon out of his property, and maybe they busted him up too much. And you said that there wasn't anybody involved who'd do a thing like that, but you hesitated a little. So you were thinking of Nephew Freddy, the head-knocker. So you came back and laid some very indirect questions on him and he convinced you he was absolutely innocent, and then you told him who had been feeding you such crazy ideas. So, lo and behold, the eyewitness was brought in and she changed her story and the sheriff let me go."

"I guess then we can . . . talk business?"

"Sure, Press. That's what I'm here for. By the way, the eyewitness identified Freddy as the killer. He heard about it by accident and took off. They're running a manhunt right now. So it was a pretty good guess."

"I got the money together, but first I have to . . . What did you say? Freddy? Come *on!*"

"He ran, Press. He took off. Check it out. Call Burgoon."

He reached for the phone, hesitated, then picked it up and ran a thumbnail down the typed list of numbers under the desk-top glass. He dialed and asked for Burgoon. "Okay, then give me Tom Windhorn. Thanks. . . . Tom? This is Press. Say, Tom, is Freddy in some kind of a . . . Huh? No kidding! But look, it couldn't really be that he would . . . Oh. . . . I see. . . . Yeh. . . . Boy, some mess. Anybody get hold of Monk yet? . . . Oh, that's right I forgot. . . . No, Tom, I don't even know what route they were taking. Monk said he was going to take his time and see the sights. Sis will be out of her mind. Tom, is everybody absolutely *positive* he . . . All right. Sure. I'll be over later." He hung up and shook his head in bewildered fashion. "I just can't believe it. He's a nice clean-cut boy."

"I'm afraid you've got too much on your mind. This is no time to talk business. We've got another deal we can work out. So let's forget the whole thing. Okay?"

"But I . . . but I need——"

"Just hang onto your fifty acres and use the forty thousand to pick up that Carbee land. The way the area is going to go, you ought to make a nice profit in a couple of years. Just sit tight."

His smile was slightly ghastly in its attempt to be reassuring. "Listen, Trav. Believe me, I can keep my mind on your proposition. I mean this is a terrible tragedy in the family and all, but it isn't going to do anybody any good for me to lose out on something."

"Maybe you won't like it anyway," I said. "Give me a piece of paper and a pencil. I'll show you how it works."

I wrote down a little tabulation on the sheet:

Carbee	200	acres	@	$2000 =	$400,000
LaFrance	50	acres	@	2000 =	100,000
McGee	10	acres	@	2000 =	20,000

Total purchase price	520,000

Cost to LaFrance:

McGee 10 acres	$ 90,000	
Carbee 200 acres	40,000	
	$130,000	130,000

Total available for split		$390,000
To LaFrance	$265,000	135,000
McGee (+ 40,000 from LaFrance)		95,000
X		60,000
		390,000

"Who is this X? What does your ninety-five thousand come out of? I don't understand this."

"Mr. X is the man we're going to meet at the hotel for lunch. The point is, I don't trust him completely. But he has the authority to buy—from one single owner—those two hundred and sixty acres at two thousand an acre. And because he's going to the top limit authorized, he wants a cash kickback, under the table. The trouble is, he wants it now. And I don't think we ought to turn it over until we get the full amount on the land. If something went wrong, we couldn't prove a thing. Right?"

"Yes, but——"

"Listen, can you get my forty thousand in cash instead of by certified check?"

"I . . . I guess so. Sure. But—"

"Then, maybe there's a way we can work it so we won't end up with the dirty end of the stick, Press."

"But what's this ninety-five thousand for you?"

"For putting this thing together. You are going to sell me a twenty-five percent share of that option for five thousand."

"The *hell* I am! I can sell that Carbee land for——"

"Forget it. Forget Calitron. You'll see why when you see the correspondence X has. If X can't deal with us, he'll deal with Gary Santo and we'll be out in the cold.

160

Why are you crying anyway, LaFrance? You get all your bait back, all hundred and thirty grand, plus a hundred and thirty-five on top. That's fifteen thousand over a quarter of a million."

We had lunch with Meyer at the hotel. He was superb. He told us where he was staying. I went to the bank with LaFrance and got the papers on our land sale signed and notarized, and he got the forty thousand cash. I drove him to the motel where Meyer was waiting, and before we went in, I unlocked the trunk compartment and dug out the little package of currency I had taped to a far dark corner. It was my total war fund, and it made me feel uneasy carrying it around. Meyer showed us the rest of the correspondence and the overlays. He took them out of the bulky dispatch case. He was properly arrogant, properly shifty. LaFrance bought the con. I could read it on his face and in the sweatiness of his hands, leaving damp prints on the papers.

"So, if we can settle the last little detail, gentlemen?"

"Doctor Meyer," I said, "We get . . . I mean Mr. LaFrance gets the point five two million check or definite confirmation from topside that it has gone through, then you get the money we agreed on."

He stared at me with a heavy, convincing contempt.

"And sue you if I don't get it, Mr. McGee? Where? In Small Claims Court? You see the correspondence. You see the authorizations. It will go through. Believe me."

"And at the last minute they change their minds. What have we got to make you give it back, Doctor?"

"There will be nothing in writing. You understand that. You have my word."

"But you won't take ours, Doctor?"

"So forget it, gentlemen. Impasse. I'll resume the negotiations for the other tract."

"There's one possible solution, Doctor, that might satisfy both sides. It would be safe for both of us."

"Which is?"

I took out the two packets of money and dropped them on the coffee table. "Seventy-five thousand dollars, Doctor Meyer."

"So?"

"Let's seal it in an envelope and we can put it in the

161

hands of a local attorney, and give him instructions about it."

"To do what?"

"I'll tear a dollar bill into three pieces. We each keep a third. The attorney is authorized to surrender the envelope to whoever shows up with the three pieces, or to any two who, between them, have all three pieces."

"Kid games!" said Meyer. "Nonsense games!"

"The extra fifteen, Doctor, is a bonus for doing it this way. Does the game sound better?"

He nodded. "A little. But you can save fifteen by giving me the sixty now."

"We'll pay the extra fifteen for insurance, Doctor."

"Sometimes being too careful is stupid," he said. "I'll play your game."

The good doctor had a fresh Manila envelope in his dispatch case. He handed it to me. I put the money in it and sealed it and handed it to LaFrance, saying, "Which lawyer do . . . "

"I think," said Meyer, "as long as we are not trusting one another, I will choose not to trust any lawyer of your selection, gentlemen. The old hotel where we lunched has a safe, no doubt. And some sort of claim check arrangement. The claim check could be torn into three portions, and the manager instructed not to surrender the envelope except for an entire claim check taped back together. Satisfactory?"

"Suits me." I said. "Press?"

"Sure." So we went back downtown in my car, Press beside me, Meyer in the rear. I parked and we went in. Meyer hung back while Press and I went to the desk. The girl greeted him by name and Press asked for the manager by name. He came out of his office.

"Can I help you, Mr. LaFrance?"

"Harry, this is sort of a wager. Can you put this in the safe for me and give us a claim check. We're going to tear it into three hunks, and don't surrender it unless you get the whole claim check."

Harry was affable about the whole thing. He took the envelope into his office and came back with the other half of the perforated tag he had affixed to the envelope. I had a five-dollar bill ready and reached and laid it on the counter and said, "For your trouble," and he gave me the tag, telling me it wasn't necessary to . . . uh . . .

"Go ahead, Harry," I told him. I turned away, and walked over to Meyer, with LaFrance hurrying to keep up with me. I tore the tag into three parts, making them irregular, and ceremoniously put a third on each of their outstretched palms.

Meyer sighed. "Games for children. An expensive game for you, my friends." We walked out and stood by my car. I offered the doctor a ride back to his motel. He got into the front seat. I closed the door and turned and held my hand out to Preston LaFrance.

"Press, I think we're really in business. I'll be seeing you in a few days. You draw up the agreement on the Carbee option."

"Sure, Trav. I'll sure do that." His expression was doleful and earnest and anxious, like a dog hoping to be let in out of the rain.

"I hope you get your trouble worked out all right."

"What? Oh, that terrible business about my nephew."

"The boy just got too eager, I guess. He knew you and his father were using every legal means to run Bannon out of business. He probably tried a different way of discouraging him."

"That's probably it. And he tried to cover up. It was sort of an accident, I'd say. Freddy wouldn't want to kill anybody. When they find him, I think if he tells exactly what happened, they might agree on letting him plead guilty of manslaughter. Monk has got a lot of leverage in this part of the state. Trav, how . . . how soon do you think our deal will go through?"

"A matter of days. Don't worry about it."

"I think I'll go over to the sheriff's office and see what's happening."

He walked away. I walked around the car and got in and drove away. "Pigeon drop, smigeon drop," said Meyer. "How was I?"

"Like a pro. Great natural talent, Doctor."

I reached into my breast pocket and took out the intact green claim check and handed it to him. He took the little tin tape dispenser out of his pocket and tore the check in thirds and stuck it back together with the tape.

I made two right turns and parked on the side street

behind the hotel. He gave me the claim check and said, "So soon?"

"Why not? While we know Harry is still in the office and we know where ol' Press is. Wait right here. Don't go away, pro."

I walked around the corner and went in the side door of the hotel and across the old-fashioned lobby to the desk. Harry was alone, sticking mail into the room boxes.

I handed him the check and said, "The winnah!"

"That was a quick one, sir."

"Wasn't it, though!"

He brought me the envelope and I said, "Harry, if you want to keep on being friends with Mr. LaFrance, you'd better not mention this little fiasco to him. He was so sure he was right he's going to be *very* grumpy about the whole thing."

"I know what you mean, sir."

I walked back to the car and drove Meyer to the motel. I gave him the forty thousand, and taped my emergency fund back into its inconspicuous place in the car trunk.

It was just three thirty. When I walked back into the motel unit, Meyer was on the phone talking with his Lauderdale broker. He hung up and looked at the figures he had scribbled down.

"I think the answer is right here, Travis. I don't think it has to come from Mary Smith. Fletcher Industries moved up one and an eighth today, to sixteen and three eighths on a volume of ninety-four hundred shares. So Janine Bannon has made eleven hundred and twenty-five bucks today."

"Today?"

"Well, so far. I mean the final returns for the day aren't in, but it will be pretty close to that. The Dow is off a little over five points. You look astonished. Oh, I see why. This morning before I left I opened her margin account with cash money, pending the power of attorney that you forgot to give me. I put in enough to buy her a thousand shares, and I got them at fifteen and a quarter."

I gave him the power of attorney. He put it in his dispatch case, and took out all the fake correspondence to My dear Ludweg and the fake reports on plant location data.

"So," he said, "it was worth the chance and now I reimburse myself out of this money and put the rest into her account to cover the order I placed for the opening tomorrow. Another twenty-five hundred shares. That will commit her account up to maximum. Then I have to go sit and stare at the tape, day after day, ten in the morning to three thirty in the afternoon. Bring me sandwiches." He waved the sheaf of counterfeit letters and documents. "When these are confetti and flushed away, my heart might slow down some you think?"

He went into the bathroom with them and I placed a credit card call, station to station to the Santo offices, and after a short wait I got Mary Smith.

The approach, to be convincing, had to be that of the male who'd been brushed off.

"McGee here," I said. "What was Santo's decision?"

"Oh. Trav. I've been *so* impatient for you to call, darling."

"I bet. What did he decide."

"I want to tell you something else first, because I have the hunch that if I tell you first, you'll hang up."

"Can you think of any good reason why I shouldn't?"

"Darling, I can think of a *very* good reason. My darned telephone was acting up. I *knew* it was you, but it just kept making a horrid ringing sound in my ear when I picked it up." Her voice was intimate, cheery, persuasive.

"Nice try, kid."

"But I'm telling the *truth! Really* I am. What could make you possibly think I wouldn't *be* there? If you want to be such a grouchy old bear, you can call the phone company and ask them if a certain Mary Smith raised absolute *hell* with them Saturday afternoon. I got the message you left at the office, and I left one for you, hoping you'd call back."

"At least you make it sound good, Miss Smith."

"Travis, I *know* how disappointed and angry you must have been."

"How come the phone company couldn't fix the phone?"

"Actually they swore there was nothing wrong with it. They tested and tested, and when I made them come back the second time, they took out the instrument and put in a new one."

"Which didn't work either. Which didn't work on Saturday night."

"I . . . wasn't there."

"You said you had the weekend open. So why didn't you hang around? How about four o'clock Sunday morning, kid?"

"I . . . I was told you'd made other plans, dear."

"By who?"

"To tell you the truth, I drove up to Lauderdale just to find you. I saw that fantastic boat of yours, dear. It must be a marvelous way of life. A man told me you might be at a party on another boat and I went there, but a very odd-looking girl told me I'd missed you and you might come back. So I waited there. You can ask those people. A lot of them are your friends, I guess. It is quite a . . . lively group. Then that strange girl came and told me that she found out you had left with another girl, so you probably wouldn't be back. So . . . you see, I really tried."

The persuasive lilt of her tone was dying away, fading back into the monotone of a deadly exhaustion.

"So even at four in the morning, you weren't home yet? I guess you had a good time."

"Not terribly. But it was pleasant. I . . . called up an old friend and she invited me over, and it got to be too late to drive back, so they put me up for the night, dear."

"So when did you get home?"

"I think it was about . . . ten o'clock last night. I spent the day with them. Why, dear? You had a date, didn't you? There was hardly any point in roaring home and sitting panting by the phone, was there? Listen, dear, I don't *blame* you for having a date. After all, it was perfectly reasonable for you to assume I stood you up, and so you said the hell with Mary Smith and her lousy steak. Don't I get any points for driving all the way up there to find you?"

I said in a marveling tone, "And all it was was a phone out of order. You know, there must be a hex on us."

"I guess there must be," she said. She sighed audibly and heavily.

"So expect a man at about nine tonight, honey. Okay?"

"Oh no, darling! I'm sorry."

"What now?"

"Well . . . I guess the hex is still working. I . . . uh . . . my friends have this little boat at their dock. They live on a canal. And they were going to take me out in the boat, and like a clumsy idiot I tripped somehow and fell headlong, right off the dock into the boat. Honestly, I'm an absolute ruin. I was waiting for you to call so that I could get out of here and go home and take a hot bath and go to bed. I've been tottering around here today like a little old lady."

"Gee, honey, that must have been a nasty fall. Where did you hurt yourself?"

She gave a tired laugh. "Where didn't I? There were a lot of . . . you know . . . fishing tackle things in the boat. I must have hit my mouth somehow because it's all puffed out, and when I looked at myself head to toe in my mirror this morning, I swear I didn't know whether to laugh or cry. I'm battered and bruised from head to toe. I *couldn't* let you see me like this. I'm a fright."

"That could be dangerous, Mary, a fall like that."

"I know. I strained my back somehow, I think. It's such a shock I guess it takes a lot out of you. My bones ache even." She sighed again. "Darling, give me time to get all well again, just for you. Please?"

"Sure. Take care of yourself, kid. Sorry our luck was running bad."

"Friend McGee, you are not one tenth as sorry as I am," and there was total conviction gleaming through the drag of her words. "The decision was yes, by the way."

"Good. How much."

"He said it depends on how it goes. At least one and a half. Maybe up to three, or anywhere in between. He said to tell you he'll be doing it through different accounts, scattered across the country. He wondered if you mind the amount being a little vague."

"I expected that. If it gets too much play from the traders, he won't be able to slow it down enough."

"Dear, may I wish us better luck next time?"

"You may indeed. Hurry home to bed, honey."

I hung up and looked into the bathroom in time to see Meyer sprinkle the last of his confetti and flush the toilet.

"The evidence is destroyed," said Meyer, with big smile and big sigh.

"And Santo has climbed on."

"May he enjoy the trip in good health. May he have asked a few friends to join him even."

I gave him my third of the other claim check and he put it carefully into a pocket of his wallet. "So tomorrow," he said, "I drive up to Broward Beach and go out A-One-A and find a place called the Annex, and at seven I am sitting at the bar, waiting for the pigeon. Correct?"

"Looking important and shifty. Correct."

"Shouldn't you ask me what it is I checked when I arrived for lunch? Don't you care?"

"I do now. Now that I know it must be interesting."

"Here is the scene. Mr LaFrance rushes to the desk at the hotel. He has the three parts of the claim check taped together. He is panting, right?"

"His hands are trembling. He can't wait for Harry to give him the money," I said.

"So Harry takes the check and he doesn't come back with a big brown envelope. He comes back with a small white envelope. Number ten. Greeting card size. The envelope I checked when I arrived for lunch, so I could get a claim check, so you could make the substitution and tear it up into three pieces and give him one."

"Meyer, remember me? I *know* all this."

"Shut up. Let me enjoy. So he asks Harry, where is the brown envelope? Where is the money? So Harry says the other fellow claimed it ten minutes after it was checked. Yes, Mr. LaFrance, he had the right three pieces stuck together. He said I shouldn't mention to you that you lost the bet. I *know*, Mr. LaFrance, this check is torn in three pieces too, but it isn't the check for the money. It's the check for this card."

"And so," I said, "stunned, bewildered, shocked, our Mr. LaFrance wobbles over to a lobby chair, falls into it and thumbs the white envelope open. Come *on,* Meyer! What does the card say?"

"Don't rush. It says on the front: 'Congratulations from the Gang at the Office.' You open it. Inside it says: 'It couldn't have happened to a nicer guy.' "

"That is very wicked, Meyer."

"But the signature. That's the good part."

"What did you do? Forge my name?"

"Not exactly. He saw your houseboat. He saw the name. Inside the greeting card he finds five playing cards

168

I took out of a deck. I threw the rest of the deck away. The five, six, seven and eight of hearts. And the king of clubs. Right? A busted flush?"

I looked at him admiringly. "Meyer, you have great class. You have an instinct for this kind of work."

"It was nothing, really. Just innate good taste, a creative mind, and high intelligence. It will make a nice signature anytime you want somebody to know who gave it to them good."

Fourteen

AT NINE that evening Sheriff Bunny Burgoon sent word out from his office that he could see me.

His chief deputy, Tom Windhorn, was planted in the same chair against the wall as before. They both looked as if they'd had a very hard day.

"From the talk out front I know you haven't gotten him yet. But have you gotten any kind of line on him, Sheriff?"

"What I got doesn't exactly boost up my spirits, mister. And it's no joy having every newspaper and TV and radio station yappin' on and on about Shawana County having a deputy that turned bad. And it didn't help any to have Monk Hazzard chewing me up long distance and telling me I was crazy as hell. But when I told him about car number three, it slowed him some."

"Where was it? I heard you found it."

"Just before sunset. The Highway Patrol chopper spotted it way over in the southwest corner of the county, run off into a marsh and bogged up to the top of the fenders. I got a call from the boys that went to check it out. There's little places along the lake shore there, spread out. They were checking all the driveways and heard somebody yelling in one of the places. Retired couple, trussed up, scared, and mad as puckered owls. Seems that Freddy drove in, knocked, real polite, a little after two in the afternoon. Asked to come in. Said it was on a complaint on the fish and game laws. Head-knocked them both, tied them up, stuck dishtowels in their mouths. The boys say it's a big tall old man, so his clothes fit Freddy

169

good enough. Left the uniform. Put on the old man's best suit, packed a bag with other clothes and toilet articles. Picked up what money they had around. Thirty or forty dollars. Drove off in the county car. Came back on foot and drove off in their two-year-old Plymouth station wagon. Said he seemed nervous. Told them he was sorry he had to do them that way. Seemed right sorry about it. The old man tongued the towel out of his mouth after a while. When he heard the boys drive down his drive, he started bellering. So we put the car and the clothes on the wire. From there he's twenty miles from the Interstate. If he pushed it hard enough, he could have crossed into Georgia before we got the word out."

"Once they calm down," Tom said, "if we get all their stuff back to them and fix up anything busted or lost, and talk nice, they might not press charges."

"We sort of reconstructed the thing with Bannon," the sheriff said. "I say he must have come across Bannon on the road, hiking out to his place and told him he'd been foreclosed and his wife had took off on him, and he must have wanted to drive Bannon back here, but Bannon just wouldn't believe him and wanted a look, so when he insisted, Freddy drove him the rest of the way out. That would account for the fat girl thinking they were talking ugly to each other. Now I'd say Bannon lost his head and tried to bust into the place that used to be his. Now that's against the law and Freddy tried to gentle him some, but that was a lot of man and if he didn't drop with the first knock, and if he rushed Freddy, that boy in his excitement just swang too hard is all. Caved his head bone in, maybe. And he knew Tom and me had chewed him for being too goddang quick with that mail-order pacifier, and I guess Freddy just lost his head is all. Having that girl see how he covered it up was just plain bad luck."

"And was he in line to be the one to come to Lauderdale and bring me back if I was picked up there?"

The sheriff looked uneasy. "That was what was planned, mister."

"I guess I would have tried to open the car door and jump out when we were going seventy-five or eighty. After I got through bounding along the pavement, nobody'd find a little extra lump on my skull."

"Now you can't be sure that would have happened that way."

"I wonder why he told anybody about hearing from his Uncle Press that I was going to be here this morning?"

"Because," said Tom Windhorn, "he knows I play golf Sunday mornings in a foursome with Press LaFrance every week of my life, and Press knew we were hunting you, and Freddy knew there was no way in the world of stopping Press from telling me. So he brought it in first. And the fool thing about it is that Press never did play yesterday. He phoned in he was feeling poorly, too late for us to get somebody to fill out, and so they stuck some old coot in with us that couldn't hit the ground with his hat."

"That poor boy just had plain bad luck all the way around," I said. "He never did get a chance to kill me."

"He's no killer," the sheriff said. "He just lost his head some."

"Nice I get to keep mine. Find the stuff he picked up out at the cottages?"

The sheriff nodded. "It was at his place, under his clean shirts. The narcotics we got packed up to mail in for analysis. No case on that because without Freddy we can't prove the chain of possession." He opened the shallow middle drawer of his desk and then held an envelope toward me. I reached and took it.

The color prints were sharp and clear. I leafed through them. They did not leave the feral and cynical impression that the posed product of the hard-core studios induce. This was a tumble of aging children, most of them rather badly nourished. In spite of their placid, dazed, beatific smiles and grimaces, they were a kind of curious sadness, in their weird, bright patterns of love-paint on the scrawn of flesh, in their protest bangles and their disaffiliated bells, crushing the flower blossoms in a dreamy imitation of adult acts that for them had all been bleached of any significance or purpose. The rites of the strobe, frozen in such a sharpness it caught forever a wistful dirtiness of knuckles, the calico of bad bleach jobs, the moles and the blemishes and the sharp, helpless angle of shoulder blade. This was not a rebellion against mechanization, or emotional fraud. This was denying life itself in all eras and all cultures, and instead of being evil or outrageous

171

was merely empty, bland and slightly saurian somehow, as though in a vain attempt to warm the blood that had begun to turn cooler in some gigantic and total regression that would take us all back through geological time, back into the sea where life began.

Said Tom, "Ain't that Arlie the damnedest sight a man would ever want to behold?"

"Unforgettable," I said, and put the envelope on the edge of the desk. "I've been waiting around to ask permission to leave your area, Sheriff. Here's the address where you can get me. I'll come back if you need me. But now I'd like to drive up to Frostproof and see Jan Bannon."

"Get your business done with Press?"

"Yes, thanks."

"Well . . . I guess there's no call to keep you waiting around. Thank you for your cooperation, Mr. McGee."

"Thank you for your courtesy and consideration, Sheriff."

When I phoned ahead, Connie said that Janine had heard the news and that she was very upset and puzzled. I said it would be well after midnight before I could make it, and she said that it had been too much of a long, hard day to wait up. I told her my day had been on the same order, and told her that everything had gone very smoothly so far.

It was ten after one when I got there and turned under the arch and through the glare of the gate light and drove to the big house. The night was cool and the stars looked high and small and indifferent.

Jan stood in the open doorway waiting for me. And she leaned up to rest her cheek for a moment against mine, with a quick, soft touch of her lips. "You must be exhausted, Trav."

"And you shouldn't have waited up."

"I couldn't have slept."

I went in and sat down into the depth and softness of a big leather couch. There were two red embers among the silvery ashes of the hearth. She wore a floor-length navy robe with a white collar. She said, "Connie left orders to give you a great wallop of bourbon to unwind on." I said it sounded great. She drifted out of sight and

172

I heard the clink of cubes and the guggle of a generous dose.

"Water?"

"Just the ice, thanks."

She brought it over and fixed the cushions at the end of the couch and told me to lie back and put my feet up. She moved a footstool close. The light behind her from the corner lamp, the only one on in the room, shone through the fine ends of her cropped black hair. Her face was in shadow.

I sipped the strong drink and told her about Deputy Hazzard. "That's what I couldn't believe," she said. "He and the older one, with the funny name. Not the Sheriff."

"Windhorn?"

"Yes. They were the ones who . . . came out with the padlocks and the notices. And he, the young one, seemed so very shy and nice and troubled about everything. There was no point in taking it out on them. They had their orders."

"Had he been out there before?"

"Several times, yes. To serve papers, and the time they checked to see about the licenses we have to have for the houseboats. A lanky boy with a long face, kind of a red, lumpy face, but sweet. But very official about what he had to do. All leather and jingling and creaking."

"That reconstruction of it doesn't fit," I said. "It doesn't fit Tush."

"I know. He never got mad that way. Not like me. I fly off the handle and want to hit everything I can reach. He'd just get very very quiet and sad-looking, and he'd walk slowly away. It's better for me to . . . to be absolutely postive once and for all that he didn't kill himself, Trav. But it just seems to be such . . . a stinking trivial way to die, to be killed by that harmless-looking young man."

"Most of the ways people die are kind of dingy and trivial, Jan."

"It just shouldn't have been that way for Tush. But how in the world did that Freddy person get Arlie Denn to tell such an ugly lie about you? She always seemed to me to be sort of dull and placid. She never seemed mean or vicious or anything. It must have been horrible for

173

her—watching like that. I would think she would just . . . have never told anybody at all, ever."

And that took some explaining and finally I managed to make her comprehend it, up to a point. But comprehension was comingled with revulsion. "But we let that wretched girl sit with our boys a lot of times! She could have taken something . . . and hurt them."

"I doubt it."

"What kind of people were those others? How old were they?"

"I'd say Roger and Arlie were the oldest. The others looked nineteen and twenty. And the one girl about fifteen or sixteen."

"What are they trying to do to themselves?"

"Drop out of the world. Hallucinate. Turn on. Dig the sounds and colors and feels. Be at one with the infinite something or other. I can't lay too big a knock on them, you know. In another sense I'm a dropout. I don't pay for my tickets. I jump over the turnstile."

"I think I've *been* dropped out somehow. For good."

"Now I am supposed to tell you about how you're a young woman still in your twenties with most of your life still ahead of you."

"Please don't."

"A guy will need you in the right way sometime."

"Tell him not to *really* need me. That's when I run like a rabbit." She took my empty glass and said, "another?"

"No. That one is going to do it."

"I made you talk too long. There's more I want to ask. But I'll wait until tomorrow."

She got up and took the glass away. I decided I'd better get up and head for bed while I could. I closed my eyes for a moment and opened them again and a high sun was shining and her middle boy was standing holding a saucer with both hands, and he had his tongue sticking out of the corner of his mouth to help with the chore of keeping the coffee from spilling out of the cup.

"Everybody's been up a *long* time," he said disdainfully. "Mom said bring you this and if I stood here, the smell would wake you up. I think it's a lousy crummy old smell and I'm never going to drink that stuff. Oh. Good morning."

My shoes had been removed, belt loosened, necktie removed, collar unbuttoned. There was a blanket over me. The lady had given me bourbon and loving care. I hoped that it would be at least another full year before I had to put a necktie back on.

I sat up and took the coffee.

"You spilled a little bit," he said. *"I* didn't."

"Like it here?"

"It's neat. Today there's a teacher's meeting, so we don't have to go on the bus. Charlie's going to let me ride on the tractor again with him. It's real neat. I gotta go." And he went—at a full run.

I dialed Press LaFrance direct at twenty after ten. I wanted him to have a lot of time to make some collections. Just as I was ready to hang up, he answered, out of breath.

"Who? Trav? Where are you? What's up?"

"Miami, boy. And I'm getting a little sweaty. Maybe we're in trouble."

"How? My God, Trav, I thought everything was——"

"I've been making some long distance calls, Press. And it looks as if everything might go through okay. I was with Doctor Meyer a few minutes ago and he as much as admitted that he might wait until Roger Santo gets back from abroad and see if he wants to make a better deal on the side, a fatter deal for Meyer. I told you he's slippery."

"But what are we going to do?"

"If we play it his way, the way he suggested in the beginning, he'll move right ahead with it. But it has to be today. He's on his way up to Broward Beach. Do you know a place called The Annex?"

"Yes, but——"

"I had to take the chance, Press. I had to move fast. I gave him my third of the claim check. Now he's going to be at the bar at The Annex at seven o'clock tonight. I told him that you would meet him there and give him his damned sixty thousand in cash for the two thirds he's holding."

"Where am I going to get that kind of money before seven?"

"The minute after you get back to Sunnydale and walk into the hotel, you'll have it back, won't you?"

175

"Yes, but——"

"Scrounge it somehow. You could pay somebody a very fat amount of one-day interest out of that fifteen extra, couldn't you?"

"But, Trav, suppose he takes the sixty and then screws us and makes his deal with Santo? What can we do?"

"Absolutely nothing. But stop running around in crazy circles, man, and *listen* to me. I'm assuming the risk. Got that? It's my money sitting up there. Give me a week and I could scrape up three or four times sixty in cash, but I damned well can't do it today. If it falls through, what are you out?"

"There's . . . maybe one possibility."

"Now you're beginning to think. I'll phone you back. How long will it take you to find out?"

"I . . . I should know by . . . you phone me back right here at two o'clock?"

The shape of larceny is, in time, written clearly enough on a man's face so that it can be read. Constant greed and sharp little deals and steals had left the sign on Preston LaFrance. There is the old saying that God and your folks give you the face you're born with, but you earn the one you die with.

I went back into the house at two o'clock and phoned him. I knew just how he had probably worked it out in his mind. Get hold of sixty thousand cash to buy the claim check to seventy-five thousand in cash. Nobody ever gets hurt taking a profit. The small towns of Florida are peppered with old boys who don't like to have too much information on record about the deals they make. And they like to keep a little leverage around in the form of cash money. LaFrance would know a couple of those shrewd old hawks. He'd hunt one up, probably put up his fifty acres and the Carbee option as security, if the bank wasn't holding them, and pay the old boy a thousand dollars or five hundred for the loan of sixty thousand in cash for a few hours. Then he'd hike the interest rate as high as he dared when he reported to me.

"Trav?" he said. "I've been dreading this call, cause there's something I hate to have to tell you."

"You couldn't get the money!"

"No, no. I got the money. I got it locked up right here in my office. I got it from a fellow that keeps cash

176

on hand. Trouble is, he knows I'm spread thin. Maybe I got too anxious. Anyway, he gave it to me good. The only deal I could make was to pay him the whole fifteen thousand. Honest to God, Trav, when a man gets the tights, all the money dries up on you. There just wasn't anybody else who'd give me the lend of it."

"Pretty damned steep, Press."

"Like you said, this is an emergency."

It was the perfect example of the philosophy behind all kinds of con, big and small: You can't cheat an honest man. I gave him a B in the course. B for Brass.

"When I get back," he said, "that old boy is going to be right there in the hotel lobby with his hand out, and there won't even be any point in unwrapping it, except he'll want to count it slow and careful, and then go on rattling home in his old pickup truck, smiling like a toad in the moonlight. Trav, it was the pure best I could do on short notice, and that's God's truth."

"Okay, then. Tote it over to The Annex and give it to Doctor Meyer, and don't lose it on the way. Then we'll just have to keep calm and wait for the corporation check to come through."

"How long will it take?"

"Ask the Doctor."

I hung up, knowing it was going to work. The secret of the big con is to move the victim, bit by bit, into increasingly implausible situations. At last, in the act of plucking him clean, you have him performing such a damned-fool act he will never understand how he came to do it, why he didn't see through it. He was blinded by the conviction he couldn't possibly lose a dime. And when he learned he'd been conned, he couldn't take it to the law. He'd have to tell them he had been taking a sixty-thousand-dollar bribe to a man pretending to be a field representative of a huge corporation. He would have to tell them he'd paid forty thousand dollars for a worthless equity in a defunct marina. If a story like that got out, every member of the Sunnydale business community would laugh himself sick. So he didn't have a chance. Poor LaFrance. Exactly the same situation he put Tush in. Smashed flat, plucked clean. No mercy for Tush. No mercy for LaFrance.

I walked out and found Connie by the equipment barn. We strolled over and sat on the mossy old stone bench under the huge banyan tree in the side yard.

I told her that our fish had gobbled the hunk of ripe bait, and the hook was perfectly set. A very greedy fish, that one.

Her weather-beaten face twisted in mocking amusement. "Maybe he's just greedy enough so your friend should be a little careful leaving that place, Trav."

"He's got a self-addressed envelope with him, and he walks right from The Annex through into the motel lobby and drops it in the slot. It's got more than enough stamps on it. It'll be solidly sealed with tape, and the money will have cardboard and a rubber band around it. Connie, again thanks. I'm going to head back."

"You come anytime, hear? Are you going to make our gal rich?"

"Let's say reasonably comfortable, if all goes well."

"And you'll have sixty more to fool with?"

"Meyer wouldn't like that verb."

"Ahh, McGee, all those poor bastards who'll wish that Tush Bannon never had a friend like you. Anyway, when things get just a little quieter—if they ever do—please let me know because then I think would be a good time for you to phone Jan and tell her that there are papers to be signed or something, any excuse for her to come down there. I'll talk her into it and keep the kids here, and when she gets down, you make her stay awhile. She needs a change. She needs to get away from the kids and away from here. She ought to get a lot of sun, and walk on a beach and swim and catch a fish and hear music and be near happy people. Okay?"

"Okay, Connie. Soon."

At eight thirty that evening the bing-bong announced that somebody had stepped over the gangplank chain and come aboard. I looked out and saw Meyer. I let him in.

He had a grin like a piano keyboard. He fell onto the yellow couch and said, "Build me one of those death-dealing in-and-out jobs named after somebody who's name escapes me."

"You'll get maudlin."

178

"So?"

"Any trouble at all?"

"None. You know, I have seldom seen or touched a greasier, grimier wad of money. I didn't know hundred-dollar bills ever got so cruddy. They must have come from a fondler."

"LaFrance was calm?"

"He stammered and sweat and his eyes bulged and he spilled his drink and mine. Otherwise, a cucumber. By now he's got the greeting card. By now he knows how it was done, by you switching claim checks as you turned away from him to walk over to me. By now he knows you picked it up ten minutes after it was checked. By now maybe he has leaned across the desk and hit Harry in the mouth. What a pity not to see him read the nice card I bought him."

"You'll get to see a certain amount of agitation."

"You can arrange that?"

"The phone is turned off. He'll be here in the morning. Count on it. Come over early. We'll play a little chess."

"I should be down watching the board. Today it moved almost too good. Volume is picking up. Very close to two points. Seven grand, practically, for the widow. I've got a friend on the floor of the exchange keeping in close touch with the fellow who maintains the position in Fletcher, and he calls me at my brokers the minute anything starts to look sour. And I should put in some orders for her out of the sixty. We'll have five days to meet the margin call. I don't think the mail takes that long from Broward Beach to here. At least not usually."

"We could be having a little game on the sun deck. The forecast is warm and bright. We invite him aboard. We have a little chat. He goes away."

"So I could phone in the first order. So it isn't as risky now in the beginning as it is going to get. Also, there is a variation of the queen's pawn opening I think I can break your back with. You know, you don't look so great."

"I brood a lot."

He finished the last of the drink in one huge gulp. He shuddered and got up and said, "Now if I can be standing by the bunk when that hits me . . ."

179

Fifteen

WE HAD PLACED the chess table and chairs near the rear of the sun deck so we could look down onto the dock. We surveyed the morning traffic between moves. At one point Hero went by, swaying his big shoulders. The usual lock of hair was combed to fall just right over his forehead. He was taking a morning saunter through the game preserves, just in case he might flush something even at an unlikely morning hour. His gray slacks were tightly tailored to his narrow hips, and the broad belt was cinched tightly around his improbable waist.

He crinkled up at us and said in his mellow bassbaritone, "Morning, gents. Nice day out today."

"Getting any?" Meyer said contemptuously.

"Can't complain, gents. It's the best season for it."

He came to a momentary point and then lengthened his relaxed stride. I turned and saw two girls in beach togs with pale northern faces and legs, heading from the dock area toward the shops. Just as they disappeared from sight beyond the palm fronds Hero was ten feet behind them and, I suspected, clearing his throat and checking the third finger, left hand. That was his quaint little conceit, his only concession to any rule of human behavior. He proclaimed it often, with great conviction and emphasis. "I hold marriage sacred, and never in my life have I knowingly courted nor touched a lady united in the holy bonds of matrimony, no sir. It's something no gentleman would do."

A little later Meyer went below and phoned his broker and came back acting less restless. "It opened up a whole point, and then a couple of pretty good blocks came on the market and knocked it down to an eighth below yesterday's close. Insiders unloading, maybe. If so, in another week or two, they'll be slitting their throats at what they could have gotten."

At a few minutes before eleven, Preston LaFrance came along the dock at a half lope. He looked rumpled. He hadn't shaved. He came to a lurching halt and stared up at us.

180

"Doctor Mey . . ." It came out falsetto, so he coughed and tried again. "Doctor Meyer!"

"Hidey, Press," I said. "How you, old buddy? Come on aboard. Ladderway up here is on the port side."

He came clambering up and came over and stood beside us. We studied the chess pieces. "Doctor Meyer!"

"Just Meyer," he said. "Plain old Meyer."

"But don't you work for——"

"Work? Who should work? I'm an economist. I live on a little cruiser that has a case of dry rot lately. If I decide to get out the tools and go to work on it, then I'll be working."

"Then there isn't any . . . offer for the land?"

We both looked up at him. "Offer?" I said. "Land?" said Meyer.

"Oh Jesus, you two were in this lousy racket together. You are a stinking pair of con men. Oh Jesus God!"

"Please!" said Meyer. "I'm trying to figure out why he moved his bishop."

"I'm going to have you two bastards thrown in jail!"

"McGee," said Meyer, "let's finish the game after the noise stops." He stood up and leaned against the rail. Meyer in his white swim trunks reminds me a little bit of a man who is all dressed to go to a masquerade as a dancing bear. All that is left to do is put on the bear head and the collar. He stared at LaFrance. "Jail? For what?"

"You two took a hunnert thousand dollars away from me! More than that! That Bannon place isn't worth half the mortgage on it!"

"Mr. LaFrance," I said, "the records will show that I paid a legitimate fifteen thousand for Mrs. Bannon's equity in the Bannon Boatel, and then I turned around and sold that same equity to you for forty thousand. And I think that your banker will remember how anxious you've been to get your hands on Bannon's ten acres on the river."

"But . . . but . . . damn it, that was because you said . . ." He stopped himself and took a deep breath. "Listen. Forget the forty thousand. Okay. You suckered me. But the sixty thousand I gave this man last night, that's something else again. I've *got* to have it back."

"You gave me sixty thousand dollars!" Meyer said in

vast astonishment. "Look. Stop standing in the sun. Get some rest."

He stood there, blinking, clenching and unclenching his boney fists. His color was bad. He smiled what I would imagine he thought was an ingratiating and friendly smile. "You took me good, boys. Slick and perfect. You made a nice score off ol' Press LaFrance. And I guess you're not going to give it back just because I say pretty please with sugar. But you don't understand. I had to put up the Carbee option to get the sixty thousand. Now, if I had it back, I could go ahead and make my deal with Santo. That's what I got to trade with, boys. We'll draw it up legal. You'll get the sixty thousand back that you stole off me, and twenty more to sweeten the pot."

"If I had sixty thousand," said Meyer, "would I be hanging around with such riffraff? I would be riding around in a white convertible with a beautiful woman in furs and diamonds."

"How can you lose?" LaFrance said. "There's no way you can lose."

"No thanks," I said. "What shape does that leave you in, buddy?"

He wiped his mouth with the back of his hand. "I just plain can't afford to get left in the kind of shape I'd be in. Why, I would be worse off than dead broke. I would be a mile underground, boys. I would be attached and garnisheed the rest of my natural life. I would never have dime one to call my own the rest of my days."

"Now you know how it feels, Press."

"How what feels?"

"How some of the people felt who got in your way. Like Bannon."

He peered at me. "You bleeding for Bannon? That was straight-out business. He was squattin' right in the way of progress, and he was so dumb it took him a long time to catch on, is all."

"It would have helped him a lot if he'd had a brother-in-law on the County Commission."

"What in the wide world is eating on you, McGee? My God, there's a whole world full of Tush Bannons stumbling around, and they get et up left and right, and that's what makes the world go 'round. I put Monk onto some good things and he owed me a favor."

"And you and Monk let Freddy Hazzard know you'd appreciate him leaning a little hard on Bannon any chance he had?"

"Now, we never meant anything like *that!*" He smiled. "You're just trying to sweat me up a little. Isn't that right? Look, boys, it won't improve the deal any. Twenty more on top of the sixty is the best I can do."

He was such a weak, miserable, unsatisfying target. He still thought he was one of the good guys. I tried to reach him, just a little.

"If you could bring in a thousand-percent profit a day, LaFrance, I wouldn't throw pocket change on the deck there in front of you. If I was on fire, I wouldn't buy water from you. I came prowling for you, LaFrance. If the thing you cared most about in the world was that face you wear, I would have changed it permanently, little by little. If your most precious possession was a beautiful wife, she'd be right down there below in the master stateroom waiting for you to leave so I could get back to her. If you juggled for a living, friend, you'd now have broken wrists and broken elbows."

"What the *hell* is the matter with you?"

"Get off the boat. Go ashore. Tush Bannon was one of the best friends I ever had. All you give a damn about is money, so that's where I hit you."

"Best . . . friend?" he whispered.

And I watched the gray appear. That gray like a wet stone. Gray for fright. Gray for guilt. Gray for despair. His mouth worked. "You . . . rooned me, all right. Ever'thing I worked all my life for is gone. You finished me off, McGee."

"Wait a minute," Meyer said. "Maybe I've got an idea."

LaFrance came to point like a good bird dog. "Yes? Yes? What?"

Meyer smiled at him benignly. "The answer was staring us right in the face all the time. It's so simple! What you do is kill yourself!"

LaFrance stared at him, tried to comprehend the joke, tried even to smile, but the smile fell away. Meyer's smile stayed put. But not one gleam of humor touched Meyer's little bright blue eyes. And I do not know many people who could have stared into that smile for very long. Certainly LaFrance couldn't. In the same soft persuasion a lover might use, Meyer said, "Do yourself a favor. Go kill yourself. Then you won't even know or care if you're broke. Maybe it hurts a little, but just for a split second. Use a gun or a rope, or go jump off something high. Go ahead. Die a little."

It is a kind of rat-frenzy I suppose, that dreadful and murderous fury of the weak ones when the door of the trap slams shut. With a mindless squalling he plunged at Meyer, long yellowed ridged thumbnails going for the meat of the eyes, knees jacking at belly and groin. The squalling and flailing and gouging lasted perhaps two and a half seconds before I clamped my forearm across his throat. I pulled him back away from Meyer, spun him and let go. He ended up against the far rail.

Obscenities are tiresome. He kept repeating himself. I cuffed him quiet and he went down the ladderway and I helped him along the way and onto the dock.

He stayed there perhaps three minutes. He was going to come back with a gun. He was going to bring friends. He was going to have my boat blown up. He was going to have it burned to the waterline. He was going to hire some boys from back in the swamps to come with their knives some dark night and turn us into sopranos. We were going to be awful sorry we'd ever messed with Preston LaFrance and you can by God believe it.

His eyes bulged and his voice had hoarsened and the saliva shone on his chin. And finally he hitched up his pants and walked away. His walk was that of a man wearing new bifocals and not being very sure of how far away the ground might be. Meyer was able to stand up straight without much discomfort, and I dabbed iodine on the thumbnail gouge under his left eye. He seemed troubled, thoughtful, far away. I told him LaFrance wouldn't make any trouble. I asked him what was bothering him.

Meyer, scowling, pinched the bridge of his nose. "Me! Did you hear me? On the sidewalk if there is a bug, I change my step and miss him. For me the business of the hooks almost spoils fishing. Me! I don't understand it. Such a rotten anger I had, Travis! Thick in the throat like a sickness. Oh, he won't kill himself. Not that one. He'll live on and on so he can whine. But it was like changing your step to squash the bug, not flat, just a little

184

squash so he can crawl a little bit, slow, leaking his juices. McGee, my friend, I am ashamed of that kind of anger. I am ashamed of being able to do something like that. I said to myself when I first got into your line of . . . endeavor, I said—forgive me for saying this to you—I said I will go only so far into it. There are things McGee does that somehow hurt McGee, hurt him in the way he thinks of himself. I talked to Muggsie. This business of the pretty little woman who just somehow happened to go off with Hero, that wasn't pretty, and you were punishing something in yourself. Now I find myself a little bit less in my own eyes. Maybe this is a bad business you're in, Travis. Is there this kind of ugly anger in a ·man that waits for some kind of virtuous excuse? Was it there in me, waiting for a reason only? Travis, my friend, is this the little demonstration of how half the evil in the world is done in the name of honor?"

He wanted help I couldn't give him. One does not pat a Meyer on the head and give him a lollypop. He had overturned one of the personal stones in my garden too, and I could watch leggedy things scuttling away into comforting darkness.

I said, "You still didn't figure out why I moved my bishop."

He sat down and fixed a total concentration on the board. He gave a little nod at last and pushed a pawn one space forward, spoiling the sequence I was planning. He pinched at the bridge of his nose again, then smiled across at me, a hairy Meyer-smile, and said, "You know, I think I must have taken some sort of a dislike to that fellow."

Two days later, Friday afternoon, Meyer came aboard the *Flush* at four thirty, just after I got back from the beach. A mass of that arctic air that Canada sends down free of charge had begun to change the day a little before noon. It had come down so swiftly I knew the grove people would be worried. There were frost bulletins on all the broadcasts. An edge in the crisp northeast breeze had cleaned the long beaches of everybody except diehard Yankees and one masochistic beach bum named Travis McGee. I had been taking out all the kinks, in the muscles in both body and brain, of too many sedentary days, swimming parallel to shore, in and out of the surf line, for all the distance, endurance and occasional speed sprints I could manage. It had been hard work to even stay warm, and I had ground away at it, breaststroke, backstroke, crawl, until on my chattering lope back to the *Flush* I felt as if I had pulled most of the long muscles loose from the joints and sockets and hinges they were supposed to control.

Any persistent idiot, like Hero, can strain away at the doorframe isometrics and build impressive wads of chunky fibrous muscle with which you can lift the front end of any sedan to make the girls say Oooo. But if you want the kind of muscle structure that will move you from here to there very very quickly, that will enable you to slip a punch, snatch a moving wrist, turn a fall into a shoulder roll that will put you back on the balls of your feet, balanced and ready, then you'd better be willing to endure total expenditure over long, active and dogged periods. I was going to be slowed down by time and attrition, and maybe it had begun, but not to a degree as yet for me to notice, nor to a degree to make me doubt myself—and doubt, of course, is more fatal than slowed reflexes.

I had the heat going aboard. Meyer drank coffee and worked on his investment figures while I hot-showered the salt away, dressed in ancient, soft, treasured, threadbare checked shirt, gray Daks, and a pair of Herter's Two-Point woodsman's shoes, of oiled, hand-treated bull hide, worn to a condition as flexible and pliable as an Eskimo wife. In the shower I had begun to raise tentative voice in song, but had remembered another day, another shower, when that same song had been interrupted by a lady named Puss handing me in a well-made sample of the drink known as a McGee. So that song clogged and died, and I dressed and made the drink myself and took it into the lounge.

Meyer looked up from his work and said, "You look grotesquely healthy, Travis."

"And your eyes look grainy, and you look tired, and how long do you have to go five days a week and sit and watch the board like a great hairy eagle?"

"Not as long as I thought."

"Indeed?"

"Sit and listen. Without a glaze in the eyes, please. Try to understand."

"Proceed."

"These Fletcher Industries earnings statements. Look, accounting is flexible. There are choices. Each one is legal. However, say there are fifteen ways to handle different things to make earnings look a little bit better. So this outfit uses all fifteen, right up to the hilt. The last published quarter, it looks like they made forty percent more money than the quarter before that. I rework the statement and I come out with earnings not even flat. But down a little, even."

"So?"

"At fifteen dollars a share it *looked* as if Fletcher was a bargain for a growth stock, selling at maybe twelve times anticipated earnings for this year. So on top of that— which you call the fundamental picture, then there is the technical picture of the stock in the market. This buying pressure improves the technical picture. It becomes very desirable. Big volume attracts attention. Today I saw how it was going, how it was reacting, and so I took the risk, and I committed her all the way. Here is where her account stands. She's got seventy-four hundred shares. Average cost per share is eighteen dollars. Today it closed at twenty-four and a quarter. So, right now, a short-term gain of forty-six thousand dollars."

"Of what!"

"She holds shares worth right now a hundred and eighty thousand, less the margin account debit. The supply is shrinking and the demand is increasing. It is moving too fast. The *Wall Street Journal* yesterday had a statement from management saying they don't know why all the big interest in their stock all of a sudden. It got out of hand too fast. I made this projection about where it is going to go next week. I have a used crystal ball an old gypsy gave me. I say a minimum eight points next week, so it will close between thirty-two and a half and thirty-seven. Traders will grab profits and get out. Usually I would wait, buy on the correction, and ride up with it again. But we get a trading suspension, maybe an investigation of corporate books. I think they used all the accounting gimmicks they could, and then they lied a little. It went up too fast and next week will be faster.

187

So I start moving her over into that nice one I found for her to keep."

"You're telling me or asking me?"

"Telling you. What else? You are the expert on pigeon drops. I am the expert on the biggest crap game in the world."

"But you have to talk to her and explain all this."

"I do? Why?"

"Because she ought to come down here."

He cocked his head. "Connie suggested?" I nodded. "I should discuss all this with her. It is only fair to her."

"And she should sign some papers, maybe?"

"Very important-looking documents." He scratched his chin, tugged at his potato nose. "One part of your thinking I don't understand. That lousy fellow, that LaFrance, it makes some sense he should go to Santo to see if he can get bailed out by maybe peddling him the option he's got on the Carbee land. So doesn't he mention you?"

"If he mentions me, it's the same as telling Santo that he was a damned fool. If he admits he's smashed and trying to salvage something, the price from Santo will go way down."

"How can you be sure of how that idiot will react?"

"I can't be sure. I just make my guess and live with it."

The freeze hit low spots well to the west and north of the To-Co Groves, hit them hard enough so that all the smudge pots and airplane propeller fans and bonfires of old truck tires failed to save the dreams of a lot of the smaller growers. They expected the same on Saturday night, but the upper winds changed and a warm, moist breath began coming up from the lower Gulf and the Straits of Yucatán, moving across the peninsula from out of the southwest, and after some unseasonable thunderstorms, the afternoon was clear and warm and bright on Sunday when Janine Bannon arrived in the car Tush and I had fixed a quarter of a year ago.

I was watching for her, knowing when she had left the groves, and went and took her small suitcase from her and brought her aboard. She had been aboard before, when I had taken the *Flush* up the Shawana River, back when the Boatel was doing well, and they had told me their plans with an air of pleasure and excitement, so she knew the layout.

She looked trim and attractive in her green suit and yellow blouse, but thinner than she should have been. The difference in her was the way the vitality had gone out of her, deadening her narrow and delicate face, making her move like a convalescent, taking the range and lilt and expression out of her voice. Even her dark hair had lost luster, and there were deep stainings under her eyes, fine lines around her mouth.

I took her back to the guest stateroom and she said, "I don't want to be a bother. I should have found a place."

"Which would be a very good trick right now. No bother. You know that. Get yourself settled in. Meyer will be over in a while for drinks and talk, and then we'll go out and find some beef, or Chinese, or whatever you feel like."

"Oh, anything is all right. Trav, it'll just be for overnight. I have to get back."

"That will depend on what Meyer has set up for you to take care of."

A little while later I heard some small clatterings in the galley and the chunk of the refrigerator door. I went forward and found her bending over and frowning into the little freezer. She turned and said, "I'd feel a lot better about all this if you'd let me earn my keep, Trav. Connie has all that help, and they have their own ways of doing things, and I feel like a parasite. You have lots of stuff here. Honestly, I *like* to cook."

"Never volunteer, lady. Somebody will take you up on it. So you're hooked."

She smiled. "Thank you. You know things, don't you? Like you know what people really want to do. Now go away and let me just potter around and find out where everything is and how everything works, all by myself."

I went in and looked at the tape labels and picked out one of a lot of classical guitar with Julian Bream and started it rolling, adjusting it to that level that is not quite background and not quite for listening only. It wasn't until Meyer was aboard and I called Janine in from the galley that it occurred to me that they had never met.

She put her slim hand into his paw, and she had that

189

speculative reserve that women seem to have for the first twelve seconds when confronted with the rather outrageous presence of Meyer.

He peered at her, shaking his head slowly in a disconcerting way and then said, "Tricked again! Janine, my dear, if I had been told you were beautiful, I wouldn't have been working so hard to make you rich."

"Beautiful! Now *really*."

He turned to me. "See? A fishing expedition even. She protests so she can hear it again. Okay, Janine. You are a beautiful lady. I am very sensitive to beauty. A man who makes children run and hide behind mommy is very receptive to beauty."

"You should see the wolf pack of little kids," I said, "following this character up and down the beach, listening to his lies."

Suddenly her dark eyes looked lively. "Meyer, you too are beautiful. I do not know how you are doing it or why you are doing it even, but if you are making me rich, I will be very pleased and grateful."

"I am doing it because McGee nags me. That is a good guitar to drink by. And how long do we stand around with no drinks?"

She cooked up a great kettle of a delicious thing that she called "Sort of Stroganoff." I found some red wine that, for a change, Meyer approved of. After she had cleaned up, she and Meyer went into a huddle at the desk over the papers he had brought over. I sat on the yellow couch, reading and digesting, hearing them with half an ear.

At last she came over and plumped down beside me, sighing. I put the book aside. "That fantastic man keeps telling me fantastic things, Trav."

"Meyer is like that."

"He says you are supposed to tell me where so much money came from to start with. I *know* you somehow tricked Mr. LaFrance into paying such a price for our place. But there's a lot more."

"He made a donation, Jan. Press LaFrance made a nice gesture."

"But . . . if you stole it from him, I don't———"

"Meyer, did he give you that money willingly?"

190

"Willingly!" said Meyer. "He could hardly wait to get rid of it. That is the truth, dear lady."

"Okay. I give up. But apparently I might end up . . . Tell him, Meyer."

"It's an estimate only. At the end of this year, after all taxes are paid, you should have, I think, about two thousand shares, free and clear, of G.S.A., General Service Associates, worth seventy dollars a share now, and more then. The dividend income will be six to seven thousand a year. All your eggs in one basket, but a very nice basket. Great ratios, great management, fantastic promise. Meyer will have his eye on the basket. With little kids, and you a young woman, you need growth and income. Tomorrow we see some people, start setting up some basic living trust structures."

"I have to stay over another night," she told me.

"Or more," said Meyer. "Depending. A three-year program and you will be on a five-figure income with a nice reserve, with insurance trusts maturing for the college expenses. The boys grow up, get married. You can go abroad, go to Spain, rich and foolish, marry a bullfighter, buy fake paintings. I'll be right here. A little trembly old man, feeling terrible because I ruined your life."

And I wondered if it was the first time she had laughed loudly and long since Tush had died.

Sixteen

ON THE FOLLOWING Tuesday night at ten thirty, after Janine had once again fed us well, I strolled with Meyer back to his boat to check on the strategy.

"A piece of genius," he said, "that call from Connie."

I had arranged it earlier with Connie, while Meyer was taking Jan to mysterious appointments with lawyers and trust officers, and Connie had called back at six and asked Jan if it was all right if she took the boys with her for a few days. She would take Marguerita with her to look after the kids. There was an Association meeting in Tampa, and then she wanted to go up to Tallahassee for a few days, and stop and visit some other growers on her way back. She'd be gone a week, and why didn't Jan stay right where she was?

"Once she gave in," said Meyer, "you noticed the relaxation. You noticed she ate better too? You noticed she laughed a little?"

"Conspiracy."

"The best kind," he said. "Today I unloaded a thousand shares of Fletcher at thirty-one and moved the funds into G.S.A. It's the critical time right now. I don't know how high the rocket goes. Ninety-two thousand shares traded today. Suppose in the morning I call her and tell her the men we have to see will be available Friday morning. No. Saturday morning. So you should move that hunk of ugly luxury before it congeals to the slip. A nice little cruise someplace."

"I'll try it. Don't count on it."

I went ambling back and went aboard and into the lounge. Janine was standing in the doorway at the forward end of the lounge, the companionway dark behind her.

"Trav?" she said, and her voice was all wrong. It was a sick sad scared voice, and the belt she was wearing was a sinewy, sun-reddened forearm. "Trav? I'm . . . sorry."

A knuckly hand appeared at her left side, at waist-level, aiming a short barrel of respectable caliber at my middle. "I'm sorry about this, Mr. McGee," he said. I could make out a tallness behind her, a relative pallor of the face against the gloom behind her.

"Freddy?" I asked.

"Yes sir."

"I'm sorry about this too, Freddy."

"Just you stand quiet," he said. The arm left her waist. A set of regulation handcuffs arched toward me, gleaming in the light, and fell on the lounge carpeting with a jingling thud.

The arm quickly clasped her waist again. "Now you move all the time like slow-motion movies, Mr. McGee. You get down on your knees and take those cuffs there slow, and you edge over slow and reach both arms around that pipe thing and put them on and press them nice and tight."

"Or?"

"I think you know the corner I'm in, Mr. McGee. It

has piled up on me, and no way to stop it or change it. I couldn't stand being locked up anyplace even for one month without being turned into some kind of animal. So I've got no choice. I'm sorry about everything, but sorry doesn't help. So do it right now, start moving, or I'll lay one slug right through your forehead, Mr. McGee."

Freddy had been worn thin. He was on the edge, and the truth was in his voice. It made me very obedient. Very humble. I moved the way the specialists move when they are lifting the fuse out of a bomb. I snapped the cuffs snugly, taking a faint remote comfort in the knowledge that given ten seconds alone in the lounge I could brace myself, wrench the stanchion loose and get my hands on the revolver in the desk.

He walked Janine out of the doorway and into the lounge. As he put the handgun away, I heard him sigh with the release of tension. He released her and gave her a little push. She stumbled forward, her body slack, head bowed in her despair. "I'm sorry," she said in a low voice.

His hand went to his hip pocket, then reached out toward her quite casually. There was a barely audible sound of impact, a hairsoftened, leathery little thopp. She took half a broken step, face emptying. She started to lift her arms to break the fall, then pitched onto her face, jelly-slack, with a tumble of cushioned bone against the lounge carpeting.

I had seen something odd in his face just as he had flicked the lead against her skull. It had been a moment of change and revelation, showing a pleasure of erotic dimensions, of sensual pleasure. It is not an unusual way for the mind of a man to turn rancid. Cops fall in love with the hickory nightstick. Prizefighters forget to pace themselves, going for the sweet knockout. It is a pull that takes some twisted ones into anesthesiology, or into preparing the dead for burial, or into scut-work in asylums. They are the dark brothers of the slackened flesh, turned on in some soiled way by a total vulnerability.

He looked down at her, stepped over her and sat in a chair just out of my reach. He yawned hugely. There was a faint family resemblance to LaFrance. He was a big, stringy, slope-shouldered boy, and he looked stone tired. He held the spring-handled tranquilizer in his right hand and gently bounced the leaden end off the open palm of his other hand. It was of black leather, intricately woven, greasy with much handling.

The only other time I had seen him was when he and another deputy had backed up Sheriff Burgoon when he had picked me up in the lobby of the old hotel.

I sat and hitched around to where I could lean my back against the bulkhead, the stanchion between my flexed knees, forearms resting on my knees.

"Why did you come here, Freddy?"

He was so exhausted his mind was moving slowly. "I remembered two days ago my Uncle Press telling me about this houseboat of yours. I was trying to sneak aboard one of the freighters heading out of Tampa. They watch them too close. I figure I can get out of the country somehow, I can get myself all sorted out and get some time to think what to do next."

"What you ought to do next is pick up that phone over there and call Sheriff Burgoon and tell him where to come get you."

"Too late for that."

"You've got a lot of friends in Shawana County. They'll work things out for you. They think you were defending yourself from Bannon and hit him too hard and got scared. They'll make sure that old couple where you got the clothes and car won't press charges."

"I tell you, Mr. McGee, it's too *late*. I had some more bad luck. That's the only kind I've had lately. There's a woman I killed not meaning to, over west of Dade City. I tunked her perfect, light and easy and just enough, and she took two steps more than she should have been able to and when she fell, it was right on a garden rake acrost her throat, and no way in the world to stop all that blood. God, there was a lot of blood! He run into the brush and I don't know if I winged him at all. Anyway, I couldn't find him and I had to get out of there. No sir, it's too late for anything but running and hiding. Things start to go wrong, they just seem to keep right on."

"How did they go wrong with Tush Bannon?"

"I was patrolling and seen him at just about first light walking the shoulder of the road, carrying a suitcase. I stopped and he said he'd come in on the bus and phoned out to his place and no answer at all. He was worried about Miz Bannon. It's easy to know later on what you should have done. My daddy had said Mr. Bannon was sure a hard man to discourage. I should have taken him in where we were holding the stuff his wife left and the letter from his wife, and told him his place was all foreclosed and sealed up with the notices and all. Uncle Press had to have that ten acres, and he was sure going to get it. It had been a real quiet night, so I decided what I'd do was run him on out there so he could see with his own eyes, without me telling him, how he'd lost the whole works for good. I think I wanted to do that because he didn't act whipped at all. He acted like he had some way out of the mess he was in. So I said maybe the phone wasn't working and took him out. We got out there and he got ugly when he figured out I had to know that he'd been all foreclosed. Then I told him his wife had left him and left his stuff and a letter with the sheriff and he called me a liar. He walked at me, half yelling at me and I tunked him on the skull. It should have taken him down, but it just bent his knees some and he shook his head and kept coming. So I knew he had a hard skull, and he was big, and he felt ugly, so I made sure the next one would take him down. I put a lot of wrist in it and I figured to lay it right onto his forehead, but he was quick for a big man like that, and he tried to snap his head back." He sighed. "It hit him right square on the bridge of the nose, Mr. McGee. That's a real bad place because it drives two little thin bones right back into the brain. I squatted there beside him in the morning light, sweaty and cold, and held my fingers on his wrist, and felt his heart go slower and slower and softer and softer and then it stopped all the way and he shivered sort of, and after a while I figured out it would seem likely he had enough troubles to want to kill himself, and figured out how to make it look like he did and at the same time cover up the places I'd tunked him. You see, I knew if I had to tell what happened, I'd get run out of police work for good, maybe, and it's the only way I feel good, with the uniform and people listening when you tell them something."

"But Arlene Denn saw you."

He shook his head slowly. "All those weird kids. I thought I was in the clear on Bannon. Then she said she
195

watched. I stood out there in the night trying to think of some way I could kill all of them. Like tunk them all on the head and an overdose or something. Or a fire. But I was on the dispatch book because they gave me the complaint. I had those pictures, and I had that stuff I took off them. She didn't want trouble. I could give her a lot. So when she was off her high and made sense, I asked about maybe if Mrs. Bannon was playing around, or if there was some friend she could say she saw instead of me. So . . ."

There was a stir beyond the yellow couch, a grunting sigh. Freddy got up quickly and went to Janine. When he bent down over her, he was out of sight. I heard the tone of his gentle voice but not the words. It sounded as if a lover were murmuring to his beloved, comforting her fears. I heard the tiny thud once more.

When he came back and sat as before, I said, "That isn't going to do her any good, Deputy."

"Or no harm, Mr. McGee. I know just where and how hard. It just kind of puts a jolt onto the brain, with hardly even a headache afterward. I'll be thinking on what I should do so I can get some sleep without worrying about either one of you. You know, if you'd only been right here on this boat when Shawana County made the request to have you picked up and held, everything would have been all smoothed over."

"Don't count on it. No matter how good you make it look, Freddy, the people I was with at the time you killed Tush would have come forward and cleared me and left you with a lot of explaining."

"By then there would have been no Arlie to change her story. It maybe would be a big mystery, but there'd be no way to get me mixed up in it."

"So Tush was an accident, and the woman with the rake in her neck was an accident, but Arlie Denn was going to be on purpose."

"You get pushed so far there's only maybe one little narrow way out of the corner. I better get you two . . ."

I awakened lame and sore, with no knowledge of time or place. Daylight came from overhead, around the edges of a hatch cover that did not fit as well as it should. I had what I thought was a hangover headache, and when I realized that I was in the forward bilge area of the

196

Flush, curled close to the anchor line well, the old frame members of the hull biting into my side, I thought that only a sorry drunk would pick that as a place to sleep. But when I tried to bring my right hand up and rub my face, it stopped with a jolting clink of chain. I turned my head and saw that my right wrist was handcuffed to one of the forward braces made of two-inch galvanized pipe, braces I had installed long ago to give her more forward rigidity in rough water. And I wasn't going to yank one of those loose, not without a chain hoist and a power winch.

I fingered my skull with my left hand and found a tender area above the right ear and a little behind it. I could not remember being "tunked," or where the conversation had stopped. My thinking gear was sluggish. It took me a long time to realize that my houseboat could not be moored at Bahia Mar. The motion was wrong. She was at rest, bow into a gentle swell, lifting and falling. Sometimes she would get out of phase with the swell and I could feel the soft tug of the anchor line snubbing the left of the bow.

I sat up and shifted and found a better place to stretch out, where no white oak ribs dug into me. I kept telling myself that Janine was perfectly all right. There wasn't a thing in my pockets of any earthly use to me. And there was nothing I could reach. I managed to doze off a few times. The motion was restful. At eleven fifteen by my watch I awoke and heard the latch on the small hatchway entrance to the forward bilge click.

Freddy Hazzard came crawling through, wearing a pair of my fresh khaki pants and a clean T-shirt. He nodded and reached back through the hatch and lifted a half bucket of water through and put it within reach. He reached again and brought in a brown paper bag and put it beside the bucket.

"Mr. McGee, there's milk and bread and cheese in the sack, and a roll of toilet paper. You'll have to make out best you can with a bucket, because I'm not about to let you loose until there's a good reason."

"Where's Mrs. Bannon?"

"She's just fine. I found some chain and a padlock, and I got her chained in the head by one ankle, and I took her some food first."

"Where are we?"

"Anchored in the flats just off Sands Key, way east of the channel, maybe twelve mile south of Miami. I had me a time working this thing out of that big marina. The wind takes it. I fished commercial about every summer I was a kid in school. Mr. McGee, I found your fuel tables in the drawer next to the chart rack. With the fuel aboard it figures out to maybe four hundred miles range. Does that sound about right to you?"

"Why should I tell you anything, Freddy?"

He squatted on his heels, balancing easily to the motion of the hull. He looked at me in a troubled way. "I got that little runabout boat in tow. That's what gave me fits getting clear of the boat basin. I've been checking her over, and I think she's got maybe three hundred miles in her because the tanks are topped off full. Cuba would be easy, but I've got the feeling it would be another kind of jail. I've been checking weather and there's a good five-day forecast. I think I could just about get to the Caicos Islands. There isn't much of any red tape or government there because, like a friend explained to me, they used to belong to Jamaica and when Jamaica went independent, the Turks and Caicos Islands weren't in that deal. I've got your papers and I can scorch them up some like this boat burned, and leave enough to read so I can pass for you where nobody knows you. I'm sorry about the way it has to be, but if I'm going to be you, I'm going to have to leave you and her fastened tight to this thing when she runs out of fuel and I open her up and let her go down. I thought of all other ways and there just isn't a one. Now, I'm telling you this, how it's going to be, but I'm not telling her because she'd come all apart. And you won't be telling her because you and she aren't ever going to see each other again. It's the only chance and I'm sorry about it, but I have to give it a try. Now you want to know why you should tell me anything. It's because when the time comes, I can lay one on your skull bone and hers too and you'll drown without knowing a thing about it. And I'll make you comfortable as I can meanwhile. Her too. But every boat has cranky ways, and when this thing isn't acting right, I want to ask you what to do and you tell me right. If you don't, you aren't either one of you going to be comfortable hardly at all. And you should know that when I was carrying her into the head and getting that chain fixed on her leg, I thought about how full-grown women like that always made me feel dumb and clumsy and afraid to even think of touching them. But since she's going down to the bottom anyways, it wouldn't matter what happened to her beforehand. I might mess with her and I might not. I couldn't say right now, but there's not so much chance of it if you act right. So right now I want to know just where to put those tacs to get the top range out of this thing."

"It isn't going to work."

"It's the only chance I've got. What rpm, mister?"

"Eleven hundred."

"Where's the switch on the automatic pilot?"

"Up on the topside controls, under the panel, over on the port corner."

"Where's your compass correction card?"

"Pasted to the inside lid of the box where the rule and dividers are."

He nodded. "I got a nap, but I need a lot of catching up. I'm going to sleep out the rest of the day and move on out of here about dusk. I'll bring you down some blankets so you can rest better, Mr. McGee."

"Don't knock yourself out with favors."

He left. It was just a wild enough idea to work, if I'd been alone aboard. But Meyer would know Janine had been aboard, and so would Connie Alvarez. They would never quit, not until they found out what happened. Small comfort.

So this had to be the time. During this long afternoon. Don't count on his getting careless later on. Because even when pooped, he wasn't careless. He's been on the run. His two shipmates are latched up tightly. The bed is deep and soft. The sea rocks him. He may never sleep as deeply again.

So get to it, McGee. Get something working, mostly your dull head. Nothing in the pockets. Escape needs tools. Like a belt buckle? Ah yes. A careful young man. The old jail training. Belt and shoelaces were gone. What have you got that's made of metal, fella? Well, you have a corroded old bucket and you have a wristwatch, and you have some fillings in the fangs, and that is it.

And if you had metal, what could you do? You might

try to pick the lock on the cuff. Think nothing of the fact that they are designed to be pickproof. Or if you happened to have a very thin and fairly narrow piece of spring steel, you could maybe work it into this little aperture where the cuff clasps together and maybe free the ratchets somehow. Except the good sets, like this one, have little knurled places designed to keep you from doing just that.

The hatch latch clicked and it opened and he shoved two blankets in far enough for me to reach them and slammed it again. Nice gesture, fella. Thanks a lot.

More appraisal. The cuff would slide along the heavy pipe bracing. They were in the shape of the letter X laying on its side, and I was cuffed to the one with its low end on the starboard side, the high end on the port. They did not quite touch at the center of the X. There was room to get the cuff between them. I could stand up, if I kept pretty well hunched over. I gave myself very good grades in the handyman department, at least in that bracing chore. I had hacksawed them to fit snugly, then slipped the collars over them, each with a base about four inches across with four big bolt-holes. Even with the biggest wrench aboard, I would have had trouble. The rust looked as solid as the steel.

Suddenly I remembered that they were just friction collars. They were not threaded on. And the lip was about one inch deep. So, if a man could put his back into it, and put enough of a bend in one of them to make it an inch shorter, it would slip out of the bolted collar and that intelligent fellow would be free.

I made a blanket pad to protect my back. I hunched under the cross pipe, got myself nicely braced and tried to bend it. I tried until the world turned jet black with little streaks of red flickering through it. I tried until my ears were full of blood roar and my jaws ached and the pipe was grooving my bones, but it did not bend a quarter of an inch, if that.

I sat down and panted for a time. My eyes stung with sweat. Impasse. The only possible way I could get myself loose, other than chewing my hand off at the wrist, was to bend the pipe brace. And I couldn't bend it.

Give me a lever and a place to stand, somebody said.

Or was it a fulcrum? Anyway, he was going to move the earth. If a reason had been given, I had forgotten it.

Sure. With a lever or a winch or a truck jack, no problem at all. I drank some milk and ate some cheese. Okay, McGee. Sit here and make yourself a truck jack out of some bread, cheese, a watch, a pail and two blankets. The old know-how.

And something went skittering across the back of my mind so swiftly I didn't catch it. A frail ghost of some kind of a frail idea. I lay back and tried to think of nothing at all, and when it appeared again I grabbed it. I shook it but it didn't have anything to tell me. It muttered something about a turnbuckle and I let it go.

There are two ways to move something. Push it or pull it. I sat up and looked at my equipment. I took one blanket and, starting at one corner, I rolled it as neatly and tightly as I could. There was a squat thick short timber brace on the port side near the bulkhead, but it was a foot beyond my best reach. I soaked the ends of my blanket rope in the water bucket. I took off my shoes and socks and stretched out and fumbled the end of the blanket rope around the brace and clapped it between the soles of my feet and pulled it through and toward me. I looped the other end around the pipe brace to which I was fastened, and pulled it as tightly as I could manage and knotted the wet ends together. I poured the water out of the bucket, put my boat shoes back on and trod upon the bucket until the side seam parted and the seam that held the bottom on tore loose. Then I stomped and folded and grunted and sweated until I had a clumsy metal club about two and a half feet long. I wrapped that up in the other blanket as tightly as I could and tied it with strips torn off my shirt. Then I stuck six inches of the padded lever between the two strands of the blanket rope and began winding.

It was easy—at first. The blanket began to twist and knot like the rubber band in a toy airplane. The timber brace made alarming creaking sounds. Each full wind took more effort. I had wrapped my lever in the blanket to try to keep it from bending. But as I began to have to hold it right out at the end to get enough leverage, it began to take on a curve. When I noticed that the pipe brace was taking on a curve too, I began to worry about what might happen when all that accumulated force was released. The sweat ran. I turned my lever. The blanket was so taut I could imagine I could hear it humming. What is the breaking strength of the average blanket?

Suddenly it was like being dropped into the middle of a threshing machine. The pipe sprang out of the collars and banged me on the shoulder. The lever spun free and hit me on the elbow and numbed my forearm and hand. The pipe spun and rang against my skull and knocked me down and tried to twist my arm off by the cuffed wrist. It was an ungodly din, and Freddy was going to come charging down. I slipped the cuff off the end of the pipe. I clawed the shirt strips off my lever and knelt by the hatchway with the raw, flattened chunk of bucket held high, silently begging him to stick his head in, and wondering if he was on the other side waiting for me to stick my head out.

So I went creeping cautiously out, holding the loose cuff in my right hand with enough tension to keep the chain from clinking. I went up through the other hatch forward and moved silently aft. I stopped every few steps to hold my breath and cock my head and listen. At the mouth of the corridor I heard a buzzing snore, deep and slow and regular. The door of the master stateroom was ajar. The door to the head was closed, and I could hear a faint clinking of chain.

Procedure:—Go to the lounge. Get the weapon from the desk. Go charging in and blow one of his kneecaps off just to be on the safe side. Liberate the lady. Head for Dinner Key and radio the police to meet us.

But again he was careful. He had shaken the place down. No 38. I checked the pilothouse and the shark rifle was not in the spring clamps where it belonged.

Revised procedure:—Silently liberate the lady and get her the hell out of there and into the *Muñequita* and when we had drifted far enough, start her up and leave in a big hurry.

Chain. So the quickest, easiest way would be with the great big nippers, a brute set with handles a yard long. And they were right where I hoped they would be, in behind the tool locker, wedged in place.

I enjoyed his snoring as I moved like a ghost past the door to the master stateroom. I opened the door to the head slowly. She was sitting on the floor. She snapped her head around and looked at me with a madwoman's face, eyes and mouth wide and round, breath sucking to scream. But comprehension came just in time and I eased in and closed the door just as silently as I had opened it. She had found some greasy medication in the medicine locker and she had greased her bare ankle and foot and had been trying to work the chain off of it. She had gouged through the skin and her greasy ankle and the floor was speckled with blood.

I slid one jaw of the nippers under the ankle chain and applied pressure. The jaws bit through and the chain fell away, rattling on the deck. I put the nippers down and helped her up. She clung to me. I whispered to her and told her he was asleep and we were going to go aboard the *Muñequita* and release her tow line and drift away. She bobbed her head in violent agreement.

When we had crept to within two feet of the partly open door we had to pass, I suddenly knew what was wrong. I couldn't hear him snoring. So I took her by the arm to try to make it a fast run, but the door swung open and there he was. I shoved her along the corridor and in the same violent effort I tried to jump him. But a big soft hot red hammer hit the meat of my left shoulder and that much impact at that close range spun me and drove me back through the open door of the guest stateroom. The spinning tangled my legs and I fell heavily, remembering as I went down an old lesson painfully learned long ago. When you are shot, you are dead. Bang, you're dead! So be dead, because it might be the only chance you have left in the world.

I heard him come in to stand over me. "You damn fool!" he said. "You sorry pitiful damn fool." And he put his toe against my hip and nudged me to see how slack I was. I swung both legs and swept his feet out from under him and clawed my way onto him, yelling at the same time to Jan to get off the boat, swim ashore, run like hell.

It was very busy work. My left arm wasn't part of me, and he kept trying to work that revolver around to get it against me, and I kept trying to stay behind him and get the cuff chain around his throat. He managed to struggle up with me, which was a demonstration of an

203

impressive amount of wiry strength, but I yanked him off balance and toppled back on the bed with him. It had taken only a very few seconds. I gave up the chain bit and got my right forearm across his throat, but he kept his chin tucked down well. I got the gun wrist with my left hand, but the left arm was getting worse by the moment, and slowly, slowly he was turning the muzzle to where he could be sure of putting the next slug in my head without even having to look back at me.

It was then that Janine came through the door screeching, and bearing on high, in both hands, the small red fire extinguisher she had apparently yanked out of the clips on the corridor wall. Screeching, face contorted, she ran directly at us, starting the great descending blow when she was at least three steps from the bed. He wrenched the gun wrist free and there was the great slamming sound of a shot in an enclosed place, and I saw her head wrench sideways as she struck her fearful blow, then a jostle of great weight made such a sickening pain in my shoulder and arm, the world shrank down to a little white thing and winked out.

I don't know how long I was out. Thirty seconds, fifteen minutes. I came struggling up aware of great urgency, aware of being pinned under great weight. Freddy Hazzard seemed very heavy. I fingered his slack throat with my right hand and couldn't find a thing. I wormed partway out from under him and saw one good reason for the weight. Janine lay spilled across us, supine, the small of her back across his loins, her dark head hanging back over the edge of the bed.

I squirmed out from under both of them and stood up. I did not want to feel any more dead throats. The left side of her head was toward me. Her hair was clotted heavily with blood. I stared at her and when I saw the rise and fall of her chest, I risked the finger on the throat, found a place going bump, bump, bump.

Then I looked at him. Nobody was going to be able to feel any pulse. He had a grooved head. Diagonal. From one temple across to the opposite eyebrow. A groove as wide as the fire extinguisher and maybe an inch deep. The eye bulged with a blank astonishment greater than any astonishment in the living world.

The faintness came over me and faded away slowly. I

stood three stories tall and I would sway in the slightest breeze. Toy fellow made of broomstraws and flour paste. My left arm hung there, and I looked down and saw the blood dropping busily from my fingertips.

Things to do, McGee. Got to take care. Got to tidy ship. Grab the buckets and brooms, men. Clean sweep fore and aft. So start moving, because you don't know how much time you have, and it might not be enough. I fingered Hazzard's pockets and found the cuff key and managed to turn it with numb fingers and get my right wrist free. The metal had rubbed it raw.

I could not make myself hurry. I felt thoughtful. It was a kind of faraway game. Amusing and not very important. I might be able to do what might keep me from falling off the edge for good, and I might not. Interesting.

On my slow way to the head I ripped my shirt off. I turned my left side toward the mirror. The entrance hole was three inches below the top of the shoulder and on the outside of the upper arm, but deep enough so that I couldn't tell if it had done bone damage. The slug had tumbled apparently, and torn one hell of a hole on the way out. I lifted my left arm with my right hand, braced the left palm against the wall and locked the elbow. I took my time putting the gauze pads on the wounds, winding it very neatly, tearing the surgical tape with my teeth.

"Nice," I heard myself say in a voice that seemed to come from the next room. "Very neat."

So I went floating blissfully to the galley. Shock. Loss of blood. Replace fluids. Use stimulants. There was a quart jar of orange juice in the icebox. I found an unopened fifth of Wild Turkey in the liquor locker. I put them on the booth table and eased into the seat and wondered what a good name would be. An Orange Turkey? A Wild Screwdriver? The white mist began moving in from the edges and I realized nobody was going to come along and serve me. I picked my left arm up by the wrist and put the arm on the table. It wiggled its fingers when I sent the message down the nerves. I drank a third of the quart of juice. I took four long swallows of the bourbon. Second third of the juice. Another deep drag on the liquor. Polish off the juice. Then enough bourbon to just begin to tickle the gag reflex.

Come on, white mist. Take another shot. Here is McGee.

But it had edged so far back I couldn't see it anymore out of the corners of my eyes. I got up without thinking of my arm. It slid off the table and flapped me on the leg. And I thought about Janine, and she had a slug in her skull, and the bump, bump, bump would be over. I picked up my left arm and turned it and looked at my watch. How had it gotten to be three in the afternoon?

Go find out. You have to find out sometime. So go take a look at her.

The throat was still knocking away like a good little engine. I tugged at her and got her off Freddy and straightened her out on the bed. I did not want to move her too much. But I did not want to take the chance of her waking up all of a sudden and finding herself right there side by side with what had been Freddy.

I got an old tarp and put it on the floor beside the bed, on his side, reached beyond him and got hold of the bloody sheet and yanked it out from under her, and tugged on it until it rolled him off and he fell onto the tarp with a lanky thudding, face-down. I left the sheet on him and flipped the ends and side of the tarp over him. I turned on the bright reading light and fingered her crusted hair apart and found where the bullet had grooved her skull in an area an inch and a half long and the same distance above her left ear. There didn't seem to be anything you could pull together or sew together. It had punched out a strip of scalp meat, hair and all, and had clotted over and stopped bleeding. I soaked gauze in antiseptic and patted the wound very delicately, then tied the pad in place with more gauze.

Then, in a moment of pure genius, I got a piece of sheeting and made a sling for myself, so my arm would stop swinging around and flapping at me. It was much better. I didn't want her to wake up and look in that tarp. I found the fire extinguisher in the corner where it had rolled. I wiped it off and put it back in the clips. I sat on the floor and put both feet against the tarp and shoved Freddy half under the bunk, where he was less noticeable.

I went above decks. We were riding well at anchor. Sea calm. Skies clear. I went below and stripped and cleaned myself up. I wasn't bleeding through the gauze. Good sign. I put a robe on. The empty sleeve flapping was less troublesome than the empty arm.

I made two giant peanut butter sandwiches and yonked them down and washed them the rest of the way with a quart of cold milk. What every healthy American kid needs after being shot.

At four thirty, after some mental practice, I warmed up the set and got through to Miami Marine and put through a credit card call to Meyer aboard his boat. She told him she had a call for him from the motor vessel, *The Bustled Lush*.

"Travis? Say, I see you must have talked her into it without too much trouble, huh? Over."

"It was spur of the moment, Meyer. Crazy wild kids taking off on a magic adventure. Over."

"Are you maybe a little smashed, old friend? Listen, I can't talk about the other thing, not with half this transmission open for anybody who wants to listen. Tell her things are going well. How about the next time you call me, make it from shore and I can tell you the news. Over."

"Will do. I don't know how long we'll cruise around. Maybe I can keep her out a couple of weeks. Over."

"It will be great for her, Travis. And it won't hurt you. Have some fun. Catch fish. Sing a little."

As soon as I signed off, the reaction began. Somehow you do what you have to do, and somehow the machinery accepts the abuse. But when you've forced your way through it, all the gears and wheels start to chitter and grind and wobble around on the pinions. I felt icy cold. I knew it was all sour. She would never come out of it. Something would be bleeding in her head and that would be the end of it. Or somebody had seen him coming aboard, or seen him taking the houseboat out. My arm would start to rot. The hook would pull out of loose sand and we'd drift aground.

I went back below and looked at her and went into the master stateroom and slipped out of the robe and into the giant bed and wished I wasn't too old to cry myself to sleep . . .

I heard her saying my name for a long time before

I let it wake me up. She sat on the edge of the bed, facing me. She wore a short beach robe and she had fashioned a turban affair out of a pale blue towel. It was night. The light was behind her.

"Trav? Trav?"

"Mmm. How's your head, Janine?"

"I'm all right. I'm perfectly all right. Trav, how badly are you hurt?" She had bared my shoulder and she was looking at the bandage.

"It's just a scratch."

"Please. How bad is it?"

"I don't think it's too bad."

"I want to look at it."

"Let me wake up. I didn't mean to sleep so long."

"Get waked up, then. I'll be right back."

She came back with a towel, a first-aid kit and a basin of hot water. I rolled onto my right side. She went to the other side of the bed, spread the towel and equipment out, and snipped the bandage off.

I heard her insuck of breath, and said, "That bad?"

"I . . . I think it looks worse than it is. I'll try not to hurt you."

She busied herself. She was very gentle.

"Travis?"

"Yes, Jan."

"He was going to kill us both, wasn't he?"

"Maybe."

"I know he was. From the way he looked at me. After he . . . I thought when you came in and snipped me loose, it was him coming back."

"Did he give you a bad time?"

"Sort of. After he chained me up, he hit me on the head again. Very very lightly, and it was just enough so everything seemed to go far away and I couldn't move or speak or see. I wasn't awake or asleep. I could feel what he was doing. Just with his hands. Sort of . . . to see what a woman was like there. And when I could move, I grabbed his hands and pushed them away. And he looked at me and blushed and then sort of half smiled and shrugged and I knew he knew I wouldn't ever be able to tell anybody about whatever he decided to do to me. I knew he'd come back . . . but it was you. And then I was sure he'd killed you like he killed Tush and . . . I knew I could kill him. I knew he couldn't stop me. And so . . . I did."

"You didn't quite make it, honey. I took care of it."

"Don't try to be sweet and protective and all. I looked at him in there. I had to touch him and turn him over to make sure. I even felt it in my hands when it hit him, a kind of looseness, the way his head went. I'm not proud of it or full of joy or anything. But I can live with it. . . . There. I think that's better than the way it was, Travis."

"Thanks," I said and rolled onto my back. She took the basin and towel and gear away.

When she came back, she stood at the foot of the bed and said, "What do we do now?"

"I called Meyer while you were still out."

"And told him about this?"

"No. I said we might cruise around for quite a while."

"You did?"

"Until we're both healed up enough so people won't ask questions. If we go back, we make statements. Everybody will want to see how much front page space they can get, how many times they can get their pictures taken with us. What good will that do you or your kids?"

"No good at all."

"Or do Freddy's people?"

"They might as well think he's alive in the world, somewhere."

"And I couldn't take that kind of hot publicity, Jan. I can't start wearing a public face. It would put me out of business. I don't need a lot of official interest. There's a little bit now. All I can handle. So we deep-six him and say nothing. Not a word, Jan. Not ever, to anyone. Can you handle that?"

Her face was quiet, her eyes thoughtful. In the sea-light there was the tangible presence of death aboard. A head-knocker whose luck turned very bad, who'd never make it to the Caicos, who'd had something rancid going on in the back of his mind, some warped thing all mixed up with darkness and helplessness and sexual assault. The sickness had begun to stir and move under stress, had begun to emerge, but his life had stopped before it had gone out of control.

She said, "What if you don't heal right? What if we have to find a doctor?"

"We have a story. We were potting at beer cans with a thirty-eight. The kick startled you. It slipped out of your hand, went off when it hit the deck."

"Does . . . anyone but us know he was aboard?"

"Not likely."

She nodded. "I'll be all right, Travis. I'll be fine."

I got up and went on deck and discovered I had completely forgotten the anchor lights. We were well away from any course a small boat might take, but a darkened boat at night invites investigation. I put us back onto legal status. We were riding well. The night was soft, the stars slightly misted. Miami was a giant glow to the north.

I stayed topside a long time. When I went below, she was curled up on the yellow couch in the lounge, sound asleep. I looked down at her and hoped that she would have enough iron in her to help a one-armed man with some curiously ugly chores. She had dark patches under her eyes. I turned off the small dim lamp nearby and felt my way through dark and familiar spaces back to the master stateroom.

I didn't really know if she could last, if she could handle it, until the next morning when I sat on the edge of the freshly made bed in the guest stateroom and watched her using the curved sailmaker's needle and the heavy thread, sewing Freddy into his sea shroud. She had cleaned and dressed my wound afresh. I had wired a spare anchor snugly to the deputy's ankles, and tucked his gun and cuffs and the black leather sap in beside him.

When she ran out of the hank of thread, and clipped it off and took a fresh end from the spool and moistened it in her lips before threading the needle again, she looked up at me for a moment. It was a flat, dark look, and made me think of old stories of how warriors dreaded being taken alive and turned over to the women.

At the end of day she wrested the anchor free when I ran the *Flush* up to it, and brought it aboard. We ran outside, creaking and rocking in the swell. I put it on automatic pilot at just enough speed to hold it quartering into the sea, and together we clumsied him up and on onto the side deck. She held the book and tilted it to catch the light from where the sun had gone down, and she read the words we thought would be appropriate to the situation.

She laid the book down and with my one arm and her two, we lifted the stiffened body upright, and as she held it propped against the rail, I bent and grasped the tarp at the feet and lifted and toppled it into the sea. It sank at once. And then I took the wheel and came about and headed for the buoy that marks the pass back into Biscayne Bay.

Seventeen

ONCE SHE ACCEPTED the need to stay by ourselves, to heal in order to avoid questions, a strange new placidity came over her. She had long times of silence, and I could guess that now that she knew what had happened, and how it had happened, part of it was over and the part about finding an acceptance of Tush's death had begun.

She began to eat well and spend some of the sun hours basting and broiling herself to the deep tan her skin took readily, and she began sleeping long and deeply, gaining the weight that softened her bone-sharp face, that filled out the long concave line of the insides of her thighs, that made her fanny look a great deal less as if it had been slapped flat with a one by six.

I called Meyer from shoreside phones. I wore the arm out of the sling for longer periods each day, reslinging it when the knitting muscle structures began to ache.

She phoned Connie when the trip with the kids was over, and Connie accepted the notion that a little more time cruising would do her good. She talked to each of the boys. They were fine. They missed her. She missed them.

Meyer eased out of the last of her holdings in Fletcher on the Wednesday, the last day of January, at a good price, and when we talked again the following Monday evening—I had phoned him from Islamorada—he said with undisguised glee that Fletcher had gotten up to forty-six dollars a share at noon, and the Exchange had suspended trading in it fifteen minutes later, pending a full investigation of a tip that the earnings reports had been misstated, that a syndicate of speculators had been boosting the price, and that the company officers had been quietly unloading all their own holdings at these false and inflated values. The word on the Street was that it might be another Westec case, and it was rumored that a Florida-based speculator named Gary Santo was deeply involved in the artificial runup of the price.

"If they ever approve it for listing again," Meyer said, "it will open at about six dollars, and even that is more than a realistic book value per share."

The next morning the *Flush* was tied up at the marina dock at Islamorada, and after breakfast I had Jan peel the final dressing off the wound. The entrance wound was a pink dime-sized dimple, vivid in the middle of the surrounding tan. She made careful inspection of the exit area, held the back of her hand against it to check for any inner heat of infection and said, "This last little piece of scab is going to come off any day now. If we could have had it sewn up, there wouldn't be so much scarring, Trav. It looks as if . . . somebody stabbed you with one of those wood rasp things."

"I got through the whole day without the sling yesterday. And I can hold that smallest sledge out at arm's length for fifteen seconds. And so I keep a shirt on till the scars bleach white and match the old ones."

"You would make a very low-grade hide," she said. "They might find three or four sections that would make nice little lampshades, but they'd have to throw the rest away."

"Just accident-prone, I guess. And you pass inspection now, lady. Keep it combed that way and you're fine."

"You see, I was aboard this funny houseboat and it got rough and I lurched and took this great gouge out of my scalp on some kind of sharp thing sticking out."

"We can head back so Meyer can help you count your money."

Late that afternoon she went below and came up with two cold uncapped bottles of Tuborg and sat close beside me and said, "A sort of an announcement, Travis McGee. There won't be another chance to talk, probably. I wish to announce that you are a dear, strange, ceremonious kind of guy, and I didn't like you very much at all before Tush died and didn't know why he liked you, and now I do, maybe."

"Tell me. Maybe I can use it."

"It made me jumpy to be alone with you, because the way I had you all figured out, you were going to comfort the little widow woman. Life goes on and all that. Let me bring you back to life, darling. A woman always knows when a man finds her physically attractive, and I am flattered that you so do."

"I so do."

"I expected some of the gooey rationalizations of the chronic stud, including how Tush would approve, and besides it's so healthy. But you have been very stuffy and proper and dear. Thank you."

"You're welcome."

"Maybe I would have gone along with it, out of some kind of self-destructive impulse. I don't know. I don't know if I was a one-man gal. I sort of think so. Maybe that part of me—the privacy part—will come alive again. Anyway, I'm glad you didn't give me a chance to make any choice. Physically I'm a lot better than I was. Better nerves. But I'm still half a person. And so damned lonely, and the world is so . . . flattened out." She reached up and kissed me under the ear. "So thanks for not trying to be God's gift to the bereaved, dear."

"You're welcome aboard anytime. You wear well."

She smiled a bitter little twisty smile and, eyes wet, took my hand and clenched it tightly. So we were a couple of kids in an abandoned barn and the big storm was hammering down, and we held hands for comfort. Tush was her storm, and perhaps Puss was mine.

On another Wednesday, the day of the Valentine, Meyer came over at high noon and interrupted my project of cutting and laying some Nautilex that was a clever imitation of bleached teak on a portion of the afterdeck.

"So I am here and I have brought you a Valentine," said he.

"Sometimes, Meyer, when you act like Porky, you make me feel like Pogo."

"Read the card."

I put down the knife I was cutting the vinyl with and thumbed his card open. Homemade. He had drawn a heart pierced by an arrow, with a dollar sign dangling from the end of the arrow. His verse said, "Roses are red; violets are blue. Unadulterated, unselfish, unrewarded efforts in behalf of even the grieving widow of an old and true friend are not like you."

"It rhymes," he said.

Inside the folded card was his personal check made out to me for twenty-five thousand dollars.

"What the hell is this?"

"Such gratitude! It hurt me to see you lose your professional standing, McGee. Like you were going soft and sentimental. So, through my own account, I put us into Fletcher and rode it up nicely and took us out, and split the bonus right down the middle. It's short-term. It's a check. Pay your taxes. Live a little. It's a longer retirement this time. We can gather up a throng and go blundering around on this licentious craft and get the remorses for saying foolish things while in our cups. We had a salvage contract, idiot, and the fee is comparatively small but fair."

"And you are comparatively large but fair."

"I think of myself that way. Where did the check go? Into the pocket so fast? Good." He looked at his watch. "I am taking a lady to lunch. Make a nice neat deck there, Captain." And away he went, humming.

And not over four minutes later a half-familiar voice said, "McGee?" I looked up from the tricky bit of fitting the vinyl at the hatch corner and saw the three of them lined up on the dock, staring at me without much affability or enthusiasm. Gary Santo on the left. Mary Smith in a bright orange minitent and a little-girl hat standing in the middle. A stranger on the right, medium tall, of that hunched, thin pallor that looks like sickness, even to the little watermelon pot, with a face like a bleached mole, glasses with massive black frames, a briefcase in hand.

"Howdy do there, Gary boy," I said. "Miss Mary."

"And this is Mr. D. C. Spartan, one of my attorneys. May we come aboard?"

"Why, surely. Please do."

I took them into the lounge. There was no handshaking going on. I excused myself and went and washed the

214

grime off my hands, pulled the sweaty T-shirt off, swabbed chest, neck and shoulders with a damp towel, put on a fresh white sports shirt and rejoined them, saying, "Coffee, folks? Booze?"

"No thanks," said Santo.

Spartan said, in a voice like a talking computer with a slight honk in the speaker system, "It might be advisable for you to have your attorney present, if you could reach him quickly."

"Now what would I need lawyers for? Somebody suing me?"

"Don't get so damned cute!" Santo said. His face looked slightly mottled and puffy, as if the facials weren't working well lately.

"Please, Mr. Santo," Spartan said. "Mr. McGee, we are facing what might shape up into a very exhaustive investigation of Mr. Santo's role in the speculation in Fletcher Industries. And it may well become necessary to have you testify as to your part in bringing this . . . uh . . . investment opportunity to Mr. Santo's attention."

"Why?"

"There seems to be an unfounded opinion that Mr. Santo knew of the precarious condition of Fletcher Industries and conspired to run the stock up, and then short it, and that this scheme was interrupted by the suspension of trading in Fletcher common. To show Mr. Santo's good faith, we will have to subpoena your trading records and show that you had taken a position in Fletcher and then went to Mr. Santo to elicit his interest, and that Mr. Santo then made a cursory investigation of the company's condition before beginning a very active trading in the common stock."

I shook my head. "Mr. Spartan, you lost me there somewhere. I never bought a share of Fletcher. I don't own any stock at all. Never have."

"Come off it, friend," Santo said in an ugly way. "You better be able to show me you took a real good bath in Fletcher. You better be able to show me you got stung."

"I've never owned a share of stock in my life!"

Spartan looked sad. He dug into the briefcase. He took out the stapled Xerox copies of the fake margin account with Shutts, Gaylor, Stith and Company. "Come now, Mr.

McGee! Surely you know that your account records can be subpoenaed from the brokerage house."

I looked at them and handed them back. "I'd say that's going to be a very confused bunch of brokers, folks. If I had to guess, I'd say these were Xerox copies of some kind of forgery, or there's somebody else with my name. I just don't know what the hell you're talking about."

"But Miss Smith can testify to what you told her and to you giving her the originals to Xerox. Do you actually want to deny that you went to Mr. Santo's offices and talked about this whole matter to Miss Smith?"

"Oh, I went there all right. I didn't have any appointment, and I had a hard time getting to talk to anybody, even this pretty little quail. Now, I suppose whatever we said was taped, just as a matter of convenience, you know, for reference. But I don't think you can introduce that kind of a tape, and even if you can, it would have to be the whole tape, not just some edited parts of it."

"There is a tape, of course," Spartan said. "And we can prove it predates Mr. Santo's interest in Fletcher common."

"Spartan," said Gary Santo, "I think this son of a bitch is too cute. I think he was working for somebody. I think he was setting me up."

"Sometimes I work for people," I said. "But not for long. Mary, you remember the long talk we had about that Gary's parcel he holds up there in Shawana County under the name of Southway Lands, Inc.?"

"What?" she said. "There wasn't anything like that."

"But, honey, you confirmed the rumor that Southway was going to sell out to Calitron for a nice price, if a fellow up there by the name of LaFrance could assemble the rest of the acreage."

"But what are you trying to *do* to me?" she asked.

"Say! If I've spilled the beans and gotten you into some kind of trouble or anything . . . I guess we didn't talk about it up in the offices. That was later, honey.'

"We *never* talked about that!"

I shook my head. "But you told me how Bannon got through to you, and you had a drink with him at the airport, and he told you how he was being squeezed and wanted Santo's help, and you decided you couldn't take a little thing like that to Mr. Santo and waste his time with a little guy who got caught in the middle."

She caught her little lip in her teeth the same way she had when talking to Tush.

I continued. "Remember, honey? You said that you thought Mr. Santo had mentioned how, up in the hotel penthouse in Atlanta, LaFrance had tried to get Santo to buy Bannon out and Santo told LaFrance that it was his problem and he should handle it? That was the same night you told me you'd give me a clean bill with Santo."

I moved just fast enough. Santo got up and got over to her and got his hand back for a slap that would have loosened her teeth. I caught his wrist. The position gave me very nice leverage. I swung the wrist back and over and down and ended up in about the same position as a pitcher after letting go of his best fast ball. Santo boomed into the yellow couch hard enough to snap his head back, and then bounced forward onto his hands and knees on the rug.

"Now just a minute. Gentlemen! Just a minute!" Spartan said.

Santo shook his dazed head. I picked him up by the nape of the neck and sat him on the couch.

I stood in front of him and said, "Fun time is over, Gary baby. I didn't get a damned word of this from pretty-pit over there. She's devoted. She's energetic. She just never got a chance to get close to me. I made sure of that. Tush Bannon was a damned good friend. Your pressure, second-hand, drove him into the ground. And it went a little wrong up there and they went further than they had to and killed him."

He stared up at me, very attentive.

"I squashed LaFrance. I would have squashed you too if I could have figured a way. But you're too big and too spread out. All I could do was sting you a little."

"A little?" he said wonderingly. "A little? You cut my venture capital right down to the nub, friend. You fixed me so I'm associated with any new stock issue and it never gets off the ground. Sting me a little! God damn you, I might never take up the slack you put in me. And all of this was over some . . . dreary little small-time buddy of yours?"

I leaned over and slapped his face sideways and back-handed it back to center position.

"Manners," I said.

I moved back to give him a chance to come off the couch. He thought it over. Then he took out a frosty-white handkerchief and patted the corner of his mouth and examined the dappling of blood.

I turned to Spartan. "Tell him how he stands if it checks out that I've never owned a share of Fletcher."

"Well . . . it would eliminate one possible way to ease the present situation."

I turned back to Santo and looked for that tinge of gray under the barbered, lotioned, international complexion. Saw a little. Not like LaFrance. Saw enough of it and enough slump of resignation. He dabbed at his mouth again and got up.

"Come on, Spartan," he said. He stopped so close in front of Mary Smith's chair there was not room for her to get out of it.

"You're fired, you stupid bitch!"

"But you heard him say I didn't——"

"You didn't do what you're overpaid to do, which is to stick close and check every little thing out. You could have saved me going into the tank for enough to buy five thousand of you for a lifetime. And that makes you too damned expensive. I'll have your office stuff packed and dropped off at your place. I'll have your check mailed. I couldn't look at you again without feeling sick."

"Gary, you just don't know how mutual that feeling is."

His arm came halfway up. "Uh uh!" I said. He lowered it and left swiftly. Spartan hurried behind him, and gave me a single despairing glance as he left.

She slumped in the chair. "Hooo, boy," she said wearily. "They told me there'd be days like this." She gave me a look through the emerald lenses. "Thanks heaps, Mc-Gee."

"I didn't exactly intend it that way, Mary Smith."

"But that seems to be the way it is. In many respects that was a very very very nice job, lad. It did have its cruddy intervals. You know, I didn't realize how much enjoyment I'd get out of seeing the great Gary Santo get clouted around. Funny. In three years he's popped me in the face three times. And I told myself that one more time, brother, and that's it. Would I have quit, though? I wonder? I am going to believe I would."

"Will he send any muscle around to teach me I can't do that?"

She looked at me, head cocked, wearing a little frown. "I'd say not. I mean if he thought you were absolutely alone in this, I think he would. But when he thinks it over, he's not going to believe that a person of your type could con him so completely. He'll think you're a front man, and I think he'll leave well enough alone. Besides, he's got a lot to think about."

"Do you think I'm a front man?"

"I am inclined to doubt it somehow. How about buying an unemployed girl a drink and then some lunch? You know. Like no hard feelings. You know, this is quite a setup you've got here, McGee. I couldn't tell much from the outside that time."

"Bourbon straight, water with no ice on the side?"

"Exactly."

As I was fixing the drinks Johnny Dow hallooed and stuck my mail under the corner of the deck mat. I gave her her drink and went out and brought the mail in, zipped through the customary junk and came upon an airmail one from Chicago in Puss's broad, round scrawl.

"Excuse a little mail-reading?"

"Sure. I'll just sit here and plan my future."

Old dear darling, I said one time that I would write it down to get it straight for you, and so I have and even have the eerie idea you might be able to read all the words between the words. The name was right. I lied about that. But the town wasn't, and Chicago isn't the town either. And there was no divorce. And I love Paul very dearly and have all along, and love you too, but not quite as much. That lousy Meyer and his lousy Law. Get a pretty girl to kiss Old Ugly and tell him he was absolutely right. You see, my dear, about six months before you met me on the beach with that living pincushion stuck into the sole of my foot, they took a little monster out of my head, maybe as big as an English walnut almost, and with three stumpy little legs like a spider. Half a spider. And the men in white dug around in my head to try to find every little morsel

*of the beast, because he turned out to be the bad kind.
So . . . I got over confusions and got my memory all
straightened out again, and my hair grew back, and I
pinned an old buddy of mine to the wall of his office and
he leveled because he has known me long enough to
know I have enough sawdust to keep me solid. His
guess was one chance out of fifty. No treatments possible.
Just go off and get checked every so often, bright lights
in the eyes, stand and touch the tip of your nose with
your fingertip while keeping the eyes closed. That stuff.
And pens drawing lines on little electric charts. I could
accept it, my dear, because life is very iffy and I have
busied up my years in good ways. But I could not
accept the kind of life that went with the waiting. Dear
as Paul is, he is a sentimental kraut type, and we had
the awareness of the damned time bomb every waking
moment. So life became like a practice funeral, with
too many of our friends knowing it, and everybody trying to be so bloody sweet and compassionate during a
long farewell party. I began to think that if I lucked
out, I'd be letting them down. So I finally told Paul
that if it was the end of my life, it was getting terribly
damned dreary and full of violin music, and I am a
random jolly type who does not care to be stared at by
people with their eyes filling with tears. So I cashed
in the bonds for the education of the children I'll never
have, and I came a-hunting and I found you. Was I too
eager to clamber into the sack? Too greedy to fill
every day with as much life as would fit into it? Darling
I am the grasshopper sort, and so are you, and, bless
you, there were dozens of times every day I would
completely forget to sort of listen to what might be
happening inside my redheaded skull. Be glad you jollied
and romped the redheaded lady as she was coming
around the clubhouse turn, heading for the tape. She
loved it. And you. And how good we were together
in a way that was not a disloyalty to Paul! He is one
of the dogged and steadfast ones. Can you imagine
being married, dear, to Janine, great as she is, and
having her know you could be fatally ill? She would
mother you out of your mind until you ran. As I ran.
But there was the little nagging feeling I was having
all too good. I kept telling myself, Hell girl, you do*

serve it. And then hairy old Meyer and his damned Law about the hard thing to do is the right thing to do. I suppose you have been wondering about me and maybe hating me a little. I had to run from you exactly when I did and how I did, or I couldn't have left at all. You see, the dying have a special obligation too, my dear. To keep it from being too selfish. I was depriving Paul of his chance of being with me, because it is all he is going to have of me . . . all he did have of me, and I was forgetting that I had to leave him enough to last him long enough to get him past the worst of it at least. The darling has not done the interrogation bit, and if he thinks or doesn't think there was a man in the scene, I couldn't really say. You would like each other. Anyway, the female of the species is the eternal matchmaker, and I have written the longest letter of my life to Janine, all full of girl talk, and about living and dying, and I have, I hope, conned her into spinning a big fancy pack of lies about the Strange Vacation of Puss Killian, because I am leaving her name and address with Paul, saying that she could tell him how I was and what happened among people who didn't know. It is a devious plot, mostly because they would work well. He is a research chemist, and perhaps the kindest man alive. Anyway, last week all of a sudden the pupil of my big gorgeous left eye got twice as big as it should, and they have been checking and testing and giving me glassy smiles, and I am mailing this en route to the place where they are going to open a trap door and take another look. So they may clap the lid back on and say the hell with it. Or they may go in there and without meaning to, speed me on my journey, or they may turn me into a vegetable, or they may manage to turn me back into me for another time, shorter or longer. But from the talk around the store, the odds on that last deal make the old odds seem like a sure thing bet. Do you understand now? I'm scared. Of course I'm scared. It's real black out there and it lasts a long time. But I have no remorses, no regrets, because I left when I had to, and Meyer got me back in good season. Don't do any brooding, because if I can try to be a grownup, you ought to be able to take a stab at it. Here's what you do, Trav my darling. Find

221

*yourself a gaudy random gorgeous grasshopper wench,
and lay aboard the Plymouth and the provisions, and
go fun-timing and sun-timing up and down the lovely
bays. Find one of good appetite and no thought of it
being for keeps, and romp the lassie sweetly and completely, and now and again, when she is asleep and you
are awake, and your arms are around her and you are
sleeping like spoons, with her head tucked under your
ugly chin, pretend it is . . .*

Puss, who loved you.

"Is something wrong?" a voice said.

I looked at Mary Smith, realizing that it was not the
first time she had asked me. "Wrong? No. Just a letter
from an old friend."

"You looked funny."

"I guess it was . . . because the old friend decided to
cancel an old debt." I got up and got the bottle and
refilled her shot glass.

She lifted it in toast. "Here's to vacations without pay
Oh, Christ, that was such a great job! Such a sweet lush
life, dear. But you know, sometimes you get an instinct
I think other things are going to go bad for Santo. I thin
he's going to strain too hard to catch up, and he'll choke
and he'll lose his style, and in a couple of years he'
be one of those whatever-happened-to people."

Puss's letter said, *"It's real black out there and it last
a long time."*

I could feel my heart fall. It dropped a certain distanc
and there it would stay.

I could look at Miss Smith as if I'd never seen he
before. She sat with a little inward smile of satisfactio
thinking of what she wished for Gary Santo. She dippe
at the shot glass for her little butterfly sips. The edge o
the minitent came to mid thigh. Exquisite legs, honey
tan and matte finish, were crossed. The light of ear
afternoon came through the window ports, highlighting th
lustrous brown-auburn fall of hair, a healthy pelt. Th
secretive lashes half veiled the vivid plastic green, th
secret half smile curved the corners of the plump mout

She got up and wandered over to look at the titles o
the sleeves of the records on the shelf by the player. "D
we get music with the booze?" she asked.

I went over dutifully and when I stood beside her, I realized she had suddenly fixed her attention elsewhere, so totally that she was unaware of me and unaware of the music. She was standing looking diagonally through the starboard aft port toward the dock, and following the direction of her intent gaze, I saw Hero ambling along, looking for fresh game, the meat of his shoulders slowly rolling, one thumb hooked into the tightness of the broad leather belt.

I looked down at her face, saw that the lips, now parted, looked almost swollen. Breathing deeply and slowly through parted lips, eyelids heavy, head nodding slightly, she watched Hero.

Then she turned to me and it seemed to take her a moment to remember who I was. In a voice pitched lower than usual, and with a huskiness, she said, "Darling, forgive me if I uninvite myself for lunch? Thank you for drinks and entertainment. Thank you for saving me from a shot in the mouth. I think I'll . . . look up those friends I have here. Some other time, dear. You have a lovely boat."

She put on her huge black sunglasses and put the empty shot glass down, and smiled and left. I went out on the afterdeck and watched her go hastily in the direction Hero had taken. Swing of the purse. Quick clip-clap of the sharp little heels on the cement. Rapid bouncing of the weight of the rich brown mane. Unseen, tented lips swinging. And, I could guess, a crawly butterfly awareness of the silky brushing of the softening thighs together, awareness of the prickling tickle of erectile tissues, of labial weights and thickenings, and a feeling of being unable to take a breath quite deep enough—as she went tocking and bobbing in her scurry to fall under the brutalizing, tireless, impersonal hammer of the Hero, to be once more the bed-beaten shoat, to be spent and lamed and emptied as before.

So I walked slowly to Meyer's boat and sat on the bunk with my head in my hands while he read Puss's letter. He finished it and coughed and honked and wiped his eyes. So I told him that we were going to take his little cruiser because it could take more sea than a houseboat, and we were going to take the *Muñequita* in tow, and we were going to go as far down the Exuma Cays as

223

the range of his boat would allow, and then we were going a lot further down in the Little Doll. I told him I was sick unto death of miniwomen, miniclothes, miniloves, minideaths and my own damned minilife. I wanted empty cays, gaudy reefs, hot sun, swift fish, and maybe some talk when it was time for talking.

And Meyer said, "So give me a hand with the lines and we'll take this crock over to the gas dock and top off the tanks."